TRAGIC
CURTAIN

TRAGIC CURTAIN

Stanley Hart Page

COACHWHIP PUBLICATIONS
Greenville, Ohio

The Tragic Curtain, by Stanley Hart Page
© 2025 Coachwhip Publications edition
Introduction © 2025 Curtis Evans

First published 1935
Stanley Hart Page, 1902-1979
CoachwhipBooks.com

ISBN 1-61646-624-3
ISBN-13 978-1-61646-624-4

ANOTHER ONE FOR THE PHILO BRIGADE

STANLEY HART PAGE AND THE CHRISTOPHER HAND MYSTERIES

CURTIS EVANS

In 1929 the prestigious firm of Alfred A. Knopf published Dashiell Hammett's tough and violent crime novels *Red Harvest* and *The Dain Curse* (*The Maltese Falcon* would follow the next year), forever altering the face of crime fiction with what reviewers dubbed the "hard-boiled" style. Yet at the very same time that Hammett commenced his great crime sweep, traditionalist American mystery writer S. S. Van Dine (Willard Huntington Wright), whose best-selling Philo Vance detective novels were published by Knopf's rival Scribner's, stood resplendent at the height of his popularity, having also in 1929 produced *The Bishop Murder Case,* the book which proved the most popular and enduring of his mysteries. Although the future of American crime writing might lie with the tough guys, what Hammett's Sam Spade or the Continental Op might have termed the "pantywaist" genteel amateur detectives were hardly down for the count. Indeed, that very same year Frederic Dannay and Manfred Lee, the two New York cousins who wrote as Ellery Queen, introduced, in *The Roman Hat Mystery,* a monocled amateur detective named, appropriately enough, Ellery Queen, a gentleman who in his studied affectations shared considerable affinity with Philo Vance, particularly in his early years in print. Five years later, Rex Stout's obese, orchid-loving eccentric genius,

Nero Wolfe, would make his first of many fictional appearances in the detective novel *Fer de Lance*. In between those epochal events in American mystery genre history, myriad Philo Vance wannabes made brief their own brief struts on the crime fiction stage. One member of this troop of toff tecs was Christopher Hand, who between 1932 and 1935 appeared in a quintet of novels by forgotten American mystery writer Stanley Hart Page.

Stanley Hart Page, who, ironically enough likely was distantly related to native Marylander Samuel Dashiell Hammett through mutual Dashiell ancestors of French Huguenot lineage, was born in prosperous circumstances in Chatham, New Jersey, on March 10, 1902, to Laurence Stanley Page and his wife Emma F. Jowett. Stanley's colorful entrepreneurial paternal grandfather was self-made millionaire coal tar king George Shephard Page (1838-1892), originally of Reading, Maine, and Chelsea, Massachusetts. Upon his death at the age of fifty-four George Page, the renowned "millionaire chemist" who was then an inmate of the New Jersey State Insane Asylum ("his mind was broken down by the worry introduced by a severe attack of the grippe" according to the newspapers), bequeathed to his four sons and one daughter the substantial fortune (about thirty-five million dollars in modern worth) which he had accumulated through his various business ventures, the best known of which today is the Vapo-Cresolene Company. This profitable enterprise with great success marketed Vapo-Cresolene, a therapeutic vaporizer used in the United States during the late nineteenth and early twentieth centuries in the hope of providing lasting relief to sufferers from such ailments as asthma, bronchitis, croup, whooping cough and diphtheria, despite the fact that the American Medical Association reported with dry derision in 1908 that "Vapo-Cresolene is a member of that

Stanley Hart Page

class of proprietaries in which an ordinary product is endowed, by the manufacturer, with extraordinary virtues."

Perhaps to salve his moral conscience George before his breakdown became a great advocate of both alcohol temperance, founding the New Jersey Temperance Association, and of universal free public-school education. He also founded Chatham's Stanley Congregational Church. After his death, Page's own rather more fortunate offspring inherited from the family patriarch his highly profitable, if arguably somewhat dubious, patent medicine business, over which they maintained firm control, with Stanley's uncle Albion Lambert Page serving as president, his uncle Henry de Bacon Page serving as vice president, and his own father, the aforementioned Laurence Stanley Page, serving as secretary. All three men additionally served as directors of the company, the remaining two of whom were Stanley's youngest uncle, Raymond Page, and his aunt, Florence Page.[1]

With a family fortune behind him, Stanley Hart Page might simply have lived a dilettante life, like the fictional Philo Vance, Albert Campion and Lord Peter Wimsey, taking a sinecure job from the firm; yet he went to work, rather, as the manager of the Montclair bureau of the *Newark Evening News* (then New Jersey's newspaper of record), after attending the Pawling and Peddie prep schools and Brown University and taking a token vagabond year out west employed as a cowboy and farm-hand. Yet in 1930, as he approached the age of thirty, he was still single and living under his parents' spacious roof in Chatham, New Jersey, the 64th wealthiest inhabitation in the United States in 2018, according to *Bloomberg News*. However, the next year he got himself an apartment in nearby Short Hills, where he found time—having been "[s]ince his boyhood . . . absorbed with mysteries and fictional detectives"—to write a pair of detective novels, *Sinister Cargo* and *The*

Resurrection Murder Case, which he successfully placed with none other than Alfred A. Knopf's Borzoi Books imprint.

Knopf evidently was on the hunt for another Philo Vance, judging from the back flap blurb description of Page's book, which boldly, if perhaps a bit precipitately, proclaimed that the author's sophisticated dilettante sculptor and amateur criminologist, Christopher Hand, already belonged in the pantheon of Great Detectives:

> We nominate Mr. Christopher Hand for a place in that distinguished company of detectives whose work has thrilled so many readers of crime fiction in both England and America. His ability as a forger, his utter disregard of such ordinary necessities as food and sleep, the fact that he is a dilettante of the arts and sciences, and his uncompromising persistence, make him worthy in every way to stand behind those masters—Sherlock Holmes, Philo Vance, Lord Peter Wimsey, Father Brown, Hanaud, Poirot, Dr. Thorndyke, Charlie Chan, Reggie Fortune and [Knopf's own] Sam Spade.

Certainly Knopf was no wallflower when it came to boosting its detective fiction to the American mystery-reading public. Beginning in 1919, the publishing firm had launched a hugely successful effort to boost the middling mainstream English novelist J. S. Fletcher as the greatest British mystery writer since Arthur Conan Doyle. In this aggressive commercial campaign Knopf made great use of the fact that President Woodrow Wilson had read Fletcher's detective novel *The Middle Temple Murder* (1919) and expressed his enjoyment of the tale.

"PRESIDENT WILSON HAS BEEN READING THE MIDDLE TEMPLE MURDER A Fine Detective Story by J. S. Fletcher," boasted Knopf's advertising in the November 22, 1919, issue of *The Publishers' Weekly*. Knopf made a similar effort with Stanley Page's Christopher Hand mysteries, though nothing was said on their part about the admitted detective fiction predilections of President Herbert Hoover, who was highly unpopular as the nation staggered through its third year of crushing economic depression.

Knopf, which published Page's first three Christopher Hand mysteries (*Sinister Cargo*, 1932, *The Resurrection Murder Case*, 1932, and *Fool's Gold*, 1933), excelled itself in the production design of the books, with each volume in the series having a striking dust jacket and an appealing uniform board design of serpentine lines. *Cargo* had dark green lines on a lighter green background, *Resurrection* blue lines on an orange-brown background and *Gold*, the fanciest of all, red lines on a faux gold leaf background. The jacket to *The Resurrection Murder Case* in particular is memorably ghoulish, but all three jackets are fine indeed.

Sinister Cargo, about endangered New York financier Robert Garrison and his retired stage musical actress spouse, begins with a miraculous country house murder and goes to some very queer corners indeed, was praised by Isaac Anderson in the *New York Times Book Review*, who in his notice avowed: "This story offers a continuous succession of thrills . . . . Christopher Hand has methods of his own. Sometimes they are more than a bit high-handed, and sometimes they are without the law, but they get results. This is Mr. Page's first detective story, but we gather that he intends to give us more stories of the exploits of Christopher Hand. We'll be waiting." In the *Saturday Review* William C. Weber was equally enthusiastic, writing, in a notice which made the book sound more like a Doyle

Sherlock Holmes or Hammett Continental Op novel: ". . . the story does stand up. . . . There are two picturesque villains named Spitz and Spawn, a variety of successful and unsuccessful attempts to kill a wealthy New Yorker and his friends, and a pitched battle finale on a little island off the Maine coast. . . ."

Sinister Cargo's weird and colorful climax on a "haunted" Maine island at times seems like an anticipation of John Carpenter's classic ghostly fright film *The Fog* (1980). For this final section of the tale the author drew on the "many summers he had spent with his family on the coast of Maine." The narrative is punctuated by a series of

wild criminal episodes which sometimes savor of pulp fiction, with Christopher Hand's slavishly loyal chronicler,
Ralph Clark, getting more pieces of the action, as it were,
than Philo Vance's poor pale shadow Van ever did. As in
Doyle's *The Hound of the Baskervilles,* Hand is absent from
a substantial chunk of the narrative but returns to the
scene to elucidate all of the remaining mysteries. Despite
their social standing Christopher Hand and Clark prove
something more of men of action than the cerebral Philo

Cover courtesy Curtis Evans

Vance and Van, at least until the late Van Dine's late Vance detective tale *The Kidnap Murder Case* (1936). The body count in the novel ends up rather high indeed.

Upon the appearance of Page's follow-up, *The Resurrection Murder Case,* the reviewer in the *Boston Transcript* huzzahed: "The many friends of Christopher Hand will rejoice to meet him again . . .The devious paths followed until the crime is brought home are sufficiently interesting to hold the attention and to make it difficult to lay down the book. . . . One reads many pages half expecting the crack of a bludgeon on one's own head." For his part A. P. Bryan in the *Lexington Herald-Leader* wrote: "Mr. Page takes the most complicated plot that has come to the attention of this reviewer in many months and weaves it into a logical and interesting, yet baffling story of mystery and adventure. . . . [Christoper Hand] eventually solves the entire mystery by one of the most ingenious devices yet introduced to detective fiction." In the *Philadelphia Inquirer,* E. W. P. raved of the novel: "Hand the investigator is brilliant, and the dénouement is breath-taking."

Page dedicated *The Resurrection Murder Case* to retired New York police captain Grant Williams, a pioneering specialist in reconstructing faces from the skulls of murder victims (Dominick La Rosa and Lillian White were two of his most noted cases) whom the press in the Twenties dubbed a "modern Sherlock Holmes."[2] The so-called "sculptor-sleuth" headed New York City's Bureau of Missing Persons between its organization in 1914 and his retirement in 1928. Read the novel to see wherefore the dedication. It is set in and around Mill Ridge, New Jersey, "a fashionable community of larges estates" located on a ridge above the Great Swamp, which sounds a lot like places where the author himself had lived, like Chatham and Millburn.

Page's third mystery, *Fool's Gold*, which he penned in 1932 and published with Knopf in the Spring of 1933, reads rather like a Sherlock Holmes pastiche, allowing for the fact that it is set in Depression-era America rather than Victorian/Edwardian England. In the novel it appears that some criminal fiend has murdered a pair of grizzled gold prospectors, who had traveled to New York to find investors in their Alaska mining concern, and purloined from them the bills and gold they had kept stashed in their money belts. Unhappily involved in the problem are the congregants of the Hendley Congregational Church, who contributed to the ill-fated venture the sum of $50,000 (over a million dollars today), constituting their life savings.

The presence of the Hendley Congregational Church recalls the real-life Stanley Congregational Church, which Stanley Hart Page's grandfather as mentioned had founded and which Stanley would attend all of his life. Along the way to the solution of the various crimes Hand confronts a locked room murder problem as well. The notice in the *Los Angeles Times* declared of the inventive novel: "[T]he reader will be caught and will hold on until the [culprits] are discovered. . . . [T]here is a trick in this tale that will almost fool an experienced student of mystery yarns." Almost! The reviewer for Kentucky's *Lexington Herald-Leader,* on the other hand, avowed that "there's no chance of [readers] beating the author to the solution," adding: "You'll be flabbergasted by the number of clues that appear and the amount of action that is jammed into a 24-hour period." On May 7, 1933, the *San Francisco Chronicle* listed the novel as the Bay Region's #6 fiction bestseller of the week.

Page's mysteries won praise as well in the United Kingdom, where the author did not even have a really prestigious publisher behind him. When the second Hand opus, *The Resurrection Murder Case,* was published by Stanley

Paul in England in 1933 (the author's name was abbreviated there, for some reason, to S. Hart Page) an anonymous reviewer for the *Manchester Evening News* roundly praised the mystery as "[a]n American thriller of the most intense kind." In the *Leicester Mercury*, the writer of the column "From My Library Table" reflected that "with the thousands of 'thrillers' that are turned out every year it is amazing that we can still be mystified over any plot. But

Cover courtesy Curtis Evans

S. Hart Page keeps us in suspense throughout and then gives us the necessary jolt at the end. . . . *[The Resurrection Murder Case]* stamps him as one those few writers who can be relied upon to give us breathless adventure and a mental puzzle."

No less a figure than British mystery writer Richard Keverne lauded *Fool's Gold,* when it was published in England the next year, humorously writing: "Quite early in the story I thought I had guessed the solution to the mystery of *"Fool's Gold".* . . . but later on the idiot police detective tumbled to the same solution, and of course it was wrong. So it was left to the Sherlock Holmesian Christopher Hand to put us both right, and Mr. S. Hart Page makes him do it in a most agreeable manner." The *Leicester Mercury* pronounced the novel a "really gripping yarn" and the Daily Mirror found it "very readable."

As has been seen above Stanley Hart Page drew upon his own privileged background for his mysteries. His Grandfather George was a noted trout angler in the state of Maine, in 1867 founding, in the remote village of Oquossoc, an angling club on the shores of Mooselucmeguntic Lake. According to *The American Fly Fisher,* George Shephard Page's "reputation and fame as a fish culturist were international in scope." Christopher Hand's detecting companion and chronicler Clark is a devotee of trout fishing, declaring in *The Resurrection Murder Case:* "I had heard of the excellent fishing in the vicinity of Mill Ridge. . . . It was with a light heart that I fell asleep that night. I visualized myself wading in a trout stream." Recalling Philo Vance's enthusiasms in *The Kennel Murder Case* (1933), George Shephard Page was also a breeder of Scottish Deerhounds. With such a background it is perhaps not surprising that one of their scions ended up writing a detective fiction series headlined by a Philo-esque gentleman detective.

Stanley Hart Page grew up in privileged circumstances in Chatham, New Jersey, along with two elder brothers, George Shephard Page and Lawrence Stanely Page, Jr., an elder sister, Elizabeth, and one younger brother, Henry de Bacon Page. Despite their fortune, there was tragedy in the family's life. One Sunday morning in January 1919 Stanley's sister Betty died at the age of twenty-one from the Spanish flu then raging around the world. At her death Betty Page, whose obituary avowed had been "universally beloved" from childhood, was doing Red Cross work and taking a "special course in domestic science" at Centenary Collegiate Institute in preparation for her impending marriage. Less than a year earlier, Stanley's brother George Shephard Page, a professional aviator, had been killed in the Great War.

Described on his 1942 draft card as 5'11", 155 pounds, brown-haired (though balding) and blue-eyed, Stanley Hart Page in late 1931, not long before publishing his first detective novel, wed Beatrice Bayard, daughter of an affluent old-money New Jersey magazine publisher and descendant of Anne Stuyvesant Bayard, sister of Peter Stuyvesant, the ill-fated seventeenth-century Director General of the Dutch colony of New Netherland. Beatrice Bayard, a lovely, doe-eyed twenty-four-year-old actress who had graduated from the American Academy of Dramatic Arts, had acted in traveling company and played small parts in two Broadway plays, the hit 1929 Edward G. Robinson comedy *Kibitzer* (2nd neighbor) and the 1928 revival of John Colton's 1926 melodrama *The Shanghai Gesture* (apprentice mouse). She had spent the summer before her marriage traveling around Europe with an auntly chaperone. She and Page were married in a small private ceremony at the Episcopal Church of the Transfiguration in Manhattan, popularly known as "The Little Church around the Corner," which liberally catered to theater folk and other bohemian types.[3]

Page credited his imaginative wife with having helped inspire him to start writing mysteries and he dedicated his first novel to her. The couple dwelt at the roughly $500,000 (in modern value) Millburn, New Jersey, home of Beatrice's parents, along with her siblings Stuyvesant and Martha. The Bayards employed a single maid, a young black woman from South Carolina memorably named Ida May Neville.

In 1933 Stanley and Beatrice produced one daughter, Martha Pintard Page, and Stanley produced two more

Beatrice Bayard Page

Christoper Hand mysteries, the aforementioned *Fool's Gold* and *Murder Flies the Atlantic,* the latter of which innovatively is set on a zeppelin flying between London and New York. It was published by a rather less distinguished concern, Alfred H. King. Despite Knopf's vigorous pushing in the press and his supposed winning of "many friends," Christopher Hand sadly had not in fact become the Next Big Thing in the way of dilettante detectives. Two years

later there followed from Page's hand, as it were, Christopher Hand's finale *The Tragic Curtain,* which was published by The Dial Press. The author appears then to have laid down his pen, at least as it concerned crime writing.

Page continued to receive press praise for his last two detective novels, however, with, for example, the *Boston Globe* labeling *Atlantic* "a tense and thrilling story that is admirable written" and the *Houston Post* avowing of *Curtain:* "It is well-told, complicated and interesting." With *Curtain* Page provided a fitting end for the series. "There is a certain ingenuity in this work, one which makes it difficult to put it down," reflected the reviewer of the novel in the *Baltimore Evening Sun.* "Mr. Page . . . has thought up a solution to his crimes which pretty completely baffles the reader until the denouement is reached. Moreover, he plays fair and doesn't break the established rules of the game."

Although his detective thus vanished seemingly without a trace ninety years ago, Stanley Hart Page himself lived on for over four decades. For years he and Beatrice were actively involved in the Chatham Community Players, who in 1941 performed Stanley's play *A Welcome Stranger,* which the Chatham Press called a "lively, uproariously funny farce." Hardly in need of money, Page retired relatively young from the news business in 1952 and passed away after a lengthy illness at the age of seventy-seven on August 4, 1979. For nine decades now Page's sleuth Christopher Hand has waited to experience his own miraculous resurrection. While admittedly, despite all the puffing from his first publisher, no Philo Vance, Christopher Hand for a very short time was a name much bruited-about in mystery-loving circles. See for yourself what you think of this clever fella.

ENDNOTES:

[1] On Vapo-Cresolene and George Shephard Page and his children, see the online accounts provided by John Langlois, "On Beyond Holcombe: Vapo-Cresolene," *1898 Revenues: United States Revenue Stamps That Financed the Spanish American War*, 12 November 2012, and by Dan Edminster, "Lamps Designed for Medicinal Purposes: Vapo-Cresolene and Schering's Formalin Lamps," *The Lampworks: An On-Line Resource for Lighting Researchers and Collectors of Oil and Kerosene Lamps, Burners and Other Trimmings*, at http://www.thelampworks.com/lw_vapo_cresolene.htm. On the AMA's 1908 report on Vapo-Cresolene, see *Nostrums and Quackery* (Chicago: American Medical Association, 1912), 626. On the overall dubiousness of Vapo-Cresolene, see James Harvey Young, *The Toadstool Millionaires: A Social History of Patent Medicine in American before Federal Regulation* (Princeton, NJ: Princeton University Press, 1961), 215. George Shephard Page, bluntly notes William D. Eddy *in Stone Pond: A Personal History* (1982; rev. ed., White Plains, NY: Plain White Press, 1988), was "colorful, eccentric and ultimately mad. . . . In the quaint phrases of his obituary, he was 'deprived of his reason and removed to the State Insane Asylum at Morris Plains, NJ'" (p. 51. n. 4).

[2] A 1936 letter writer to *Time* detailed the Lillian White case:

> In April 1922, acting Captain Grant Williams of the New York City police department was imported to Rockland County, handed a skull and other bones found on Cheesecock Mountain and asked to solve the mystery of its presence there. Sterilizing the skull, he placed it on an artificial neck made out of a curtain pole shaved down to fit the opening of the spinal column. Inside the skull on either side of the pole, he wedged two radio tubes to hold the head steady. The other end of the pole he fitted in a stand made of a soap box.

Greasing his fingers, Williams then coated the
skull with modeling clay. He spread it thinly, following the contour of the bone evenly. Gradually he applied other layers, feeling his own jowls
& forehead for guidance. The length of the nose
he determined by measuring the distance between
the bridge and the roots of the upper teeth: its
contour by following the curve of the nasal bone.
To get the fullness of the cheeks he held a pencil
from the cheekbone down to the jawbone and allowed a little for normal rounding. He used the
same instrument to determine the set of the eyes,
holding it slantwise from the eye socket to the
cheekbone. . . . The brows he determined by beginning at the inside corner of the eye socket and
following around the upper edge of the bone; the
fullness of the lips by the protrusions and reces-
sions of the upper and lower teeth. And so on. . . .

Until, 56 hours later, when he had dipped the
flesh-colored clay in wax, inserted glass eyes and
dressed the victim's original hair, which providen-
tially had been recovered near the skull, he had
before him the snub-nosed, sullen face of a tem-
peramental Irish girl.

The rebuilt corpse was subsequently identified as Lillian White, an inmate of Letchworth [a
New York residential institution]. The identification was upheld by Justice Arthur S. Tompkins of
the New York Supreme Court; and her murderer,
Joseph Blunt, was subsequently caught in Maine.

[3] The Church of the Transfiguration was built and consecrated
in 1849. During the New York City draft riots of 1863, Rector
George Hendric Houghto, gave shelter to African-Americans
who were targets of a draft-protesting white mob. Houghton
was said to have turned the rioters away, sternly admonishing:
"You white devils, you! Do you know nothing of the spirit of

Christ?" The church's nickname came about thusly: In 1870 the rector of the Church of the Atonement refused to conduct funeral services for a deceased actor, airily telling his friend, famed thespian Jefferson Farjeon (grandfather of English mystery writer Jefferson Farjeon), "I believe there is a little church around the corner where they do that sort of thing." Farjeon allegedly responded: "If that be so, God bless the little church around the corner!"

I

A SHOT

Breaking off a chain of idle musings, Mr. Ralph Clark, finger-print expert and general assistant to Mr. Christopher Hand in the latter's criminologic work, leaned forward in his chair and snapped on the table-lamp. The soft glow pervaded the living-room, sending long shadows into the corners and across the walls.

Hand had been cooped up in his laboratory since luncheon. As he had slept all morning, Clark had seen almost nothing of him all day. Now, with the light all but faded out of a dreary, wet day in late October, the laboratory door, firmly shut until then, was abruptly opened. Immediately the air in the living-room became tainted with the vile odor of chemicals. A brilliant light fell through the door and along the carpet, putting to shame the feeble efforts of the table-lamp. The snap of a switch blotted out all view of the laboratory as suddenly as it had appeared. Hand stalked into the living-room.

Mastering a pained expression, and with a pronounced and audible sigh, Clark twisted about in his chair. He sniffed significantly.

"The laboratory door, Hand, please!"

Hand grunted, spun about, and jerked the door shut. He was by no means in his best humor. Nor had he been for some time. The reason was apparent in Clark's records:

their services had gone unsolicited for a fortnight. As far as Hand was concerned, the unaccustomed inactivity was beginning to fray nerves whose existence would have been doubted by those who knew him well.

The unwholesome atmosphere of the laboratory thus having been repulsed, Clark sighed with satisfaction and settled comfortably back into his chair. Hand strode irritably to the center of the room. The skirt of his lounging robe flapped about his long, lean and powerful legs, very much as though it, too, was displaying a disagreeable mood. He stopped and stood, tall, legs apart and hands thrust into the pockets of his lounging robe. Over his long, sharp features was stamped a half ludicrous expression of petulance.

All at once his gray eyes, until then squinting moodily, flew wide open and stared incredulously at Clark's goldfish bowl, resting in its customary place on the pedestal under the window. With a faint stirring of embarrassment, Clark also directed his gaze to the bowl. Every vestige of dust was washed from it, inside and out, and the bowl sparkled as, clearly as the fresh water that had just been put into it. Clark's newly-acquired goldfish were swimming inquisitively about, carefully inspecting their new domain.

"Goldfish!"

Hand breathed the word as though, for the first time in his life, he were doubting his eyesight.

"Beauties, aren't they?" asked Clark hopefully.

"Goldfish! Who in heaven's name put them into that bowl?"

"Well, after all, it is a goldfish bowl. My cat has wandered off; so I thought it would be safe to keep goldfish again."

Hand gazed sternly at his friend. "If you are going to keep goldfish in that bowl, will you tell me where I am to keep my matches?"

Hastening to open the table-drawer, Clark produced a tin cracker box. He opened it and displayed the matches that filled it.

"There you are! Out of sight, and yet they're easy to get at. Much better than the old idea of keeping them in my goldfish bowl."

Hand shook his head dubiously. "Goldfish?" he muttered. "First that abominable hound dog. It was really a blessing when the beast contracted hydrophobia, even though I was forced to shoot it when it leaped at me as I lay on my bed, its eyes blazing and its jaws dripping! Then that wretched cat. And now—goldfish!"

"At least," chuckled Clark, "you won't find them curled up in your chair."

"The next thing I expect to see is a parrot. I tell you, Clark, if you ever bring a parrot on these premises I'l—"

Christopher Hand flung himself violently to the floor. Almost instantly there was a lurid flash, a shattering report, and the glass leaped in scintillating fragments from the window, some splashing into the goldfish bowl and the remainder descending to the floor with a further crescendo.

Crawling out of the range of the window, Hand leaped over beside it and peered warily round the sill. Drawing his pistol, he thrust his head and shoulders through the window. Two shots crashed out. He quickly sprang back to the center of the room, turning a beaming face upon Clark.

"Someone tried to shoot me down!" he cried, as he sped across the room. "I hit him, but I didn't stop him."

The rooms of Hand and Clark occupied the second floor of a small building on the lower west side of New York. At the back a flight of outside steps led down into a court at the rear of the house. Down these steps Hand flew in pursuit of his would-be assassin. Clark, as soon as

he had collected his wits, followed him to the head of the
steps. But by that time the blackness below had swallowed
up his friend. He reflected that Hand was sneaking about
down there with a drawn revolver. In his hand Clark held
his own weapon. If he followed Hand down into the court,
it seemed to him, one or the other of them might acciden-
tally get shot. Shuddering under a cold drizzle that spread
a clammy mantle about him, he started back through the
rooms, intending to gain the street and reconnoiter from
there. He entered the living-room at a lively pace. And
then he started so violently that he all but dropped the
pistol from his hand. A shadowy form stood in the gloom
over near the door to the outside hall.

"Oh!" a low, rich voice exclaimed. "How disappoint-
ing. You nearly jumped out of your skin."

Clark dimly made out that his impromptu visitor was
a girl. He felt like something that has not quite come up
to expectations.

"Is there anything I can do for you?" he stiffly asked.

"I'm sorry," said the girl impulsively. "I shouldn't have
said that, of course; it just slipped out. But I thought you
weren't supposed to be startled by anything at all."

All was clear. Clark melted from his icy attitude.

"I fancy," he smiled, "that you are under the impression
that I am Mr. Christopher Hand. I'm not. I'm his lodging
companion, Mr. Clark."

"What a stupid mistake!"

"Eh?"

The girl gasped and then smothered a laugh. "Oh, I'm
sorry, again," she said. "I'm determined to get into hot
water, aren't I? You see, I had expected to find Mr. Hand
here. Is he in?"

"No," replied Clark, with a shake of his head, "he is
not in. He is out chasing after a fellow who just shot at
him through the window."

The girl evinced no astonishment. Presently she laughed, a low bitter laugh that carried softly across the room.

"I might almost think I were home," she remarked. "Do you suppose it will take Mr. Hand long to catch the man who shot at him?"

"Either he'll find him in a very few minutes, or he'll not find him at all. At any rate, I think he'll be back before long. Won't you have a seat and wait for him?"

She nodded and moved slowly over toward the table. She wore a long black raincoat, that had given her figure a rather ominous appearance, and a little black felt hat was pulled down over her chestnut hair. The lamplight beat softly upon her face, revealed her pretty mouth and the rich color of her cheeks, and reflected warmly from the depths of her large brown eyes. There was something suggestive of wistfulness about her eyes, and the curve of her lips was just a little bit cynical. A lithe, supple body moved gracefully underneath the raincoat. Clark watched her with growing interest.

"I shouldn't stand," he said, at length, "right in front of that window. That is the window the shot came through."

She glanced quickly at it, but more with curiosity than with uneasiness. Disdaining Clark's warning, she slowly unbuttoned her raincoat and laid it back, revealing an attractive dark frock with a soft white collar. Clark offered her his chair. She rewarded him with a frank, warm smile, a smile that invited good fellowship. She slipped quietly into the chair and glanced at the broken window.

"How did it happen?" she asked, a note of excitement in her voice.

"Well, I was sitting right where you are now, and Hand was—"

"Oh!"

The girl stared wide-eyed at Christopher Hand, standing silently in the door to the bedrooms. He had moved

like a ghost, and in the half-light he looked not unlike
one. His long white face shimmered; his gray eyes seemed
to possess an incandescence of their own. Clad in the dark
lounging robe, his tall body all but blended completely
into the black background.

"Did you get him?" cried Clark.

"No. We have a caller, I see."

"Yes. This is Miss, or—"

The girl rose. "Miss Bernice Holloway," she supplied.
"I am very glad to meet you, Mr. Hand. What on earth
have people been shooting at you for?"

Hand bowed with a cold smile. "There are," he said,
"two points about the affair that are obscure. One is the
identity of the person who did the shooting, and the other
is his reason for having done it."

"My," exclaimed Bernice, "that must be nice!"

"Well," said Hand enthusiastically, "it presents a nice
little problem."

"What are you going to do?"

"I fancy Clark and I will investigate it somewhat. The
man had access to the building next door. He dropped
a rope from the roof of it and slid down to a level with
our living-room window. After firing at me he slid to the
ground and rushed down the alleyway to the court out
back. I'm sure I wounded him before he reached it. We
may pick him up in one of the hospitals. Someone may
have seen him lurking about here. What can I do for you,
Miss Holloway?"

"What? Oh, I came here to consult you."

"Upon what?"

The girl peered uncomfortably about. "Could we have
more light—do you mind?" she asked. "It seems so spooky
in here with just that table-lamp. I'm getting quite used
to the idea of people lurking at windows, and all that, but

I think it would be ever so much more cheery if we had another light going."

Clark switched on the overhead light. Hand strode over to the window and drew the curtain over it. Then once again he turned to Bernice.

"Do I understand, then," he demanded, "that someone has been threatening you?"

"Not exactly that. Perhaps it would be better if I started at the beginning and told you exactly what has happened."

"An excellent idea."

Bernice dropped her eyes. The expression of wistfulness became more pronounced about her soft lips. Clark shook his head, sadly and quite unconsciously.

"To begin with," she said, "my great-uncle is Leander Holloway."

"Oh, yes," murmured Hand. "The old railroad magnate."

"Yes. My father, Phil Holloway, is his nephew. Uncle Leander, of course, has several millions in his private treasury, but dad hasn't. Poor dear, I guess he's broke; he always was before he went away. I don't know where he is. He went away eight years ago, and I've heard from him only once—four years ago. The letter was from South America, telling my brother and me how sorry he was and asking us to forgive him. And now—now I almost wish—almost hope that he is dead!"

A tremor crept into her voice. She closed her eyes to stem a flow of hot tears. Hand came quickly to her rescue.

"Perhaps," he said quietly, "I can assist you through this difficult recital. I should be glad to try. It may seem odd, but I have a rudimentary knowledge of the affair that I believe you have come to see me about. You see, I chanced to dine last evening with Police Inspector Gerrity. He gave me a few of the details."

Bernice drew her fine eyebrows into a frown. "Inspector Gerrity!" she cried. "He's the one who has caused all the trouble. He makes me nervous. I wish you'd tell me what he has in his mind."

"Let's leave what he thinks until later," smiled Hand thinly. "For the present let's concern ourselves with what he knows. Perhaps you can augment it. This is what I learned from him last night. There was recently an attempt upon Leander Holloway's life. That is no secret; the newspapers were full of it. There is reason to believe that the attempt was made by one of the old gentleman's relatives. These relatives are not numerous. There is your father, and his two children, yourself and your brother, Roderic Holloway. Then there is another nephew, Robert Bradshaw; a bachelor and your father's cousin. The only other nephew, Randolph Holloway, is dead. He was also your father's cousin. Randolph Holloway left a son, Ludovic Holloway, who is near death from tuberculosis, and his widow, Mrs. Eleanor Holloway. That is all, I believe."

"Yes, that's all of us."

"If you'll pardon my saying so, Gerrity has investigated you all rather thoroughly. We'll begin with the nephews. Without mincing matters, your father was addicted to gambling. His luck was ever bad. In time his uncle became disgusted with him and cut him off. After making a futile attempt to support his motherless children, your father consigned you and your brother to Leander Holloway's care and disappeared."

Bernice smiled pitifully and shrugged her shoulders. "Yes," she said. "All that is perfectly true. But poor Rod didn't get much care from Uncle Leander. He's on the stage, you know, although he hasn't had a part in some time. He went against Uncle Leander's wishes when he took up the theatre. As a result he got the same treatment dad got—cut off. I don't say they both didn't deserve it, but they're both such peaches. Poor dad—he's just a big boy who never could take life seriously. He was a pal to Roddy and me."

She smiled up at Hand. Again Clark sadly shook his head.

"I understand," said Hand, "that you support your brother from the allowance your great-uncle gives you. Very commendable."

"I don't support him," she softly corrected; "I just share with him, that's all."

"I see. Well, to proceed. Ludovic Holloway started out on a promising career in the railroad industry under his great-uncle's patronage. It didn't last long. He turned to wild living and ended up by wrecking both his career and his health. His mother plunged into a social whirl. Between them they used up what money they had, or very nearly so. I understand that your great-uncle turns a deaf ear to their entreaties for financial assistance."

"Yes, they're out too. Poor Uncle Leander doesn't get much comfort out of his relations."

"Nor do his relations out of him, if I may say so. The only one we have not touched upon is the last nephew, Robert Bradshaw. He is in the real estate business. Your great-uncle still backs him on a venture now and then, but Robert Bradshaw has never been a highly successful man in business."

"Well, I really couldn't say."

"But Inspector Gerrity could—and does. Now the facts of the attempt upon Leander Holloway's life are these. Ten days ago he was being driven in Central Park in his barouche, following a custom of long standing. It was quite late in the afternoon. The carriage was proceeding slowly down the west drive near the north end of the park. Without warning a shot was fired by someone concealed in the shrubbery at the side of the road. Whether the horses saw the fellow skulking in the bushes or not, the fact is that they started up violent just before the shot was fired. To this sudden lurch of the carriage Mr. Holloway undoubtedly owes his life. The bullet barely missed him."

"Yes," said Bernice indignantly. "And Inspector Gerrity thinks it was my father who fired the cowardly shot! It's not only absurd; it's abominable."

Hand frowned. "He has his reasons. Shortly after the report of the shot was heard, a man clambered over the park wall, not far from where the shot was fired. He dropped to the sidewalk, crossed Broadway, and disappeared down one of the cross streets. This entire procedure was observed by another man. This witness, according to Gerrity, has identified the man as your father."

Bernice cried out. Her hands fluttered to her breast. "I can't believe that!" she gasped.

"Take it for what it's worth," shrugged Hand. "This witness is a disreputable character. He is a professional gambler, and he knew your father—slightly. Gerrity has ways of flinging out his nets to catch just such fish. I have been thinking it over. Your father and Robert Bradshaw are first cousins. Do they resemble each other?"

Bernice's mouth opened and her eyes grew round. "They do look something alike!" she exclaimed. "What are you thinking? Do you suppose this witness mistook Cousin Robert for dad?"

"It is too early," smiled Hand, "to form any conclusions. I must remind you, too, that you haven't said exactly what you wish me to do for you. I assume, of course, that you wish me to prove that it was not your father who made that attack on your great-uncle's life."

"You're right about it, too," she said quickly. "They all think dad did it, and that he'll do it again. Cousin Robert is particularly sure that dad is guilty. He's been saying all along that poor dad is probably lurking about, waiting to get a chance to shoot Uncle Leander through the window, or something like that."

Hand took a turn up and down the room. The girl followed him with her eyes. Finally he stopped before her.

"It is possible," said Hand, "that someone desired to get me out of the way tonight, so that you couldn't retain me."

"Oh, no!" cried Bernice. "You can't mean that they tried to kill you—that—that shot through the window was intended to kill you so that you couldn't help me out!"

"Precisely," snapped Hand. "Did anyone know you were coming here?"

"Yes—yes, they all knew it. I threatened to retain you when they first started to blame dad."

Hand smiled. "At any time did you announce definitely that you were going to retain me?"

"Yes, just this afternoon. Cousin Robert called a meeting of the clan at Uncle Leander's house. He told us all that he had inside information that the police knew dad was hiding in town. Imagine! He said he wanted to make an earnest appeal—if you please—to any of us who knew where dad was hiding to warn him to get away. I lost my temper and told him, and all the rest of them, that I was coming right over to see you."

"And did you come right over to see me?"

"Well, no, I didn't. Cousin Robert persuaded me to go with him to his office. He tried to talk me out of retaining you. He said the family has been subjected to enough publicity as it is."

"How did your Cousin Robert seem?"

"He was as nervous as a cat. I could tell."

Hand, characteristically thorough, questioned the girl further at great length, hoping to draw forth significant information that she had either considered too insignificant to relate or had merely neglected to mention.

And as they talked, a man on the other side of town
halted on the wet pavement before an apartment house,
on the upper side of West Fifty-seventh Street just off
Fifth Avenue. His coat collar was up, with his chin buried
in it, and his hat was pulled down low over his eyes. This
was very plausibly a protection against the rain, but it
effectually concealed his features. Through the glass-
paneled door he peered sharply into the small lobby of the
house, and made sure that there was nobody there. Then
he briskly entered, still with his chin buried in the collar
of his coat. He ignored the elevator and chose a flight of
stairs instead. On the second floor he stopped cautiously
and gazed up and down the hallway. Again he made sure
that he was alone. Striding diagonally across the hall, he
halted before the door of an apartment and quickly drew
a key from his pocket. He knew that the key would fit the
lock in that particular door; he had tried it on a previous
occasion, an occasion when he had been just as particular
that no one observed him.

The man silently let himself into the apartment, which
was a vacant one, and carefully closed the door. A small
electric torch guided him through the apartment to the
kitchen, situated in the rear of the building. He knelt before the one window in the room and slowly raised it.

The window looked across a black chasm to the rear of
an old brownstone house on West Fifty-eighth Street, one
of a short row of such architectural relics. Furthermore, it
looked directly at the bright rectangle of a window in the
back of the old house, and through it, because the curtain
was not drawn over the window. A little room, therefore,
was exposed to view—the study of an old man whose name
was still a by-word in the realm of commerce.

The man at the window finally rose and swiftly left
the apartment. Behind him, in the kitchen of the vacant

apartment, he left evidence of his visit. He had not closed the kitchen window again. And on the floor beneath it, completely invisible in the blackness, lay a little exploded brass cartridge shell.

2

THEORIES

"Well," said Christopher Hand, satisfied that his client had no further useful information to give him, "the case that you present me with is purely a routine matter. Gerrity is charged with the protection of your great-uncle, of course; we have nothing to do with that. There is but one way for me to convince you and your relatives that your father is not threatening Leander Holloway's life. It becomes our duty, Clark, to find Phil Holloway, or to learn his fate."

"But," cried Bernice, "how on earth can you do it?"

Hand smiled. "It may take a little time," he said. "But there is a good chance that it will not be long before we have results. We shall have to trace him. We have means of doing that. We shall cable to—"

He was interrupted by the strident ringing of the telephone. He snatched up the instrument and placed it to his ear. He answered; then he turned to Bernice and held the instrument out to her. She took it wonderingly.

"Hello—What!—Roddy!—This is ghastly!—Is he dead? —Oh, Roddy, this is perfectly horrible!—Yes, yes, I think he'll go over with me; we simply must get to the bottom of this!—Yes, g-good-bye Roddy."

Her eyes were wide with horror, staring unseeingly. Hand gently took the telephone from her and, replaced it on the table.

"That was your brother?" he asked softly.

The full import of what she had just been told suddenly went crashing through Bernice's intellect. She gasped and placed her hand over her mouth. Then she leaped to her feet and clutched Hand by the arm,

"Mr. Hand!" she cried. "Cousin Robert Bradshaw has just been shot dead!"

This startling information made wreckage of Hand's chain of reasoning. Clark, too, was taken completely by surprise. He showed it; Hand did not. His only reaction was a narrowing of the eyes.

"That was your brother on the phone?" he demanded.

"Y-yes," sobbed Bernice, but she controlled herself the next instant.

"How did he know about this tragedy?"

"Horace Forschell called him—trying to reach me. Horace is Uncle Leander's private secretary."

"Then how did Mr. Forschell know of it?"

"Because Cousin Robert was killed at Uncle Leander's house."

"Indeed! By whom?"

"H-he didn't know! That was all he could tell me!"

Hand's eyes narrowed even more. Bernice tensely watched his face, hoping to read some sign of encouragement there. Her dreadful doubts about her father had increased a hundredfold. But Hand's austere features remained inscrutable.

"I think," said he, "that we should proceed immediately to Leander Holloway's house."

"It's in West Fifty-eighth Street," said Bernice quickly, "right across from the Plaza."

"Yes, I know," said Hand.

He strode over to the closet and snatched up his hat. Bernice, unable to contain herself, ran over to the door and opened it. Clark frantically donned his hat, raincoat and overshoes. He barely caught up with the other two as they were boarding a cab at the curb.

Rain was falling steadily. The reflection of myriad lights transformed the pavements into turbulent streams of black and gold. Objects, large and small, passed back and forth, like restless specters. The cab swung out from the curb and joined the eerie parade. Hand turned his head.

"Miss Holloway," he said.

"Yes," she replied, from the depths of the seat-corner.

"Have you seen your great-uncle's will?"

"Have I seen it? Why, no, of course not."

"I daresay these relatives of yours are down for some quite handsome bequests, in spite of the fact that they don't get along with the old gentleman so well."

"I daresay," said Bernice dryly, "that I'm down for one myself."

"It would seem logical," murmured Hand.

"But," she quickly pointed out, "I'll bet you mine that poor dad is not down for a penny. That's what I told the others. He has no motive for—for anything."

"Hum-m," mused Hand, ruthlessly, "that could be argued both ways. He would certainly be benefiting his children considerably if he hastened their inheritance."

Bernice retired farther into her corner and remained silent. They rode in silence for several minutes.

"The secretary, Horace Forschell," said Hand, "is a young man of parts, I believe."

"Horace?" said Bernice. "Yes, he is."

"You are quite well acquainted with him?" asked, Hand.

There was a short but, nevertheless, a protracted silence.

"Quite well," replied Bernice.

"Thoroughly reliable?"

"Of course he is! Poor Horace. He's in something of a spot, isn't he? I suppose he'll be thoroughly investigated."

Clark supposed he would be, too. Hand made no comment. The taxicab turned into West Fifty-eighth Street and continued almost over to Fifth Avenue. There it pulled to the curb before an antiquated brownstone building. To the left was the great esplanade of the Hotel Plaza. Ahead a steady line of cars moved up and down Fifth Avenue. People trudged by through the wet.

As usual, Hand paid no attention to the cab driver, who was paid off by Clark. All three of them mounted a flight of stone steps, rising abruptly from the pavement to a vestibule erected at an altitude that suggested a speakers' rostrum more than it did the entrance of a private house. Through the glass panel of the door to the vestibule they caught the glint of a policeman's buttons. He opened the door and confronted them. He was inclined to be professionally gruff. Then he recognized Hand and Clark.

"Hello, Mr. Hand," he grinned. "Howdy, Mr. Clark. You know, I had a hunch you two'd show up."

"The inspector here, Martelli?" asked Hand.

"Yes, sir. He's upstairs with Detective Courter. Step right in, Miss, out o' the damp."

As she passed before him, the policeman regarded Bernice admiringly. They entered a small and rather dark front hallway. Bernice led the way up a steep flight of stairs to the second floor. At the head of them a corridor extended to the rear of the house. It branched round the stair well and continued to the front. They were immediately met by a tall, slim young fellow. A pale mustache adorned his upper lip. He was blond, with a sallow face, and wore rimless eyeglasses.

"Miss Holloway!" he cried. "Your brother got in touch with you, then?"

"Yes," replied Bernice quickly. "Did he have it right? Cousin Robert has really been shot?"

He nodded. "I'm afraid he had it straight," he said.

"I presume that this is Mr. Forschell," said Hand quietly.

The young man peered sharply at Hand. "I am Horace Forschell," he said. "I am Mr. Holloway's private secretary."

"So I understand," said Hand.

"This is Mr. Christopher Hand," said Bernice. "And this is Mr. Clark."

"Very glad to know you," said Clark, amiably.

"Can you tell me where Inspector Gerrity is?" demanded Hand.

Again Forschell nodded. "It seems," he said, "that Miss Holloway was far ahead of the rest of us. This was work for you, sir. She was for retaining you over a week ago. I'm afraid she was persuaded not to. Too bad, Miss Holloway, that you didn't do it anyway."

"I'm keeping Inspector Gerrity waiting, I think," said Hand, curtly.

"Oh—I see," said Forschell, somewhat taken aback. "I really didn't know I was detaining you gentlemen. The inspector is in Mr. Holloway's study."

"Is—is that where Cousin Robert is?" asked Bernice.

"Yes," replied Forschell. "The body—nothing has been touched."

"Where is Uncle Leander? How is he?"

"He's in the front living-room. He's quite upset, of course. He was present when it happened. A pity, too. He would be glad to see you, Miss Holloway."

"An excellent idea," cut in Hand. "We will join you with your great-uncle shortly, Miss Holloway. And now, Mr. Forschell, I shall be very much obliged if you will direct me to the study with no further preliminaries."

Forschell nodded coldly and struck off toward the rear of the house. Bernice hesitated, and so did Clark. Then, without a word, the girl hurried off toward the front, and Clark followed after Hand and the secretary. Forschell halted in the gloomy corridor and indicated a closed door almost at the end of it. Hand thrust it open and stood momentarily in the light that flooded through it. Then he and Clark stepped into the study and confronted Inspector Gerrity and Detective Courter.

Gerrity stood huge and ponderous in the center of the small room. He chewed ferociously on a black cigar, with his massive jaw protruded pugnaciously. His keen blue eyes darted a glance at Hand and Clark from under his heavy black brows. In appearance, and in many respects in methods, he was the exact antithesis of Hand. Yet between these two there was mutual admiration and warm friendship; their one characteristic in common was a strong disinclination to reveal that they were imbued with these emotions toward each other. Of Clark, on the other hand, they were both frankly fond. From a professional standpoint, however, he did not altogether enjoy their esteem.

Beside Gerrity stood Detective Courter, a wiry little man, intensely alert. Across from the door stood an empty chair, directly at Gerrity's back. To the left was a flat-topped desk scattered over with papers. On it burned a reading-lamp, the only illumination in the room. Drawn up to the desk was a swivel chair, facing across the desk toward the door. One side of the desk was flush with the wall. At the other side, facing the black square of a window at the back, stood a leather easy chair. And in this chair sat a man—quietly. The brilliant light of the reading-lamp splashed down upon his legs, crossed comfortably one over the other. It picked out his left elbow resting upon the arm of the chair. He was a large man, inclined to portliness. Almost exactly in the center of his forehead, an inch above the bridge of the nose, there was a little round hole from which had flowed a trickle of blood. His eyes were wide open, fixed and staring blankly. His jaw hung down, giving the face an expression of weird, rigid astonishment. He was clad in a dark overcoat, and beside him on the floor lay a soft felt hat. The man was dead.

For a few moments the group in the room stood as silent as the corpse of Robert Bradshaw, Gerrity eyeing Hand. Hand glanced over everything in the room, rapidly. His crisp voice finally broke the stillness.

"Well, Inspector, I see that your patient has got worse."

Gerrity growled in reply. "How do you mean, worse? He's not worse; he's dead, blast it!"

"That chap in the chair? I don't mean him in particular. We are not unlike those in the medical profession, you and I. We are called in upon a case, and in a sense that case is our patient. We employ all the skill and all the science at our command; and then, if the patient gets worse, it's not a bad idea to call a consultation, eh?"

"I wish you wouldn't be so damned frivolous, Hand! This is serious business—it's murder!"

"Hum-m, appears that the shot came through the window. Nothing so unusual about that tonight."

Clark hastily directed his glance to the window. He saw with a nasty start that it was broken. He had been intimately associated with just such a smashed window not long before, and the sight of this one made him remember it poignantly. A few jagged fragments of glass still clung to the frame. For the most part, however, what had once been the window pane lay in glinting pieces on the floor.

"That's right," said Clark, with a glance at Hand. "Windows seem to be danger points tonight."

Inspector Gerrity eyed them curiously. He took the cigar from his mouth.

"I don't get you," he said. "In some parts of New York, I grant you, it wouldn't be so surprising for a bullet to come through a window. But not on Fifty-eighth Street just off Fifth Avenue, blast it!"

"I was speaking," Hand reminded him, "of this particular night. A bullet crashed through our living-room window not over an hour ago. Fortunately, our bullet crossed
the room and hit nothing but Clark's meerschaum pipe on
the mantel."

Clark started excitedly. "I didn't know that!" he cried.
"It escaped me. Of all the luck!"

Gerrity quickly learned all that Hand could tell him
about the episode. He frowned thoughtfully for several
moments.

"So," he said, "you are retained by Bernice Holloway. I
tell you, it appears that her father is behind all this."

"And," said Hand, "I don't need to tell you that if he
is, I'll help you prove it. To date the only evidence that
incriminates him is the word of that gambler, McNader,
that you told me about. Unless you have uncovered something new since last night."

"Not a thing," said Gerrity, with a shake of his big
head.

Hand strolled past Gerrity and sprawled into the empty
chair. He thoughtfully lighted a cigarette.

"Then," he asked, "what have you learned since you got
here?"

"Precious little," growled Gerrity. "I didn't get here
much ahead of you. First I looked this fellow over. They
had a doctor here—thank fortune I got here before he had
a chance to mess things up. I just let him make sure that
Bradshaw was gone."

"Good!"

"He sits right there, just as he was when he was shot.
Nothing has been disturbed. I've sent for the medical examiner, and there are finger-print men down in the car waiting for me to get through. Well, after looking things over
in here, I interviewed the old man. The story is this. Old
Holl—"

"Be accurate, Inspector."

Gerrity paused and glared down at Hand, who kept his gaze quietly upon the floor.

"Of course I'll be accurate!" snapped the inspector. "Well, it was like this. Old Holloway got a note from Bradshaw this morning, the nephew asking his uncle to grant him an interview tonight at six o'clock. Just mark the unusual hour."

"I have."

"Well, Bradshaw showed up. The note had asked that no one be present at the interview, and that the whole thing be kept secret. Old Holloway was waiting for him here, and as soon as Bradshaw arrived he got right down to business. He wanted a loan. He's a real estate operator—or he was—and he wanted to buy an option on an office building down town. It was a big one. They sat—"

"One moment, Inspector. What office building was it?"

"What? Well, I didn't get that."

"Proceed, Inspector."

"Well—blast it, where was I? Oh, Mr. Holloway was sitting in that chair at the desk, with his back to the wall. You see how it is situated now—the swivel chair, I mean. Bradshaw sat just as you see him, facing the window. All at once the glass smashed out. Bradshaw gave a start—just a little start—and then he collapsed back into the chair. That's when he got that little round hole in his forehead. Old Holloway set up a clamor. Forschell and Holloway's old manservant, Simeon Slack, rushed in here. The old gentleman, of course, was pretty badly shocked. Forschell and Slack got him out and sent for the doctor. Then Forschell called headquarters and reported this thing to me. When I got here the old fellow was in a pretty state of nerves. After the doctor gave him a sedative he gave me the information I've just given you."

"Have you seen the note Bradshaw sent his uncle?"

Gerrity pulled an envelope from his pocket. He turned it over and pointed to the post mark.

"It was mailed last night," he said.

He gave the envelope to Hand, who extracted the note from it. It read:

> Dear Uncle:—
>
> I have a request to make. Please don't turn me down this time before hearing my case. I shall call on you tomorrow at 6 P.M. and explain everything. I shall enter the back way, and I'll appreciate it if you let no one know of my visit.
>
> > Your nephew,
> > Robert

After scanning the note Hand turned it over to Clark, who read it carefully. Then he gave it back to Gerrity. Hand got briskly to his feet.

"Look this fellow over," he muttered.

A long stride took him beside the dead man. Gerrity stepped over beside him. He tilted the table-lamp shade so that the light shone full on the face of the corpse. The inspector squinted expertly at the wound in the forehead.

"Twenty-two calibre did that."

"Obviously."

"Didn't bleed much."

"No; a wound of that sort doesn't."

"Killed him instantly."

"Undoubtedly. Accurate marksmanship, Inspector."

Hand whipped about to face the window. Dropping to one knee, he peered sharply through it. Gerrity bent down and did likewise.

"That building back there," mused Hand, "could have afforded an excellent vantage point for a sniper who wanted to shoot into this room."

"Not only could," grunted Gerrity, "but I'll bet it did."

Hand rose quickly to his feet and turned toward the corpse. Clark had been busy. He had smeared the fingers of the corpse with lampblack, while Courter eyed him with uncertainty, and was busy getting Robert Bradshaw's finger-prints on an impression card. He rolled the last finger over the card as Hand turned from the window.

"By the way, Inspector," said Hand, "I don't believe you've searched this man yet."

"I haven't," replied Gerrity. "Courter and I were about to do that when you came in."

"What is your theory, Inspector? Surely you have formed a hypothesis to account for this man's murder."

"Of course I have. You remember I asked you to mark the unusual time set for the interview between this man and his uncle? Well, it's important—very important. There is without question a man seeking to murder Leander Holloway. And he knows Leander Holloway's habits pretty thoroughly. I have learned that Leander Holloway for years has been accustomed to read in this study before dinner. He is always here at six o'clock. The murderer knew that! He got into that building out back and was at a window that looked into this room. Bradshaw had the misfortune to be here. He sat in full view of the window, right where he's sitting now. The shade of the reading-lamp, the only light in the room, cast the light down so that it didn't fall on Bradshaw's face at all. The sniper looked over here and saw him, and because Bradshaw's face was in a shadow, the man thought he was Leander Holloway. He fired at the dark outline of the man's head and—killed Robert Bradshaw."

Hand silently rubbed his chin. Then he peered sharply at the inspector.

"Without doubt," he said, "you have touched upon one or two items of the utmost importance. You didn't mention the curtain of that window. It must have been drawn."

"The curtain was up. That also is customary with the old man."

"Well, there is nothing wrong with your theory, Inspector. The worst of it is that it is the only theory you have. My policy is to construct as many of them as possible and balance them against each other, amassing every atom of evidence in support or derogation of them all, until the correct one achieves such conspicuity that the minimum possibility of error exists."

Gerrity scowled. "What other theory is there?"

"I have no doubt that, after we have more facts in our possession we shall be able to produce a number of them. At the moment, I think, we have another piece of evidence here."

Hand spun about and took a quick step over to the corpse of Robert Bradshaw. He crouched, in his quick, furtive way, and jerked back the right side of the man's unbuttoned overcoat. Protruding above the inside pocket of the coat was the handle of a pistol. Hand whipped out a glove and drew it on. Then taking the butt of the pistol gingerly by thumb and forefinger, he withdrew the weapon and laid it on the desk. To the muzzle of it was attached an odd, cumbersome appliance. Gerrity glared at the pistol.

"He had a gun!"

"So he did, Inspector. And it was equipped with a silencer. Inspector, did you give McNader an opportunity to confront Robert Bradshaw?"

"No."

"You missed a trick very neatly there. McNader said he saw Phil Holloway leap over the wall up in Central Park

just after Leander Holloway was shot at. Bradshaw and
Phil Holloway were first cousins. They once looked a good
deal alike. McNader had not seen Phil Holloway for at
least eight years, and the probability is that he never knew
him very well. Is it not conceivable that he saw Bradshaw
leap over the wall and mistook him for Phil Holloway?"

"Well, maybe it is."

"We can, of course, still confront McNader with Bradshaw's corpse. But all the man's facial expression, his manner of walking, all such characteristics are gone forever.
Even so, we may yet make the identification."

Gerrity flung his arms out in a gesture of exasperation.
"But it doesn't make sense," he objected. "Bradshaw has
been murdered; he couldn't have been back of any of this!"

"Nonsense, Inspector," retorted Hand. "You speak
without reflecting. Suppose Bradshaw, after failing in one
attempt, came here to murder his uncle with a silenced
pistol. He arranged this visit without anyone's having
knowledge of it. But suppose someone did penetrate his
plot, and sent a bullet through that, window, killing the
potential murderer and, thereby, preserving Leander Holloway's life.

"It will require checking up. We must determine whether it is possible to enter and leave this house through the
back without running the risk of being seen. But there,
Inspector, you must admit that my theory is quite as
ingenious as yours. And we must also admit that neither
of them is anything more than a theory."

3

TRAILS THROUGH THE NIGHT

Inspector Gerrity frowned down at the dead face of Robert Bradshaw. Shifting his cigar viciously to the opposite side of his mouth, he glanced up at Hand.

"Well," he growled, "I must admit there's a thing or two to support your theory. But, by thunder, there's something to support mine, too!"

"Decidedly, Inspector," agreed Hand. "I have no doubt, as I said before, that there will be other theories presenting themselves. And there will be much to support them. Let's finish searching this man; we may find something quite as significant as the pistol."

Gerrity nodded and motioned to Courter. The detective quickly emptied Bradshaw's pockets. He produced the customary heterogeneous mass that men usually carry about with them. Gerrity and Hand took an interest in but one object, a notebook. But they found that it contained nothing but business appointments and other notations that Bradshaw had entered in it.

"Well," said Hand, "I intend to investigate the rear entrance of this house."

"That suits me," said Gerrity. "It will take us to the back yard, and from there we can get to the building across the way. Courter, you go down to the front hall and wait for Dr. Richards. When he comes bring him up here to view this body. I reckon, Hand, that this door across from the one to the hall will take us to the back entrance."

Hand jerked it open and found that it led to a flight of dark stairs. Followed by Clark and the inspector, he descended them to a little square hallway, as black as a pocket. Clark whipped out his electric torch and turned it on, its powerful ray striking the inspector full in the eyes. Gerrity squinted painfully.

"Turn it down, Clark!" he yelped. "Blast it, you're always doing that!"

"Excuse me, Inspector," said Clark. "I didn't know you were there."

"See this door?" asked Hand, indicating with his own torch one right across from the stairs.

"Can't see a thing yet," gloomed Gerrity. "I'm half blind."

"It must lead out of doors," said Hand.

He opened it and found that he was right. Another door beside the stairs, he discovered, led down into the basement. A third in the side wall gave entrance into the kitchen. This last had a spring on it to keep it closed.

"It would be simple," averred Hand, "for a man to gain that study upstairs without being seen."

"Sure," agreed Gerrity. "Let's get over to that building across the way and see what we find there."

"Don't touch the doorknobs," cautioned Clark. "We may find some helpful finger-prints on them."

He pulled on a glove and gingerly opened the outside door for his companions. They went out to a small porch and descended some steps to the ground-level behind the house. Hand flashed his torch about. It revealed a wild tangle of brambles and bushes surrounded by a high board fence. Picking out what appeared to be a path through the entanglement, Hand led them off toward the rear of the property. They made their way with difficulty to the fence on the farther side. There was no gate or door in it.

"We're stuck!" grumbled Gerrity. "Now we'll have to claw our way back through this stuff, go through the house, and all the way round the block!"

Hand flashed his light about. "This used to be a rose garden," he mused.

"Well," sniffed Gerrity, "it's a barbed wire entanglement now."

"Ha! I believe I see a door over there."

"I see the house; that's good enough for me!"

"Undoubtedly there's a path leading to that door in the fence."

"Path my eye! We're supposed to be on a path now, aren't we? And the infernal thing isn't—ouch! There, I'm clawed again!"

"Have patience, Inspector. I can't get by you; if you and Clark will retrace your steps no doubt you'll reach a path to the left."

Muttering and grumbling under his breath, the inspector followed Clark back along the overgrown path. He halted at length, disdainfully indicating what had once been a gravel path. Thorny branches from the bushes on either side almost met over the center of it, wet and glistening in the light of his torch.

"There," he said disgustedly. "Looks like a rabbit-hutch!"

Hand forced his way by them, the brambles pulling at his coat. He turned briskly into the old path.

"Come on," he said. "I'll break a way for—"

His voice stopped abruptly. He swung round, flashing his light rapidly in all directions.

"What's eating you now?" demanded Gerrity.

Hand did not immediately reply. His light ceased its maneuvering and remained directed at the ground, as though he had forgotten about it.

"Someone," he said thoughtfully, "has invaded this old garden, and not long ago. The branches along this path are all dragged in the direction away from the fence, as though by someone's forcing his way through them."

Gerrity's eyes narrowed. "You're right, by thunder," he said.

"But," objected Clark, "I don't see the connection with this case. A man couldn't shoot through the study window from here and hit anybody. Not unless the man he was shooting at were glued to the ceiling."

"No," grunted Gerrity. "And he wouldn't stick round here afterward, anyhow."

"Well," said Hand, "there doesn't seem to be any sense in standing here getting soaked. Come on."

They pulled and tugged their way through the brambles to the door in the fence. Hand opened it without trouble. They stepped through into the rear yard of the house next door. A quick circle of Hand's torch revealed that the space was clear of shrubs. It showed, also, that no fence surrounded it.

"This is better, eh?" said Hand.

"My coat is torn," grouched Gerrity.

They picked their way over to the building behind Leander Holloway's house. They located the superintendent of it in the basement. He was a little man. He thought they might be looking for an apartment and at first was very amiable to them. He said his name was Snedick. But when he was given a glance at Gerrity's badge he became highly agitated.

"I want a list," said the inspector gruffly, "of the tenants in the rear apartments on the second floor. Might as well let me see those on the third floor, too. Make it snappy."

Snedick scurried into his apartment and returned with the list. It revealed that there was an unoccupied apartment on the second floor. Hand and Gerrity immediately pounced upon Snedick, who was scarcely more than half the size of either of them, and ordered him to conduct them to the vacant apartment. They entered it and stood peering into the darkness of the empty rooms. Snedick said that the electricity in the apartment had been turned off. Hand and Gerrity got out their torches and flashed them about. The desolation of an empty dwelling, be it house or apartment, struck an uncomfortable sensation into Clark's heart. They proceeded on through a living-room and dining-room and out into the kitchen. Gerrity's light circled about, momentarily passed an open window, and then flew back to it.

"See that?" he cried.

They moved swiftly over to the open window, leaving Snedick mystified behind them in the dark. Clark now got out his torch and directed it on the window sill. Hand and Gerrity peered out of the window into the rainy night, across the way to the bright rectangle of the window in Leander Holloway's study. They could see the slumped figure of Robert Bradshaw's body sitting in the chair, facing them.

"Not such a difficult shot, at that," mused Gerrity.

"No," replied Hand.

Hand stepped back from the window and flashed his light on the floor beneath it. He stooped quickly and picked up a little exploded cartridge. He flipped it into the palm of his hand and directed his light on it. Gerrity moved over beside him and peered at the cartridge.

"Twenty-two calibre," grunted Gerrity.

Clark was still at the window, playing his light over it. "You know," he remarked, "there are plenty of finger-prints on this window."

"Yes," said the inspector, turning to regard it, "Heaven knows whose they are. I'll have my men look it over and get pictures; you don't have to bother with that, Clark."

"And while you're at it," suggested Hand, "you might have some of your fellows go through the building to look for somebody who might have seen the assassin enter this apartment. That's a routine matter that we can well afford to spare ourselves. Well, Inspector, I think that I shall go round and have a talk with Leander Holloway."

"Good," said Gerrity. "I'll go with you. I've already ordered some more men down here; they should be at the house when we get there."

They left Snedick, to his vast relief, to lock up the apartment. As they were leaving the building, Hand made a remark that upset Clark and astonished the inspector.

"So my client," he said, "lives in this building."

"Didn't you know it?" demanded Gerrity.

"Not until this minute."

"Well, by thunder, I didn't hear anyone tell you."

"No; because my eyes told me. I saw her name beside one of the door buttons as we passed through the vestibule."

Gerrity shook his head. "Those eyes of yours," he grinned, "are always up to something. Yes, she lives here, on the third floor, and her brother lives with her."

They started up the street toward Fifth Avenue, their hands deep in their pockets and their heads pulled into their overcoat collars. Clark was wishing that murder investigations, like baseball games, could be called off on account of inclement weather. As they turned the corner and approached Leander Holloway's house, Hand and Gerrity stopped so abruptly that Clark ploughed into them from the rear. A young man was leaping up the steps of the house. He was halted at the vestibule by the policeman. There ensued a voluble discussion between the two, a discussion that was presently interrupted by the inspector.

"The police," he said, as he mounted the steps, "are in charge of this place. You'll have to give an account of—oh, it's you Mr. Holloway."

"Hello, Inspector. I know what's happened. It's all right for me to go in, of course."

"Well, I guess so. This is your client's brother, Hand. Come on."

They all entered the front hall, where Roderic Hollo-way greeted Hand and Clark. He was a handsome young fellow, with the same deep brown eyes as his sister. He was not more than average height, but he was well set up and carried himself with an air of grace and assurance. He was dressed in the height of fashion—spats, gloves, derby hat and black overcoat, and he carried a highly-polished, slender cane.

"Just getting on the job, Mr. Hand?" he asked, with a tilt of his handsome head.

"We have been here for some time," replied Hand, rather coolly. "We are about to have a few words with your great-uncle. Won't you accompany us?"

Gerrity eyed Roderic in none too friendly a manner. Then he swung abruptly about to face Courter, who was standing quietly in a corner of the hall.

"Dr. Richards not here yet?" he demanded.

"No, sir," replied Courter. "Lieutenant Perkins was here a few minutes ago. The doc is on his way to a dinner party, and the lieutenant is locating him."

"Well, I guess he'll be here pretty soon," said the inspector. "I'm glad he's good-natured. You stick with him to see whether you can help. And when he gets through, tell him I'd like a word with him."

They started up the stairs, the Inspector and Hand first and Clark and Roderic behind them.

"So Cousin Robert got it in the neck," mused Roderic.
"Found the monster who did him in, Mr. Hand?"

"Afraid not," replied Hand, shortly.

"Any—ah—clues lying about?"

"Yes; several."

"Suppose someone is pretty thoroughly enmeshed by
now."

Hand made no reply to this at all. Roderic placed the
back of his hand to his mouth.

"Your friend's a communicative sort, eh?" he whispered
to Clark.

Clark smiled and shook his head. Roderic shrugged his
shoulders and climbed the rest of the stairs in silence.
They turned down the narrow hallway toward the front
and entered the sitting-room. The old man sat in a large
chair beside a heavy oak table in the center of the room.
He was feeble and shrunken. On either side of his huge
nose two little blue eyes, deep set in his withered face,
gleamed brightly. His loose lips had been robbed by time
of all their character. But his jaw still jutted out in the
pugnacious manner for which it had always been famous.
His dome-like head, fringed with white hair, bulged out
over his eyebrows. On one side of him sat Bernice, and on
the other stood Horace Forschell.

Leander Holloway glanced sharply up. Bernice rose,
with bated breath, and stood beside her chair. Gerrity
stepped forward, directly in front of the old man, and
indicated Hand.

"Mr. Holloway," he gruffly announced, "this is Christopher Hand. Miss Holloway has retained him to investigate this matter, and I am always glad to collaborate with
him."

Old Holloway glanced reprovingly at Bernice. His
shriveled white hands, almost like those of a skeleton,
twined and untwined restlessly in his lap.

"You didn't tell me, Bernice," he said. "It's a pleasure to meet you, Mr. Hand, though I should have preferred a more pleasant occasion."

Leander Holloway's voice was amazingly rich and strong.

"It is," bowed Hand, "a distinct pleasure to meet you, sir. I am an old admirer of your accomplishments."

"That so?" chuckled the old man. "Well, I'm a real old admirer of yours. My inability to do things myself has made a vicarious reader of me. I have just been reading of that singular case of yours aboard the Airship Jupiter. Marvelous things, those dirigibles. That is the travel of the future. Ah, if I were only young once more!"

"Yes," nodded Hand. "It's a pity that you can't do for the airship what you did for the railroad."

Suddenly old Holloway craned his neck and glared across the room. "Is that Roderic I see there?" he demanded. "Yes, by Jackson, it is Roderic. I'm seeing a lot of my relatives tonight!"

Some of young Mr. Holloway's aplomb left him. He twisted his cane and glanced aside.

"Didn't know whether to come over," he said lamely, "but I finally decided to."

"Now, Mr. Holloway," briskly began Gerrity, "Mr. Hand and I—"

"Yes, yes," broke in the old man excitedly. "How are you getting on? Have you uncovered anything?"

"I'm afraid," replied Hand, "that the case is still a trifle puzzling. But there is a point or two that I think you could clear up for us. Your nephew, according to his letter to you, requested you to keep the matter of his visit tonight a strict secret. Did you carry out his wish?"

Mr. Holloway ground his jaws together, a process for the purpose of adjusting his false teeth. Then, quite energetically, he shook a finger at Hand.

"I did!" he said firmly. "I couldn't imagine what he wanted with all that secrecy, but I was willing to let him have his way about it. I asked Robert what he meant by it, when he got here tonight, but he absolutely evaded the question. Why, it almost appears that he prepared his own murder!"

"It is most extraordinary. As I understand it, then, no one in this house besides yourself knew that you were conferring with Mr. Bradshaw in your study."

"Not a soul. He came in the back way, as he had asked permission to do, and he came right up to the study. I am always alone there at that hour."

"Where were the servants?"

"Simeon, my man, told me that they were all on the first floor. Simeon's been with me fifty years—Simeon Slack. Absent-minded beggar!"

Gerrity noisily cleared his throat. "I checked that," he said. "The cook, the maid, Slack and the housekeeper were all on the first floor. Neither the chauffeur nor the coachman was here at the time. The others heard the window smash, and then they heard Mr. Holloway cry out for help."

Hand turned to Horace Forschell. "And you?" he asked.

"I had stepped out," replied Forschell. "But I was in the house when Mr. Bradshaw was shot. I had just returned."

"Your story's all right," growled Gerrity. "I had one of my men go over to the Plaza to check on it. The clerk says he knows you and that you got some cigarettes just before Bradshaw was shot. He established your alibi, all right."

Forschell's eyebrows went up. "Alibi?" he said stiffly.

"Just a matter of form," said Gerrity, with a wave of his hand. "No offense."

"You say," asked Hand, "that you were in the house when Mr. Bradshaw was shot?"

Forschell passed a hand delicately over his blond hair. "Did I say that?" he retorted. "If I did, I was slightly mistaken. I must be positively accurate, I see. When I returned from the Plaza, I came into the house and heard a commotion upstairs. I rushed right up, fearful lest something had happened to Mr. Holloway."

"What did you see?" Hand shot the question so abruptly that it disconcerted Forschell.

"What did I see?" he repeated. "Why, the first thing I saw was the cook and the housekeeper, all a-flutter, outside the study door. I brushed by them and in the study, to my relief, I saw that Mr. Holloway was all right. He was supporting himself by holding to the desk. Mr. Bradshaw seemed to be dead. I got Simeon to help me get Mr. Holloway in here; then I called for the doctor. I also informed the police and Mr. Roderic Holloway."

"Horace did very well," commended Leander Holloway, slowly nodding his head. "I thank God he got back when he did. I was badly shaken. It seems horrible that this should have happened right before my eyes. Dr. Hartshorne gave me a sedative, which has helped a great deal."

The old man closed his eyes and gently rested his head back against the chair. Bernice quietly stepped forward and stroked his forehead. He smiled faintly, raised his hand, and affectionately patted her arm.

And as they talked, a man rapidly crossed Washington Square. His coat collar was up, with his chin buried in it, and his hat was pulled down low over his eyes. This was very plausibly a protection against the rain, but it effectually concealed his features. He turned down a street and continued on until he was abreast a small restaurant. He turned briskly into an entrance beside it in the same building and mounted a flight of dark stairs. A few minutes later the proprietor of the restaurant thought he

heard an automobile backfire. He went to the front windows and looked out into the street. No automobiles were
in sight.

4

QUENTIN MORLEY

Christopher Hand frowned thoughtfully for a moment. Then he glanced sharply at Leander Holloway.

"Mr. Holloway," he asked, "what did your nephew discuss with you before he was shot?"

The old man opened his eyes and peered wearily at Hand. "He hadn't time to tell me much," he softly replied. "It was a real estate venture. He mentioned an option on an office building down town. He was just about to give me the details when that shot put an end to his life."

"Did he ask you to back the scheme?"

"No. But I had expected him to."

"Were you inclined to favor such a proposal?"

"I was not!"

"Did you tell him that?"

"No. But I would have."

"Would you mind telling us why you didn't intend to grant his request, Mr. Holloway?"

The old man darted his finger at Hand. "I didn't think much of my nephew's business acumen—never did!" he snapped. "He frittered away a good deal of money that he got me to advance to him. Ludovic is the only one of the lot who ever had any business sense. And look how he used it! Dragged his name in the mud and wrecked his career and his health with his wild orgies! Disgraceful young fool! He had—"

"Uncle!" cried Bernice, smiling behind his back.

"I entrusted my name and my reputation to him!" shrilled old Holloway, becoming more agitated. "I put him in a position of influence, and he disgraced my name! I'll have nothing more to do with him! He's a disgrace, I tell—"

"Uncle!" Bernice cried again, now becoming alarmed. "You poor dear, you mustn't get yourself all worked up. Your nerves are in terrible shape from all this, and you know Dr. Hartshorne told you to be quiet."

"Nonsense," he muttered.

Bernice shook a finger playfully at him. "Besides," she said, "you know very well you'll help poor Luddy."

The old fellow fidgeted petulantly in his chair. He grumbled and growled under his breath. Bernice covered a smile.

"I want nothing more to do with him," he sulked.

"Beg pardon, Mr. Holloway," said Hand, soothingly. "Could you tell me what building Mr. Bradshaw spoke—"

"Ah, there you are!" interrupted a voice from the doorway.

They turned about to behold Dr. Richards, the police surgeon, stalk into the room. As he glanced from Hand to the inspector, the doctor wore a peculiar expression on his pleasant face. His black overcoat was unbuttoned, revealing that he was dressed in evening clothes. Behind him Detective Courter was displaying a purple countenance.

"Look here," demanded the doctor, "are you fellows getting down to playing jokes on me?"

"Inspector!" blurted Courter. "That body in the back room is gone!"

Inspector Gerrity said something quick and profane under his breath. As if by reflex action, he spun about and leaped for the door. With the agility of a cat, Dr. Richards got out of his way, and Courter discreetly flattened himself against the wall. Then everybody converged upon the door. A stampede down the hallway ensued.

Gerrity charged into the study and stopped short. He glared at the empty chair where the corpse of Robert Bradshaw had sat. From the narrow hallway came the voice of Leander Holloway, high and tremulous.

"What has happened?" he cried. "What has happened? Don't stop me, Bernice; I must see what has happened!"

"Horace, help me!" cried Bernice. "Uncle, you must come back with me!"

Forschell wriggled out of the group at the study door and disappeared. Gerrity twisted about.

"If Dr. Richards will step inside," he said curtly, "we'll ask the others to remain outside. Courter, get some men and search the grounds back of here. Send in a general alarm."

Dr. Richards entered the study. Clark closed the door on the disappointed face of Roderic Holloway.

"Well," asked the doctor, "what's it all about?"

Hand shrugged his shoulders and nodded toward the chair beside the desk. "There was a dead man," he said, "sitting in that chair when last we were in here. I must say that I don't feel very proud about this. Do you, Inspector?"

More sulphuric undertones emanated from the inspector. He stared fixedly at the empty chair, as though to make sure of his eyesight.

"It seems," mused Hand, "perfectly evident how this body was removed. There remains no doubt that a man was lurking among those old rose bushes out back when we passed through the garden. That door over there, Doctor, leads to a staircase, which in turn leads to a back door of the house. Anyone could steal up here and remove the body without being seen."

"Yes, blast it!" exploded Gerrity. "But what for?"

Again Hand shrugged. "You can't convict a man of a crime," he said, "unless you produce the evidence of it. There is nothing new in doing away with a body."

"But we all saw Bradshaw sitting here dead," objected Gerrity. "And besides that, Dr. Hartshorne examined him and pronounced him dead."

Dr. Richards shook his head. "I agree with Hand," he said. "From what I gather, the murderer didn't know a doctor had pronounced this man Bradshaw dead. He simply removed the evidence of murder, and I'm inclined to think you'd strike difficulties in convicting him even now without it. Well, if you fellows can't provide me with a corpse have to run along. You got me out of an engagement as it was."

"Go ahead, Doctor," grunted Gerrity. "Sorry about this."

"All right," laughed Dr. Richards. "Good luck, you fellows."

He went out and closed the door. Hand dropped to his knees and commenced peering sharply about.

"What are you looking for?" asked the inspector disgustedly.

"Well," smiled Hand, "You are standing on a piece of paper that was not here before."

Gerrity leaped aside and glared at the floor. A folded piece of note-paper lay on the rug, an innocent thing anywhere else, but here a sight to send the blood pounding in the inspector's temples. He pounced upon it. Flipping it open, he read it tensely. Hand slowly rose and brushed the knee of his trousers.

"Interesting, Inspector?" he asked.

"Is it!" crowed Gerrity. "Here, I'll read it. The date is of yesterday, and it's addressed to someone named Quent. Funny name, eh?"

"I should say," replied Hand, "that it's a contraction of the name Quentin. It is derived from the Latin, and means the fifth."

"So?" said Gerrity, without much enthusiasm. "Here, let me read this to you. It says: 'Dear Quent—Now don't start gnashing your teeth just because I can't go out with you tonight. Yes, I'm going out to dinner with Horace, your hated rival. I told you he had asked me, and he looked so pitiful when I suggested a postponement that I just had to give in. He's a nice boy, even if you do think he's a fiend in human form. I really do feel sorry for him. Hope you had loads of fun on your trip and sorry, old boy, to have this waiting for you when you get back—Bern.' I'm inclined to think that is your client, Hand."

"Perfectly sound," agreed Hand. "Let me read it. Yes, it is written in a feminine hand. Not very expensive paper. Those quick upward movements of the pen denote a person of impulse—the pen has sputtered twice, you see. Shouldn't be surprised, Inspector, if my client wrote this note. Gives us a decided advantage if she did. I think we might inspect those back stairs now; we should have done it before."

He gave the note back to Gerrity and opened the door to the back stairs. With the aid of his torch he clearly made out wet tracks on the steps. Gerrity and Clark followed him down. As they emerged through the back door they were confronted by Detective Courter.

"I think," he said, "that the body was carried through this old rose garden and out through a door in the fence over there. I noticed the bushes have been bent that way, as though something was carried through them—something bulky."

"No doubt of it," said Hand. "Inspector, do you notice that alleyway between the buildings on that other street?"

"I do," replied the inspector. "I get you; a car, eh?"

"It would be the very place to leave it."

"No doubt about it. Courter, get some men and see whether you can find anyone who saw a car parked in that alleyway. If you can get a description send it right in to headquarters so they can broadcast it. You get the idea; the fellow left his car in the alley, stole the body, carried it to the car, and drove off with it."

"Right, Inspector."

Courter disappeared in the gloom, thrusting his way through the brambles. The others returned to the study and passed right through to the front sitting-room. They found Bernice vainly striving to interest her great-uncle in a tray of food. Forschell and Roderic looked on apprehensively. Behind his master's chair stood Simeon Slack, a wizened little fellow with a face like a walnut and a pair of black eyes as alert as a squirrel's. Gerrity walked directly over to Bernice and handed her the note he had picked up in the study. She took it wonderingly.

"Did you write that?" demanded the inspector.

"Why—why, yes," she stammered. "Where on earth did you get it?"

Gerrity ignored the question. "Who did you write it to?" he shot.

"To Quent Morley, of course," said Bernice, hesitatingly. "But how did you get it?"

"We got it," slowly replied Gerrity, "on the floor of Mr. Holloway's study. It was dropped by the man who stole Bradshaw's body out of there; no doubt about that!"

Bernice gasped and her face blanched. Roderic scowled at the inspector.

"There can't be anything in that," muttered old Holloway. "This Quentin Morley is a dissolute young rake. One of Ludovic's fine friends! He hasn't the courage to do a thing like that."

Bernice bit her lip and said nothing. Roderic scowled more than ever. Forschell appeared embarrassed.

"Where does Morley live?" demanded the inspector.

There was a protracted silence. Old Holloway glanced sharply over at Bernice.

"I suppose you know, Bernice," he said bitterly. "Tell the inspector."

"I'll tell you, of course," she said. "But first I want to know what you intend to do."

"I shouldn't answer the question at all, Bern," loftily advised her brother. "After all, the whole thing is a whole lot of your business, and none of theirs."

"Keep quiet, Roderic!" snapped old Holloway.

Hand smiled and turned suavely to his client. "There is no reason to become excited over this," he said. "Frankly, I suspect that someone was intent upon guiding our attentions to Mr. Morley. That letter was lying too obviously in sight. My advice, Miss Holloway, is to let us get the matter cleared up as soon as possible."

"Very well," said Bernice, "I'll take you to see Quent."

"Ah—ah—see here!" exclaimed Gerrity. "That won't be necessary, Miss Holloway. It won't be necessary at all!"

Bernice tossed her head and stared coolly at the inspector. "Just the same," she said, "if you want to get there you'd better let me take you. I have no doubt you could find Quent sooner or later, but if you want to see him in a hurry—"

She shrugged her shoulders indifferently and sat down. Clark smiled approvingly at her. Again the old man peered sharply at her.

"Bernice," he admonished, "you keep out of this! It's bad enough without having you mixing yourself up with the police. And I don't want you associating yourself with that worthless Quentin Morley I've told you a hundred times!"

Bernice smiled, went over to the old fellow, and put her arms about his neck. "Please forget all about this, dear," she said. "And do eat something."

"I'll eat nothing," he snorted. "Simeon, take this tray out!"

Simeon started forward. Bernice shooed him off.

"Leave the tray here, Simeon," she commanded.

"I'm bein' drove crazy," cried Simeon shrilly. "First it's take it away, and then it's leave it be!"

"Simeon," cried old Holloway, "I won't stand for any temperament! Mr. Hand, how was my nephew's body spirited away?"

"It seems apparent," replied Hand, "that it was carried out the back way and through the rose garden."

"What in tunkett," abruptly demanded Simeon, "would anybody want with a dead man?"

"Keep your oar out of this, Simeon!" snapped old Holloway.

"I know my place," retorted Simeon, "and I ain't said nothin' yet I shouldn't of!"

"Simeon," shrilled Holloway, shaking his finger at his man, "I've told you for fifty years I'll have no temperament! And take this tray out of here!"

"No!" said Simeon. "I ain't a-going to! You got to eat!"

Bernice and Roderic quickly left the room. Clark went out with them, exchanging a grin with Bernice. The argument between Simeon and old Holloway waxed hotter. Gerrity and Hand followed the others out into the hall. They all descended the stairs, the voices of the two old men clamoring shrilly above.

"Poor Horace," snickered Bernice. "That will go on for a half hour."

They left by the front door, Gerrity last. He paused beside the policeman on guard there.

"I want no one admitted to this house," he sternly instructed the guard. "You understand that?"

"Yes, Inspector."

"That goes for everyone. You may let me in, or any other superior police officer. Mr. Forschell, of course, may come and go as he pleases, or any other member of the household. But aside from that, not a soul goes in or out. Understand?"

"Yes, sir."

"Say," called Bernice, from the steps, "you're going to get in Dutch with Uncle Leander if you don't watch out. I can just see him letting you keep everybody out of the house. Suppose I wanted to go in?"

"Well," growled Gerrity, "for the present the orders I just gave you are the ones you go by. I'll arrange matters more satisfactorily afterward."

Gerrity slowly descended the steps, a huge and imposing figure. Roderic, resting with debonair ease on his cane, glanced at him with an amused smile.

"I say, Inspector," he drawled, "must say you have the front of the house impregnable, but it occurs to me that all the dirty work has been at the back."

From under his heavy brows Gerrity glanced with vexation at the splendid, nonchalant young man. He had taken the back of the house into full consideration. But it did not please him any to have the young man calling it to his attention in that fashion. He walked deliberately by the group and up to his car, parked at the curb. The others followed him, Hand beside the inspector. As they approached the car, from under the instrument board issued the dry, staccato voice of the announcer at the police radio station.

"—body would probably be stuffed into the rumble seat, which would be closed. Stand by."

The voice stopped. The inspector's chauffeur, leaning over the side of the car as he stood on the curb beside it, caught sight of Gerrity and straightened smartly.

"Quick work, Inspector," he said admiringly. "They just put a description of the car over the air."

"Good!" grunted Gerrity. "Hear that, Hand? They must have found someone who saw a car parked in that alley. Where's Captain Dykeman, Kelly?"

"Have him in a second, sir," replied the chauffeur.

Kelly reached into the car and pressed the electric button of the siren, producing a short whine. Captain Dykeman produced himself from between the buildings as though he had been on a wire. He strode quickly up to the inspector.

"Captain," Gerrity briskly addressed him, "I want this house carefully guarded, from now until I give orders to lift it. I expect another attack on that old man's life almost any minute. For the present allow no one into the house except Mr. Forschell and Mr. Holloway's servants. I want a man at the front door, one at the back door, and one in the house. Pick these men carefully! Eight-hour shifts throughout the day and night. And I want every one of 'em a good shot! Tell 'em to be ready to shoot; I'll stand for the consequences."

"Yes, sir," enthusiastically replied the captain.

They all crowded into the inspector's car, Roderic included. Gerrity sat in front beside Kelly. Bernice perched herself on Roderic's lap. Clark caught himself regarding Roderic with unconcealed envy. Bernice and her brother were amused by his look; whereupon Clark flushed, managed an embarrassed smile, and felt exceedingly foolish. Hand sat silent, gazing vacantly out the window. The inspector hitched himself petulantly about to face Bernice.

"Well, Miss Holloway," he demanded gruffly, "where do we go?"

"McDougal Street," she replied, benignly. "I'll show you where to go then, Inspector."

They proceeded rapidly down Fifth Avenue, Kelly keeping the siren going. Clark was having trouble keeping his eyes off Bernice's face. She finally noticed it and smiled at him. He was disconcerted for a moment; then he smiled up at her. She found herself liking Clark immensely. He kept himself in the background, almost shyly, and she found that she could confuse him so deliciously just with a quick glance of her big brown eyes. Yet there was something in his own blue, kindly eyes that told her he was capable of intelligent and bold action should it be required. Ralph Clark, she mused, was all on the surface. She could read him clearly, and instinctively she felt drawn to him. She felt that she could read Gerrity, too, and in his blunt intelligence she found nothing to warm her to him. Hand was an enigma to her. He stirred her curiosity. More to satisfy this than for any hope of getting any information out of him, she abruptly broke into his reverie.

"Have you made no headway, Mr. Hand," she asked, "toward clearing my father of suspicion?"

Hand slowly turned his head to look at her. "The case," he smiled, "appears to be considerably too complex for any sort of solution at this early date."

"But have you made any headway?" insisted Bernice.

"Oh, yes," replied Hand. "But events have been crowding themselves upon us so rapidly that we have scarcely had time to evaluate them. And then we have had no opportunity for mental research into the various significances of the clues that have fallen into our hands. So far we have been rushing rather blindly to keep up with the action that surrounds us. Very shortly I hope to be able to call a halt in order to fathom our position in relation to what we have found."

"Oh," said Bernice, rather weakly.

"If you can give us an unbiased opinion," smiled Hand, "just what sort of person is this Quentin Morley?"

"A big kid," she chuckled. "It's absurd to think Quent is wrapped up in anything sinister. He drinks too much for his own good, to be sure, and he gets into all manner of scrapes. If he got the chance he'd pull a chair out from under the French ambassador, but he wouldn't disturb an alley cat if it were asleep in his favorite chair. Quent's an author, or he would be if somebody would accept his work. He has a rich uncle some place who keeps his body and soul together."

"From the way Mr. Holloway spoke," said Clark, "I gathered the impression that Mr. Morley didn't possess a soul."

Bernice laughed. "He's not in Uncle Leander's good graces," she said. "But that's mainly because he's a friend of Ludovic's. He and Luddy did do some awfully fast stepping. Poor Luddy is finished up with that, though."

The police car shot through Washington Square and into McDougal Street.

"Now where?" demanded Gerrity.

"Slow down a bit," cautioned Bernice. "We're almost there. Pull up to the curb in front of that little restaurant."

They got out to the sidewalk before the restaurant. Bernice glanced over it to a lighted window.

"Quent's there, all right," she said. "Inspector, please don't be rough. One look at Quent will convince you that he's no murderer."

She led them to an entrance beside the restaurant and up the stairs to a dark hallway. Bernice halted them before a rickety door. Light streamed from beneath it and through several cracks in the panels. They listened for a moment without hearing a sound on the other side of it. Gerrity reached forth and banged energetically on the door. There was no response.

"Guess you were mistaken, Miss Holloway," he said gruffly. "It appears that Mr. Morley is out."

"He sleeps like a rock," offered Roderic. "I'll wager he's asleep now. We can go in and see; he never locks his door."

Brushing by Gerrity, he grasped the knob and thrust the door open. His body stiffened.

"My God!" he hoarsely cried.

Bernice Holloway screamed.

On the floor of an untidy room before them lay a large young man. His mouth gaped foolishly. Blood oozed from a hole in the center of his forehead. His glassy eyes seemed to be gazing straight at the ceiling with the vacant stare of a dead man.

5

HEADWAY

Like a man stealing upon another unawares, Inspector Gerrity approached the corpse on the floor. Hand seized Roderic's arm.

"Take your sister out," he ordered.

Pressing a hand to her mouth, Bernice stared with horror at the body of Quentin Morley. Clark took her by the shoulders and gently guided her away from the door. Gerrity spun about and called after him.

"Clark," he said briskly, "tell Kelly to take Miss Holloway and her brother home and then to return here and wait."

"Thank you, Inspector," said Roderic huskily. "I appreciate your thoughtfulness for my sister."

He followed Clark and Bernice down the stairs. Hand knelt beside the corpse. He peered at an object clutched tightly in the right hand of the dead man. It was a blue, blunt automatic. Gerrity closed the door of the room and stepped back beside him.

"Wonder if he left a note," mused the inspector.

"You are assuming suicide, Inspector."

"Looks like it, doesn't it?"

"It does indeed. You'll have to discommode Dr. Richards again."

"Yes. I guess headquarters will know where to reach him now. I'll set them after him. And this time, by thunder, the body will be here for him to examine! Wonder where the phone is."

"Over on the table by the window. If a note was left it should be there too, I should think."

Gerrity crossed quickly to the table. On it were several pencils, two sheaves of manuscript paper, and the telephone. Beside the table, on the floor, was a portable typewriter in its case. Gerrity uttered a subdued cry of triumph. He snatched up a bit of paper from the table and scanned it with avidity. He lowered the paper and smiled over to Hand.

"Here it is," he said. "The note. Always relieved when these fellows leave a note; simplifies matters tremendously. It was doubly kind of him to leave this one. Clears up some of our difficulty."

"Related to the case, then."

"It is. Morley stole our corpse, Hand."

"What were his last thoughts, Inspector?"

The inspector frowned a little at the note. "He could have gone a little further," he said, "without hurting my feelings any. But I'm not bad at reading between the lines. This note is not addressed to anybody, which, if young Mr. Morley had wanted to be real nice he could just as well have done. It just starts right off, and it says: 'I'm thoroughly sick of the whole dirty business. I went through with my end of it and God knows why I did. He's in the river and I almost threw myself in after him. But there's more than one way to usher yourself out of this rotten world, as you've seen by now. I'll be waiting for you in hell's fire.' It's signed *Quent.*"

"I'm glad," said Hand quickly, "that your car is no longer parked below here."

"I get you," nodded Gerrity. "It's up to us to set a trap. Morley expected his pal to come here and find him; the note indicates that. We've got to make everything look innocent. I'll lock the door. We'll make him knock to get in. When we open the door for him he'll get the shock of his life."

After locking the door he snatched up the telephone and got headquarters on the wire. He told them to summon Dr. Richards and ordered a squad of four detectives to report at Morley's apartment, instructing them to enter cautiously and unobtrusively. Hand and Gerrity then proceeded to search the apartment thoroughly. They uncovered nothing that commanded their interest. Neither did Morley's pockets produce anything significant.

The apartment was small and blandly untidy. It was just such a place as Hand would have lived in had he not elected to share lodgings with Clark, who managed, but not without effort, to foist upon him a modicum of neatness in their home surroundings. It was at once a despair and an anomaly to Clark that his friend's precise mind could produce such chaos in their rooms.

Gerrity glanced disdainfully about. "Can't understand," he said, "why people come down here to live like this."

"It is," smiled Hand, "a matter of temperament that you will never understand, Inspector. Some people's personalities bask in surroundings of this sort. I think Mr. Morley was a man after my own heart."

"You would," grinned the inspector.

In a detached sort of way, Hand walked over to the writing-table and sat down in a chair drawn up to it. Gerrity sat down in a chair across the room and stared steadily at the corpse, as if in deadly determination to have it there when the doctor arrived. The knob of the door turned. Although neither of them moved another muscle, Hand's and Gerrity's eyes darted to the door-knob. The door strained against its lock. Then there came a soft knock on it. The two men slowly rose and drew their pistols. Hand moved silently to the door and, as the inspector stepped cautiously to his side, he unlocked it. Their pistols came up together and Hand threw the door open.

Clark stood in the hallway, peering uncomfortably at the muzzles of the two pistols.

"Oh," grunted Gerrity, shoving his pistol back into his pocket.

"Ah, ha," said Hand, doing likewise.

"I hope everything's all right," ventured Clark, peering now at the body on the floor. "I see that you still have the body."

Hand motioned him to enter and closed the door after him. Clark appeared a trifle guilty.

"You deserted us," accused Hand.

"Where did you get to?" demanded Gerrity.

"Well, you see," hastily replied Clark, "Miss Holloway was —"

"So!" broke in Hand, his eyes twinkling.

"I hope you took good care of her," said Gerrity solemnly.

"Go to the devil," said Clark. "The poor girl was terribly shocked. Frightfully shocked!"

"And nobody to look after her," observed the inspector, "except her brother. Fortunate thing you were here, Clark. By the way, is my car parked outside?"

"Right outside," Clark assured him, glad of the chance to change the subject. "I told Kelly to wait."

"Then," said Hand, "go do it again, and this time tell him to wait down at the end of the block, around the corner out of sight. Then come back again, old boy."

Clark departed swiftly. When he returned he found Hand sitting at the writing-table and Gerrity occupying a chair across from him. He locked the door at the inspector's request and gazed vainly about for a chair for himself. Then he knelt beside the corpse and proceeded to get the late Mr. Morley's finger-prints.

Hand found that one of the sheaves of paper on the table was an unfinished manuscript. Morley had added his last efforts to it that very afternoon. Hand idly glanced over it, turning the pages with his thumb. His interest suddenly quickened. He bent over the manuscript and rapidly inspected each page. Then taking in his fingers the last page that Morley had written on, he deliberately folded it and placed it in his inside coat pocket. Gerrity watched him quizzically. But he said nothing.

There came another tap at the door. This time three detectives were found standing in the hall. Gerrity hastened them inside and closed the door again. He rapidly outlined what had been discovered. Since it was the first time Clark had heard of the suicide note, he took a lively interest in it. The three detectives nodded.

"Now," Gerrity told them, "it seems apparent that our man was expected here tonight by Morley. Griffith, you stay in this room, with the light on and the door locked. Snyder, you station yourself in a dark corner of that hall out there. Reilly, you hang out across the street and follow anyone who enters this building through the door at the foot of the stairs. The doctor will be along soon. Stay here until you're relieved."

Having arranged matters thus, the inspector, Hand and Clark left the building and walked quickly down to the inspector's car. They climbed into the back seat.

"Inspector," said Hand, "what do you contemplate doing now?"

Gerrity thoughtfully rubbed his lip. "Well," he confessed, "I don't exactly know what to do. I've got Leander Holloway about as thoroughly protected as I know how. Everything is all set at Morley's rooms. We seem to have followed whatever light there is to the point where it has faded out."

"That," conceded Hand, "is true so far as the light we have followed is concerned. I must say that I don't regret it, even though all that it illuminated was tragedy. But we can, at least, attempt to create a little light for ourselves. The time has come that I mentioned to Miss Holloway, I think, when we could very well pause for a little research. Should you care to visit my rooms?"

Gerrity gave him a glance and a nod. "All right, Kelly," he said; "we'll go to Mr. Hand's."

The car shot away. It was the joy of Kelly's life to get to a destination in the shortest possible time, whether there was any reason for it or not. Gerrity and Hand both approved of Kelly's habit. But Clark regarded it with alarm. Whenever he got into the inspector's car he was always prepared to give thanks if Providence elected to allow him to get out of it again with his natural property intact. He never survived the ordeal without an unfortunate alteration of his mental poise. And on a wet night such as this one, the alteration was quite violent. They rode in silence. Hand was deeply absorbed, as was Gerrity, and Clark could scarcely jam enough air up and down his throat in order to keep alive. Words were not possible with him. They arrived before Hand's and Clark's lodgings several minutes before in all safety they should have. Kelly settled down to wait. The others went on up to the rooms. Hand and Gerrity discarded their wet hats. Clark laboriously got out of his raincoat and overshoes. Gerrity bit the end from a cigar and lighted it. As he started to lower himself into a chair, Hand stopped him.

"One moment, Inspector," he said. "If you sit in here, you sit alone."

Gerrity slowly raised himself. "I don't get it," he complained.

"Clark and I shall be busy in the laboratory. I have developed a theory, Inspector, and I wish to put it to a test immediately. We have not got under the surface of this case."

"Well, I wouldn't dispute that."

"We have not wanted for evidence. It has literally been thrown in our path. I am inclined to suspect it as being deliberately deceiving."

The inspector pondered at some length. "I've learned enough," said he, "not to believe everything I see."

"Precisely. Shall we go into the laboratory?"

Without waiting for a reply, Hand turned and stalked across the living-room. Followed by the other two, he strode into the laboratory and switched on the powerful light. Then he turned abruptly to Gerrity.

"Let me see that suicide note."

The inspector took it from his wallet and silently handed it over. Hand stepped briskly over to the bench and sat down on a stool. Laying the note down before him, he pulled a gooseneck lamp to him and turned it on, directing the brilliant light down upon the note. Then he screwed a watchmaker's magnifying glass into his eye and bent his head over the note found on Morley's writing table. He examined it thus until Clark and the inspector were convinced he had turned to stone. But then he twisted the gooseneck so that the light shone full at his face. He held the note up before his eyes, dropped the magnifying glass from his eye-socket, and peered searchingly at the handwriting, his eyes glittering in the strong rays of the light. After several minutes of this intensive scrutiny, he placed the note back on the bench and laid beside it the page he had purloined from Morley's unfinished manuscript. There ensued a long and painstaking comparison of the handwriting on the two sheets of paper. For a half hour Gerrity and Clark tensely watched him. Abruptly Hand grimly nodded and glanced up at them.

"Inspector," he said, with his eyes glinting, "I can say in perfect confidence that Quentin Morley died at the hands of a murderer."

Gerrity raised his hand deliberately and pointed at the note. "Forgery?" he asked.

"Forgery," affirmed Hand. "You will wish corroboration, but I am convinced that Morley never wrote that note!"

"No," growled Gerrity; "if you say he didn't, then I'll swear he didn't. It's fairly evident, is it?"

"It is excellent forgery," replied Hand. "No amateur, this fellow! The ordinary faults of the forger are present, but in a far lesser degree than in a good many specimens I have scrutinized. Not very noticeable—but he has pressed down a trifle too heavily upon the pen. And he has not altogether escaped the obsession to go back over the work to improve upon it. But it is admirable work!"

Gerrity held his cigar forgotten before his lips for several long moments. "I'll be damned!" he said at length.

"And now," said Hand, "let me have that letter of Bradshaw's."

Gerrity's jaw dropped. "Bradshaw's—letter?" he asked incredulously. "Surely that's no forgery!"

"I mean to make sure. Let me have his notebook, too."

Hand took the letter and the notebook from Gerrity and laid them before him on the bench. Then he glanced up smartly at Clark.

"Examine that suicide note for Morley's fingerprints," he ordered.

"Hardly necessary, is it," objected Clark. "If you've determined the note is nothing but a forgery, of course Morley's finger-prints are not on it."

"Examine it, Clark," insisted Hand. "And don't let my deductions induce you to be careless."

Clark nodded and picked up the note. He worked with gold dust and microscope while Hand worked with fiendishly brilliant light and magnifying glass. Gerrity browsed between them, peering alternately over their shoulders, and growled unconsciously in his throat. Hand completed his task first. As he lifted his head Gerrity peered sharply at him.

"Well?"

"This work is not as good as the other."

"Forged, then!"

"Unquestionably. As I say, the forger was not quite so careful with this effort. He considered, no doubt, that this letter would never be suspected. Here you are, Clark, when you get through with the note examine this letter for Bradshaw's finger-prints. Fortunate thing, old boy, that you got them before his corpse was spirited away. Found any of Morley's on that note?"

"Not a one yet."

"I don't think you will. But make certain, Clark, make certain."

Gerrity strode up and down the little laboratory, growling worse than ever. He stopped and glowered at Hand.

"Blast it all!" he exclaimed. "I get the slant all right on why the suicide note was forged, but I'm hanged if I can add the other one up and get anything that looks right!"

"The answer," mused Hand, "is not one to be arrived at in an instant. I think, however, that it quite definitely indicates that Bradshaw was lured to his death, and that Leander Holloway was not the intended victim, after all."

"But," protested the inspector, "how did a fake note sent to Holloway lure the man it was supposed to come from to his death? The whole blasted thing is the craziest stunt I ever barked my shins on!"

Hand set a match to his pipe. "Hold on, Inspector," he chuckled. "You are being guilty of letting this singular murderer mislead you. That is precisely what he desires.

In fact, I begin to suspect that his whole plot is predicated upon that as an essential. I am beginning to see—"

His voice trailed off to silence. He pulled reflectively on his pipe for several moments; then he forgot to do even this. The pipe went out. Hand apparently was gazing straight through the wall. The inspector was about to speak. Clark glanced round at him and checked him. Gerrity frowned and glanced silently at the floor. Minutes seeped away.

"Inspector."

Gerrity jerked his head up and fastened his eyes sharply on Hand.

"Inspector, I think I have penetrated the darkness somewhat. Not much, but somewhat."

"Let's have it."

"First, of course, we must go back to the motive."

"Well, that's no mystery, anyway. It's the old story, of course, of a potential legatee attempting to hasten his windfall. The poor old gent has become the target of someone who is mentioned in his will. But there's one more who could be after him—Phil Holloway! No doubt Phil has been cut out of the will, if he ever was in it, but his children haven't. His motive is probably the strongest, for he surely owes his children a lot. At any rate, to name them over, we have Phil Holloway, Bernice and Roderic, Ludovic and his mother, Eleanor Holloway. That's only five; one of 'em is at the bottom of this!"

Hand got his pipe going again. "I can find no fault with that, Inspector," he said. "But the enormity of the plot escapes you, I think. Unless I am wrong, of course, which is altogether possible. According to my theory, when you state that one of these people is anxious to acquire his inheritance before the time nature has set for it, you state only a portion of the fact. What would you say if he were intending to receive not only his own portion, but the portions of all the other legatees as well?"

Gerrity started. He stared at Hand.

"What!" he exclaimed. "You mean that this fellow is systematically exterminating everyone mentioned in the will but himself?"

Clark nearly upset the microscope. "Look here!" he cried. "If that's the case Miss Holl—all these people should be protected!"

"Exactly!" snapped Hand. "Inspector, I suggest that you go to the phone at once and have headquarters detail a guard to each one of them."

"I'll do it, by gad!" shouted Gerrity, as he leaped through the door.

"Just a minute!" said Hand sharply. "You might just as well make this a two-edged weapon, Inspector. Detail a detective to each one of them, by all means. Tell them that they are to protect the lives of the persons to whom they are detailed and—to prevent any one of those persons from taking the life of another. The best way for them to do both is to keep all these people ignorant of the fact that they are under guard."

"You're right!" growled the inspector.

As he gave his instructions to headquarters, Clark strove mightily to get his mind back on his fingerprint work. At length the inspector set the phone down and returned to the laboratory.

"Well," he said, "everybody will be covered very shortly—everybody but Phil Holloway!"

"Yes," sighed Clark, "but he wouldn't harm his daughter. I mean—what I meant to say was that it's a point that we shouldn't overlook."

"His son, too," grinned Hand, "would seem to be safe from damage from that quarter, don't you think, Clark? You are neglecting your work, my boy."

"Look here," said the inspector, "your theory is very loosely held together, after all, Hand. I don't think Quentin Morley was due for any bequest from old Holloway, and he was the second victim."

"Yes, I know," said Hand quietly. "But Miss Holloway was interested in him. There is nothing to prevent taking a possible elopement into consideration there, and such a thing might very well have wrecked the complete consummation of the plot."

"Miss Holloway," said Clark firmly, "merely felt sorry for Morley. I'm sure that—"

"You are still neglecting your work," grinned Hand.

"It does seem," mused Gerrity, "that your reasoning is pretty flimsy there."

Hand nodded. "It would be," he retorted, "if my reasoning were based purely on the possibility of an affinity between Morley and Miss Holloway."

"I think it's ridiculous!" snorted Clark.

"But," went on Hand, "there is another consideration. Morley was on intimate terms with at least three members of the family. He may have discovered something that it was not wholesome for him to discover. All this is pure hypothesis, of course, but it may lead somewhere."

"Well, I agree with you," said Gerrity. "But let's get back to that letter of Bradshaw's—or the one that was supposed to be his. How in blazes could it have lured the man to his death?"

"Here again we merely hypothesize," pointed out Hand. "The forged letter did not, of course, summon Bradshaw to his uncle's house; it merely set the stage for the murder. It induced us to believe at first that Bradshaw was there merely by coincidence when the shot was fired through the window. And from that we were naturally led to the conclusion that Bradshaw died by mistake, and that it was Leander Holloway who was the intended victim. Thus we were led,

Inspector, to throw all our protective powers in the future about Leander Holloway, leaving the others to this fellow's mercy. Leander Holloway's turn would come last."

"Seems logical," agreed Gerrity. "The forged letter was sent to Leander Holloway, and that accounts for his expecting his nephew there tonight. But what drew Bradshaw there?"

"A spurious telephone call would do it," replied Hand. "And one would reasonably expect with Bradshaw dead no trace of the call would be left behind. But there may be a trace, nevertheless. We shall have to see whether we can determine Bradshaw's exact movements and by going back over the trail, we may encounter someone who heard him receive such a call. Surely it must have been a puzzling one to him. For that reason, if his part of the conversation was overheard, it would have been marked. It is far too late in the night to work on that now. But I shall proceed with it the first thing in the morning."

Gerrity wrinkled his brow. "It's headway, anyhow," he said gruffly. "And I'm with you on it. I haven't laid all my cards on the table, Hand, and I'm a little ashamed of it. Here's my last one. Phil Holloway has returned to this country. He was in New York the day Leander Holloway was shot at in Central Park!"

"I wondered," said Hand softly. "You picked up his trail through the immigration officials?"

"That's it," replied Gerrity. "He came in from the Argentine. He landed in New York the day before that shot was fired at his uncle. He registered at a hotel, and the morning after that attack on Leander Holloway he disappeared. I haven't been able to tie it up, but it's a fact that during that time his son and daughter were out of town on a house party."

"Good work, Inspector," nodded Hand. "Well, at least we are getting some threads into our hands. If only one of them is genuine it should lead us to the core of this affair. Finished, Clark? What's the report?"

"Everything negative," replied Clark. "There are none of Morley's finger-prints on the suicide note, and there are none of Bradshaw's finger-prints on the letter."

"That settles that, then," said Gerrity. "Well, I think I'll get along and see that all our defenses are in shape."

Clark and Hand accompanied him to the door. As he was leaving, the inspector turned smilingly to Clark.

"Maybe," he said, "I should double the guard on Miss Holloway."

Running his fingers through his hair, Clark shook his head. "It would suit me," he said.

"Don't worry, old top," said Gerrity, his smile fading. "Well, Hand, thanks to you we've learned a lot. And your theories were interesting, if nothing else."

Hand smiled and glanced down. "I may have some more for you in the morning," he said. "Good night, Inspector."

Not long after Gerrity had gone, Clark was nervously getting ready for bed. Christopher Hand sat in his easy chair in the living-room, a circle of light cast upon him by the table-lamp. A curl of smoke rose from the bowl of his pipe. There was no other motion anywhere in the room, save the curtain gently swaying at the broken window.

6

A WALK THROUGH THE PARK

Clark was up early the next morning. He had slept very badly, the night having been punctuated by some agonizing dreams. Throwing on a dressing gown, he hastily left his room and found Hand just about to go out.

"Where are you off to?" he demanded.

"Ho, Clark!" cried Hand, turning at the door. "Up, are you? The inspector and I are going back over Robert Bradshaw's trail. I just had him on the phone."

"Not Bradshaw!"

"Scarcely. I'm afraid you're not at the height of your powers, my boy. A cold shower should sharpen you up, and get your eyes open beyond the halfway mark."

"What happened during the night?"

Hand shrugged. "The sun succeeded in getting round the earth and coming up over us again. Not many minutes ago, either. But that is about all that appears to have happened. This task of ours is not going to be very interesting. Tedious job, but necessary. I thought I'd let you sleep. However, if you'd like to come along I'll wait."

"Matter of fact I—ah—thought I wouldn't. Think I'll just sit around this morning, Hand."

"Excellent—and give her my best regards. And look here!"

"I—ah—what?"

"Nothing about her father, mind you! That is Gerrity's affair; he expects our confidence. You may report fully on anything we have uncovered. I really wish that sometime this morning you will look in on old Leander Holloway for me."

"I'll go over right away if you wish."

"Not necessary, Clark. But you might drop in later on. You will probably connect up with the Inspector and me there during the course of the morning. See you later."

Hand went out and closed the door. Clark remained in the center of the room, pulling at his lip. He passed up and down for several minutes. Then he smote the back of an easy chair and snatched up the telephone. He gave a number that he had looked up the night before and retained in his head. Several seconds later a sleepy voice answered his call.

"Hello."

"Is—is that you, Miss Holloway?"

"Oh, yes, I think so. Wait till I look."

"How's that?"

"Oh, it's you, Mr. Clark! Goodness, what's happened, right in the middle of the night like this?"

"Nothing. I was worried about you. You're all right?"

"It's almost too early to tell, yet. But I think so."

Clark grinned. Then he drew a long breath. Then he laughed gayly.

"By Jove, I'm relieved to hear that!"

"Haven't you been to bed?"

"Yes. I just got up. I was—well, I just wanted to make sure that you were all right."

Bernice turned the phone aside and giggled. She settled back on the pillow and pulled the covers up under her chin, one slender white arm extended out to hold the phone.

"Hello!"

"Yes, Mr. Clark?"

"Oh. I thought you were gone—or that something happened."

"Something did happen; I pulled the covers up. It's cold, and I just have a nightie on, you know."

"That's—ah—yes."

Bernice giggled again. "You're so naive, Mr. Clark. But I like you immensely for it."

"I say, do you? Then I shall become perfectly child-like!"

"This morning?"

"Yes, this morning. How about a walk through the park? It's a beautiful morning after the rain. Clear and crisp."

"I think it would be lovely. But when? It's awfully early, or doesn't that matter?"

"That doesn't matter at all!"

"All right; I'll be waiting. Good-bye."

"Good-bye."

Clark hung up the phone and, somewhat beside himself, inadvertently knocked it on the floor. He picked it up again and took a long breath. It had been many a year since Ralph Clark had made a date with a girl. He had gone to war when scarcely eighteen. Later, at college, he had discovered that charging across No Man's Land was a simple thing compared to preparing to entertain a young lady. After two or three terrible evenings, when his tongue had become hopelessly cloven to the roof of his mouth, he had avoided all females as he would have the plague. This was one thing that had endeared him to Hand.

But now Clark went whistling merrily off to his shower, pausing long enough to give a flourishing punch to the bell-button that would signal his landlady to start his breakfast. He was dressed and waiting before Mrs. Flemming appeared with the tray. She found him humming a lively air, adjusting his tie before a mirror, a mirror that

Hand had placed judiciously for quite a different purpose. His greeting was hearty and profuse. Mrs. Flemming
beamed upon him.

"Ah, Mr. Clark," she said, "'Tis the fine lookin' man
that you are. With them lovely soft eyes that can glitter so
elegantly once in a while and your jaw."

Clark flushed. "Do you really think so, Mrs. Flemming?" he earnestly asked.

"I do! A pity you ain't got a mustache like my Tim,
before the Lord took him, God rest his soul! There ain't a
girl wouldn't drop dead at the sight of you."

"Oh, really now, Mrs. Flemming!"

"Don't I know. Just because I'm four times the size I
was when I got Tim, me eyes is the same, ain't they? Come,
set down to your breakfast. Mr. Hand been out all night
ag'in? More's the pity, for 'twas a night fit for nothin' but
snakes—the b'astes!"

"No, Hand was here. He's gone off already, though."

"Without his breakfast! He'll be killin' himself with his
didoes!"

Mrs. Flemming departed murmuring dire predictions
concerning the health of Christopher Hand. Clark devoured his breakfast. He took a cab and was soon pushing
the button outside Bernice's door. There was an exclamation of dismay from within, and Bernice flung the door
open. She was wearing a peach-colored negligee that literally dripped with lace. The sun beaming in a window at
her back made a rich halo of her lovely hair. Her cheeks
and lips were as fresh as morning roses, and her eyes were
wide in mock horror.

"So quick!" she cried. "Why, you just hung up!"

"I—I—"

Clark could say nothing. In fact he could do nothing,
except just look at her. The roses bloomed even more riot-

ously in Bernice's cheeks. She gazed at him softly, and reaching out, she took his arm and guided him over the threshold.

"Oh, good morning!" said Clark, explosively.

Bernice laughed. "You're so darned refreshing!" she said. "Now, you sit still and look at the pictures while I dress. I've just had a snack of breakfast; so I'll be ready to go with you in a jiffy."

Her feet, in little mules that seemed to be mostly vivid green feathers, seemed literally to fly across the floor. Clark slowly lowered himself into a chair. He sighed and smiled dreamily. Bernice took an amazingly long time, but still Clark sat and smiled. Finally she burst forth, wearing a little black hat and tying up the belt of a polo coat.

"There," she cried, "wasn't I quick?"

"Just like lightning," stoutly affirmed Clark.

Bernice opened the door and halted abruptly. "Oh," she said, "what about poor Roddy?"

"Poor Roddy?" inquired Clark. "What's the matter with him?"

"He's still asleep," replied Bernice. "Who will get his breakfast?"

"I know that one," grinned Clark. "Roddy will."

He took her arm and waltzed her out of the apartment, shutting the door none too gently behind them. Bernice laughed. They went down in the elevator and out to the street. The old apprehension of a miserable silence the whole time he was in the company of a girl had plagued Clark all the way over. Now it had entirely disappeared; in fact he had forgotten all about it. They talked gayly as they walked rapidly up Fifth avenue. But as they crossed Fifty-eighth Street to enter the park, the foreboding old mansion of Leander Holloway frowned down upon them. Bernice glanced nervously over at it.

"I wonder," she said, "if—"

"Everything's all right," cut in Clark quickly. "Hand told me so before he left this morning."

"Where has he gone?" asked Bernice.

Clark told her of the events of the night before, valiantly resisting a potent urge to give her Gerrity's information about her father.

"Then Quent was murdered!" Bernice's voice broke. "I'm afraid! I'm afraid that someone—something has all of us on a frightful list—something that doesn't seem human!"

Clark gripped her arm. "No harm shall come to you!" he said grimly.

Bernice caught her breath and looked up at him. Clark did not see her; he was staring straight ahead.

"You don't look," said Bernice, "like the same man who came into my apartment this morning. Somehow I feel safe with you."

Clark halted abruptly and swung about to face her. They looked straight into each other's eyes. "You are safe with me," he said evenly.

They scarcely moved for more than a minute. Then, quietly, they walked on again. Finally Bernice looked up at Clark once more.

"Is there really," she asked, "someone who wants to—to kill us all. I have a ghastly feeling that we are all caught in an invisible net! It's horrible!"

"Heaven only knows what it is," replied Clark. "But then, you must feel the confidence that I do. Hand and Gerrity are the perfect team. Hand is the scientific reasoner. Gerrity is deficient in that respect, and he's intelligent enough to realize it. But there is none so proficient as he in coordinating all the mechanics of police work. He it is who sends forth those myriad filaments that go out from police headquarters, many to all parts of the world. Hand is uncanny in detecting physical clues scattered on or near the scene of a crime, clues that even escape the inspector. And with those clues and the material that the inspector is able to glean, by a process of scientific reasoning and deduction Hand can penetrate the screen of mystery to an amazing degree."

"It sounds perfectly marvelous," said Bernice, not without some degree of uncertainty. "But results do come so slowly!"

Clark squeezed her arm. "They'll come fast enough pretty soon," he assured her lightly. "Let's think of something more cheerful. Let's talk about you. Do you like living in New York?"

Bernice shook her head and smiled wistfully. "I don't know just how it's possible," she said, "to be lonesome in New York, but I am. I think I always have been. Do you like to live in New York?"

"Hate it! Detest it!"

A laugh escaped from Bernice's parted lips. "Then why do you go on living here?"

"Because Hand will live nowhere else."

"Oh, yes. I suppose you do find more work here than any place else."

"That's true. But you couldn't pry Hand out of New York anyway. I'm very fond of Hand. And it's wonderful to be able to study him at his profession as intimately as I'm privileged to do. It has been my one interest in life for several years now. You see, I get nothing material out of the association. I have an income that is quite sufficient I have also inherited a ranch in Texas that I'd like to live on."

"That would be wonderful!"

"Nothing better! Riding, fishing and shooting! And it's near enough so that a car would get you to Fort Worth in a little over an hour, if you suddenly craved the city. A trip to Europe or South America now and then, too, just to provide the proper variation to life."

"Gorgeous!"

Thus auspiciously launched, for the first time in his existence Ralph Clark poured into a dainty ear a complete record of his past and a delineation of his hopes for the future that was not so complete. The status of his emotions of the moment he studiously avoided mentioning. Bernice listened attentively. She said nothing with her lips but, to Clark's immense gratification, much with her eyes. She walked close to his side, supple and graceful. Clark knew that his feet were on the ground, but surely his head was in the rose-flecked and fleecy clouds that hung in the spicy air so far above the turmoil of the city. At length they walked in silence, a silence that Clark strangely reveled in. Their steps took them back toward Leander Holloway's house. Bernice glanced across at it. Abruptly her mood changed.

"Well," she sighed, "I wonder what's happened there."

Clark took his pipe from his mouth and looked at her. "Why, nothing, I imagine," he said. "What makes you wonder?"

"Oh, I don't know. I just keep expecting something dreadful to happen. Let's drop in and see whether everything's all right."

Clark nodded in agreement. They struck across in front of the Plaza. Suddenly, as they were about to cross the street to the house, Bernice halted Clark. Again he took his pipe from his mouth and looked sharply at her. She was peering across the street to the vestibule of Leander Holloway's house. He followed her gaze and saw a man descending the steps. He was bundled up as though it were the middle of winter, with a heavy overcoat and a woolen muffler wrapped tightly about his neck. His shoulders were sagged. His face, even from across the street, looked as pale as the clouds in the sky. But there was not even the faintest tint of pink in his sunken cheeks. He was muttering to himself, as people in weakened conditions do when emotionally aroused, even when they are as young as he was. This was Ludovic Holloway.

"Oh, Luddy," called Bernice.

Ludovic glanced across and saw her. He hesitated a moment; then he shuffled across the street to join her. His remarkably brilliant eyes snapped angrily in the pallid background of his face. He scarcely paid any attention to Clark when Bernice introduced them.

"What are you doing out, Luddy?" demanded Bernice anxiously. "You know you're not supposed to be. And I suppose you walked over, too."

"Yes, I walked over!" snapped Ludovic, savagely. "Why shouldn't I. Suppose I did cave in; I'd be damned well out of this! And now the old devil has shut his door to me! He has a policeman there, if you please. I was turned away like a common beggar!"

"Oh, no!" cried Bernice. "The policeman couldn't have understood."

"He did understand!" fumed Ludovic. "He told me his orders were not to let me in! He'll pay for this, the old fool! I haven't long—"

He was seized with a violent attack of racking, dry coughing. Bernice's eyes filled with compassion. She took Ludovic gently by the arm.

"Go home, Luddy," she said softly. "I'll speak to Uncle Leander. You must go to the mountains, and I know he'll take care of it. Take a taxicab, now, and go on home."

"Haven't the price," muttered Ludovic bitterly.

"Never mind that, old man," said Clark. "We can finance that, all right. There's a cab—ho, taxi!"

Ludovic drew his wasted frame erect. "Thank you," he said coldly; "I'll walk."

"Just a loan, Mr. Holloway," smiled Clark. "A dollar will do it, eh? Pay me back anytime. Here's your cab."

"Thanks," thickly muttered Ludovic.

He got into the cab and was driven off. Bernice sighed and shook her head. She flashed Clark a glance of gratitude and they crossed the street. A policeman stepped out of the vestibule as they started up the steps, and peered stolidly down at them.

"How do you do, Stacey," said Clark. "Are the Inspector and Hand here yet?"

"No, Mr. Clark, they ain't," replied Stacey. "Was you plannin' to go in, you and the young lady?"

"Yes," grinned Clark. "That is our fell intention."

Stacey was inclined to be garrulous, whenever he got the chance. He perceived that a chance was at hand. He explained that he would endure anything for Mr. Clark, barring death, and he would endure even that if it were painless. But he pointed out that if he let the young lady into the house, the demise that he could expect at the hands of the inspector would not be a painless one. Mr. Clark could go in, he would take a chance any day on the inspector's condoning that, but the young lady must not pass the portal he was set to guard. In vain Clark expostulated. At length Bernice ended the controversy.

"Never mind," she said. "I'll go on home. You go in, and when Inspector Gerrity gets here try to get him to change these silly rules."

"All right," agreed Clark. "But I'll walk around with you."

They left Stacey victorious and circled round the block to Bernice's apartment house. At the entrance she turned warmly to him.

"This has been wonderful," she said.

"Indeed it has!" vigorously concurred Clark.

"It's done me a world of good," she said. "I can't thank you enough. Hope I'll see you over at Uncle Leander's before long."

"I'll move heaven and earth to get you in! We must take another walk or—or do something else before long. It's been the greatest pleasure, Miss—"

"Why don't you call me Bernice?"

"By Jove, may I! And my—ah—my name is—"

"Good-bye, Ralph."

She laughed gayly and whisked through the door. Clark thrust his hands into his overcoat pocket and inhaled deeply of the fresh air. He turned abruptly and strode back to Leander Holloway's house. Stacey stuck his head out of the vestibule and peered anxiously down upon him. Seeing Clark's beaming countenance, the policeman's face cleared. He liked Clark.

"There you are," he said heartily. "You look twice as cheerful now, Mr. Clark. It's a relief, ain't it, to be able to shake a skirt when she's clawing onto you like that?"

Clark tripped on the steps. He shut his mouth with a snap and stalked stiffly into the house without a word to Stacey. The policeman removed his cap and dubiously scratched his head.

7

THE POLICE IN CHARGE

Hand and Inspector Gerrity were on a hot trail. It was the trail of the late Robert Bradshaw, and they had been on it for several hours. But until a few moments before, it had been cold and unproductive. It had led uneventfully all over town, and had required the keenness of both of them to follow it, finally turning from cold to hot in the dingy office of a money-lender. They were there following a slender clue when it happened. The man, Mr. Gutzon, had willingly admitted to them that, unfortunately, he held Robert Bradshaw's note for a small loan.

"When did you see Mr. Bradshaw last?" asked Hand.

"Just yesterday afternoon," replied Gutzon. "I went around to his office to see about liquidation, you know? It looked very bad. His stenographer—he had none any more."

"Did you see Mr. Bradshaw?"

"Yes. He could do nothing about the note."

"Did he happen to get a telephone call while you were there?"

This question had been fruitlessly put to everyone they had interviewed.

"A telephone call? Why, sure, he had one. Nothing important, I guess. I wouldn't have noticed, but I was impatient to talk to him. He had a lawyer inside talking to him. The lawyer wanted money, too, and I—"

"Just a minute!" barked Gerrity. "The telephone call's what we want to hear about. What did you overhear?"

Gutzon appeared astonished. "Why, Officer, not much. It was just something about his family. His uncle. He's very rich."

"Tell us exactly what you overheard!"

"Oh! Not much, Officer. I heard Mr. Bradshaw ask why his uncle hadn't called him himself. Then he said something about he thought it was funny but he'd be there. That's all."

Gerrity glanced meaningly at Hand. "It's enough," he growled.

"Who was the lawyer," asked Hand, "who was talking with Mr. Bradshaw while you waited?"

"Sidney Malloy," replied Gutzon. "You know him? He's in the Stallman Building."

"Very well," said Hand abruptly. "Thank you very much."

Twenty minutes later they walked in upon Sidney Malloy, Attorney at Law, who was not altogether unknown to either of them. Gerrity hoped some day to have him in the Tombs.

"Hello, Sidney," he said.

Malloy glanced up from some papers he was scanning on his desk. He chuckled.

"Hello," he said. "You look like a couple of undertakers."

"Maybe we are," growled Gerrity. "Sidney, let's have the low down on Robert Bradshaw."

"Then you really are a couple of undertakers, aren't you?" said Malloy, cheerfully. "Bradshaw's bumped off, eh? Inconsiderate of some guys. I have a client who'll lose some money, and I'll lose a fee."

"All right," snapped Gerrity; "spill it, Malloy!"

"Nothing much to spill," smiled Malloy. "Bradshaw was up to his neck in debt and—"

"And you were putting the thumb-screws on him, eh?"

The lawyer grinned crookedly. "It's not my business how the debts are contracted. My job is to see that my clients are paid."

"No sense of trying to pull that stuff on us," said Gerrity. "We're up on your game, you know. This time it's likely to be serious. What hook did you use on Bradshaw?"

"I fancy it would be a woman," said Hand.

Malloy sat back in his chair and frowned. "I think," he said, "that I should warn you two to be more careful in what you say to me. I wouldn't like to have to institute proceedings—"

"Shut up!" Gerrity leaned across the desk and glowered fiercely into the lawyer's face. "Come clean, Malloy, or I'll take you in, by heaven I will!"

Malloy squinted at him for a moment. Then he shrugged his shoulders and smiled his crooked smile.

"Don't get excited, Inspector," he said. "Bradshaw wronged a poor young woman. She came to me. Any man with a spark of humanity in his breast would have gladly done what I did. My fee was to be very small—hardly enough to cover my expenses."

"Yeah?" drawled Gerrity, expressing no credulity at all. "Well, let that go for now. We'll look into all that very thoroughly, and don't forget it! You were driving him; we know that. You drove him to the point of taking a shot at Leander Holloway."

"That so?" said Malloy. "Well, if you know, why ask me?"

Gerrity glared at him for several long seconds. "All right," he snapped. "As I said, we'll let that go for the present. But there's something we want right now. You were in Bradshaw's office yesterday afternoon."

"What of that?" asked Malloy imperturbably.

"Bradshaw received a telephone call."

"That's right."

"What was Bradshaw's end of the conversation, as well as you can remember it?"

"It was a personal call. Very short, too, and Bradshaw seemed to be puzzled by it. I think I can quote what he said. He answered the phone and listened a while. Then he said: 'Yes, I can stop in then, but if my uncle wants to see me, why doesn't he call me himself?' He listened again, and then he said: 'Why does he want me to do that?' At last he said it seemed very funny, or something like that, but he promised to do whatever he'd been asked and hung up. That's all there was to it. Now then, you fellows, never say that Sidney Malloy ever shirked his duty as a citizen. I am for justice, first, last and always, and the blinder it is the better I like it."

He grinned at Hand, who smiled and shook his head. After a stoney, lingering glance at Malloy, the inspector turned deliberately away from him.

"All right," he grunted. "But I'm not through with you, Malloy."

The inspector stalked out of the office. Hand leaned across the desk to the lawyer.

"Did Bradshaw," he asked confidentially, "take that shot at the old man up in the park, Malloy?"

"I wouldn't know," grinned Malloy. "But I can tell you what I think, and I wouldn't do that for everybody, Hand. I think he did."

Hand veiled his eyes and nodded. "And you're not an idle thinker," he said; then he turned abruptly and followed the inspector.

"What did you ask him?" inquired Gerrity.

Hand pushed the button for the elevator. "He thinks Bradshaw fired that shot at Holloway up in the park," he replied.

Just then the elevator stopped for them. They rode down in silence and did not break it until they were on the sidewalk. They got into the inspector's car.

"What do you say we look things over," suggested Gerrity, "up at old Holloway's house."

"Good idea," nodded Hand.

Kelly started up without waiting for further instructions.

"Well," growled Gerrity, "We've cleared up the telephone call. Your deduction was correct. I have a very good idea who probably called Bradshaw, too. Proving it is not going to be so easy."

"But we are a step nearer it, Inspector."

"No doubt of that. And then we've established a motive for Bradshaw's having made an attempt on his uncle's life."

"And we've come very near to proving that he actually did."

"Yes, blast it, but Bradshaw's dead himself! The only threat to Leander Holloway seems to have gone with him. And yet I seem to be expecting more deviltry all the time!"

Hand stared blankly at the floor of the car. "So do I," he said.

They found Clark chatting very agreeably with the old gentleman. The two sat at the table in the upstairs sitting-room. With keen interest Holloway glanced up at them.

"Well!" he cried. "Come in, gentlemen, and sit down. Mr. Clark and I are most anxious to hear what you have to report. He has told me of your mission. You seem to have fathomed the case very adroitly."

"Then," said Hand, "you no doubt realize that your nephew was sent here by deceit last night."

"Yes," mused Holloway. "I see it all very clearly now. Last night, during the brief space of time that we talked, I thought Robert and I were at cross purposes. I see now that we were. I thought he had asked to come to see me, and he thought I had requested him to call. He had mentioned to me a day or two before that he had perceived a wonderful opportunity in real estate. He had hinted that he would like my backing. That was what made Robert a fool! He wouldn't come right out with a proposal!"

"Did you discuss it last night?"

"Well, hardly that. I asked him point blank whether he wanted to discuss the deal he had mentioned before. He said he was eager to. Just then the shot came through the window and killed him."

"We have learned," said Hand, "that someone called him at his office yesterday afternoon and asked him to come up here to see you."

The old man's eyes shone with admiration. "Remarkable!" he exclaimed. "You must tell me exactly how—why, there's Bernice."

The inspector spun about to face the door. With an exclamation of pleasure, Clark leaped to his feet. Hand also turned to the door. And there stood Bernice, smiling mischievously at the inspector.

"Look here!" exclaimed Gerrity. "How in blazes—I mean—I mean, how did you get in?"

Bernice calmly drew a red enamel cigarette case from the pocket of her polo coat. She placed a cigarette between her lips and lighted it. Nonchalantly blowing a cloud of smoke in Gerrity's direction, she walked right by him and stopped before Holloway. The old man grinned up at her in keen delight.

"Going to forgive me, Uncle," she smiled, "for disobeying you last night? I'm frightfully sorry."

The grin faded from the old man's face. He jerked his head about petulantly. But in the end he was forced to smile. He patted Bernice's hand and glanced proudly about at the three men.

"What would you do," he chuckled, "if you had a grand-niece like that? I shouldn't forgive you, my dear, but I guess I'll have to."

"See here, Miss Holloway," sternly demanded the inspector, "how did you get in here? I left orders for no one to be admitted."

"You did?" cried Holloway, in sudden anger. "Why, that's impertinent of you, sir! I resent it! This is my house!"

Gerrity colored. "I did it for your own protection, Mr. Holloway," he said. "I'd like to know, Miss Holloway, how you got by my police guard?"

Bernice smiled to herself. She leaned against the table and flicked her cigarette at an ash tray. Clark could not have kept his eyes off her if he had tried, and he was not trying.

"I came in the back way," said Bernice. "The policeman out there was amusing himself by trying to entice the cook's cat out from under a rose bush. I'm afraid he didn't see me. The cook's cat is a lawless thing and wouldn't, of course, have anything to do with your policeman. I almost bumped into another policeman in Uncle Leander's study. He was half out the window watching the other one down in the garden. The part of him that I saw couldn't see me. I just tip-toed across to the door and—here I am."

Old Holloway chuckled delightedly. Gerrity was filled with mortification. Behind the inspector's broad back, Clark was silently clapping his hands for Bernice's benefit. Hand glanced at his friend, and his eyes twinkled.

"Oh, Bernice," cackled Holloway, "you're just as lawless as the cook's cat. If you were only a man, Bernice, if you were only a man! I'd make the world sit up and take notice of you!"

"Well," said Gerrity, "I think I'll be getting—"

A hoarse shout came from below. It was followed by the sounds of someone's rushing up the stairs. A door opened

somewhere and another shout rang out. Gerrity quickly
drew his pistol. And then Ludovic Holloway scurried into
the sitting-room. He collapsed against the table, his bony
hands clutching for support. He turned his livid face over
his shoulder and glared by the astonished inspector to the
door. His strength seemed entirely spent. Two policemen
charged into the room.

"Try—to keep me out—would you!" panted Ludovic.
"Uncle, I tell you—my blood is on your hands if—"

"Say!" bellowed Gerrity. "What's the matter with you
men? How'd this fellow get in here?"

"This fellow sneaked by me," complained Stacey, "while
I was talkin' with the woman. Here she is!"

Eleanor Holloway, plump and red of face, forced her
way between the two policemen. She looked frenziedly at
her son, who lay gasping against the table.

"He's dying!" she shrieked. "You've killed him! He's going to—"

"Be quiet, Eleanor!" testily ordered the old man. "The
boy will be all right if you give him a chance to get his
breath. The young fool should know better!"

Eleanor Holloway drew herself up and glared at the
uncle of her dead husband. She pressed her lips ominously
together.

"Oh!" she exclaimed. "How can you sit there and watch
him dying before your very eyes? Your own flesh and blood!
You, who have millions let him die for the want of a few
paltry dollars!"

The old man scowled up at her. Bernice stepped quietly
up to Eleanor and took her hand.

"Please compose yourself, Cousin Eleanor," she entreated. "Uncle Leander will look out for Ludovic. He'll
see that he's taken care of."

"Then why doesn't he do it?" demanded Eleanor, jerking
her hand away. "This is none of your business, Bernice.

You're taken care of. He supports you. Where would you be, with your good-for-nothing father deserting you?"

Bernice winced. Then she smiled her wistful smile and moved over behind Holloway's chair.

"Uncle!" croaked Ludovic. "You've got to give me the money to go to the mountains! I won't need much. I can't stay here and die like this! For God's sake, help me! I can't stand it another minute, dying like a rat caught in a trap!"

His hysterical voice sent a chill through Clark. Ludovic dropped his head into his hands and fell to sobbing. His mother continued to glare at Leander Holloway. Almost automatically everyone's eyes turned upon the old man. He sat immobile, his chin sunk upon his chest. For a long minute he remained thus, while an oppressive silence filled the room. Finally he slowly raised his head and glanced coldly at Eleanor.

"I have no affection for Ludovic," he said. "He has no one to blame but himself. And perhaps—you. You squandered your husband's fortune, and you allowed Ludovic to ruin his health."

"How can you—" angrily began Eleanor.

"Be still!" snapped Holloway. "You had better take your son home and have the doctor for him. I will think this whole thing over and let you know. In the meantime— good-bye!"

Eleanor Holloway quivered with rage. Her eyes blazing, she took Ludovic by the arm and led him out, the two policemen stepping respectfully aside for them.

The house boasted a small elevator of the personally-operated type. It made the stairs unnecessary for Leander Holloway's aged legs. Moreover, it was a consuming pride and joy to Simeon. He used it at every opportunity, and often when an opportunity was tardy in presenting itself he was prone to manufacture one. His room, as well as those of the other servants, was on the third floor. According to the cook's computations Simeon traveled up to it on an average of sixteen times a day, and as many more trips down again. Gus Staub, Leander Holloway's chauffeur, estimated that Simeon had traveled eighty-nine miles on the elevator since it had been installed.

At the moment Simeon had a legitimate reason for using the elevator. The mail had been delivered a half hour ago. It was high time he took it to the

master, and, he would have done it before this had he not been kept busy in the kitchen. He emerged to the front hall and picked up the mail, including a thick, rectangular package. He stepped over to the elevator. To his astonishment it was not at the first floor. He could have sworn that he had left it there. It was all the more astonishing because Simeon was the only one who ever used it. Holloway always insisted upon his old manservant's piloting him up and down in it. The other servants were skeptical of it and used the stairs. But Simeon was very absentminded. He pushed the button and waited. He was diverted by Ludovic and his mother, who descended the stairs and left the house. Stacey came down right after them and stationed himself once more in the vestibule. Simeon did not notice that the elevator took longer to reach him than it should have, had it come only from the second floor.

8

DEATH STALKS INVISIBLE

There was a silence for a moment in the upstairs living-room after the mother and son had angrily departed. Hand glanced keenly at Leander Holloway.

"Where is Mr. Forschell?" he asked.

The old man glanced up from a frowning reverie. "Horace?" he said. "He's down at my brokers'. If you want to make some money, Mr. Hand, I could let you in on a little secret."

"Afraid I'm too busy," smiled Hand, "to keep track of the market."

Simeon stalked into the room and laid the mail on the table. Gerrity's eyes were at once glued on the oblong package. He poked viciously at it.

"What's that?" he demanded. "It might be a bomb!"

"Well, it ain't," snapped Simeon. "It's a book."

"I didn't ask you," growled Gerrity. "How do you know it's a book, anyway?"

"Because he's always a-getting' 'em," retorted Simeon. "And why don't you say who you're askin' such foolish questions?"

"Tush, Simeon, tush!" admonished Holloway. "Yes, Inspector, it's a book. I have an anonymous admirer who sends them to me. He knows that I enjoy reading. I am a prolific reader. Very little else that I can do, now. I

wouldn't know what to do without it. In my prime I was
an active man, Mr. Hand. I slept five hours a day, and the
other nineteen I put to good use!"

"Your energy was legend."

"There was excitement in living! With a word or two
I moved mountains of human affairs. I shaped the desti-
nies of men and huge industries. I begrudged the hours
of sleep, for every waking hour was a fascination! And
now—now I am in a cage, a cage from which there is
no escape. I am hedged about with infirmities. I devour
the newspapers, reading of the surge and sway of mighty
affairs. Always the urge is upon me to get my hand back
on the throttle. My arm—my arm is too weak to support it
there. Men like I am can live too long, Mr. Hand."

"Well, well. But few men are happy to have the interesting life to look back upon that you have. Your days
should be filled with excitement merely by living over the
stirring episodes of your career."

"Bah! A man who lives in the past is a living ghost!
Life lies ahead; nothing but ashes lie behind. I still throw
a grapnel into the future—there is always the market, I
thank Providence! For the rest, there are my books. Artificial, but at least it is enough to keep me from going to
decay."

He sat brooding in his chair. Bernice slipped over to
him and put her arm about his shoulder. Horace Forschell
walked into the room.

"Ah, good morning, gentlemen," he said. "Mr. Holloway, Mr. Sinclair is at the door and that policeman won't
let him in."

"Eh!" exclaimed the old man. "Jasper is being refused
admittance? See here, Mr. Inspector, you are making a
prison of my house!"

"Well," grinned Bernice, "the prison's full of holes,
then."

"Miss Bernice," cackled Simeon, "she got in. Policemen are all dunderheads!"

Gerrity glared evilly at him.

"Simeon, you are impertinent," accused Holloway.

"I ain't," said Simeon.

"I say, Mr. Holloway," broke in Hand, "why not have the policemen stop people at the door until you have decided whether you want them to come in? The policeman within the house can keep them under surveillance while they are here. Is that suitable, Inspector?"

Gerrity was only too relieved to have a settlement of the matter. "It's all right with me," he said. "What do you think, Mr. Holloway?"

"That would seem to be a perfect arrangement," replied Holloway. "But for heaven's sake, Horace, tell Jasper to come up."

"I'll attend to it," said the inspector.

He soon returned with Jasper Sinclair, Leander Holloway's attorney. The lawyer was short and portly. He had a splotched, pudgy face and was quite bald. He peered inquisitively about the room through heavy eyeglasses. He nodded to Holloway.

"Just stopped in to see how you were," he said. "I must say you are being given ample protection. The police are to be congratulated."

"Not if you'd a-been here," chuckled Simeon. "It's been awful!"

"Say, blast it!" exploded Gerrity. "Will you lay off the police?"

"Simeon, keep still," ordered Holloway.

Clark and Bernice caught each other's glance. They turned away to hide a smile.

"Glad to see you, Jasper," said Holloway. "You must stay to luncheon. And you other gentlemen as well. Simeon, go tell the cook to prepare for guests."

They all accepted save Bernice. To Clark's disappointment, she declined in order to go home and get Roderic something to eat. She said good-bye to them and left the room. Forschell followed her out.

"Bernice," he said plaintively, "we were supposed to have a date last night."

"Oh, yes, Horace," she said, "but that dreadful murder of Cousin Robert! I couldn't go out last night."

"No, of course not," agreed Forschell. "But how about tonight?"

"Please, Horace, don't ask me for tonight."

"All right."

She saw the disappointment in his eyes and quickly relented. She took his arm impulsively.

"Don't look so gloomy," she smiled. "We'll make it tonight."

"Fine!" cried Forschell. "You're an angel, Bernice, really you are. You're the most beautiful—"

"Listen," she laughed, "I haven't time to hear that all over again! See you tonight, Horace, about eight-thirty. 'Bye."

She ran lightly down the stairs. Forschell stood at the head of them and gazed down at her with shining eyes. She turned back at the door and waved gayly. Then she was gone. Forschell smiled to himself and slowly descended the stairs.

Soon after, the others slowly followed old Holloway out of the sitting-room. He shuffled down the hall to the door of his bed-chamber. There he halted and turned to them.

"I'll meet you downstairs in a moment," he said. "If you see Horace tell him to send Simeon up for me."

They found Forschell staring out of a window into Fifty-eighth Street from a parlor at the front. He departed when Sinclair repeated Holloway's request.

"I'm very much worried about Mr. Holloway," confided Sinclair to Hand, Gerrity and Clark. "Do you feel that he is in any danger?"

"I really think he is quite safe," replied Hand.

Sinclair glanced nervously about. "There seems to be," he said, "an ominous atmosphere in this old house. Perhaps its just because it is so old. I've always thought it rather gloomy. I came here many times as a child. My father was Mr. Holloway's attorney until his death a few years ago."

Holloway soon joined them. The sudden influx of guests for luncheon was having a distressing effect upon the staff in the kitchen. The old man called Simeon twice, demanding an explanation for the delay. Simeon's patience, no better than his master's, also gave out.

"Here I am ag'in," he exclaimed, "right in the middle! Cook's fussin', and you're fussin', and I'm in the middle!"

"No temperament, Simeon!"

"I ain't in a temperament; I'm mad! I'm good and mad!"

A maid timidly announced luncheon, bringing an abrupt end to the conflict. The tiff was forgotten as easily as it had occurred. Holloway led his guests into the dining-room. He took Hand by the arm and expressed a keen interest in the detection of forgery. Hand replied with a rather technical dissertation on the subject. They arranged themselves about the table, Hand at Holloway's right.

The dining-room was one to command immediate interest. The heavy black oak furniture was old and richly carved. The walls were of the same wood, paneled and extending high to the ceiling, where the black beams were all but indistinguishable in the subdued light. Oil portraits, mellowed with age, looked down from the walls, their heavy, gilded frames glinting dully. In one corner stood a china-closet containing myriads of wine-glasses of every description. Only the white napery of the table,

snowy under the light from a chandelier, relieved the dig-
nified, comfortable atmosphere of the room. It was, alas,
the dining-room of a bygone day, when ladies and gentlemen knew how to enjoy a formal dinner.

The maid set cups of bouillon before them. Sinclair was
a man with a robust appetite. But his spoon was in action
only a second before Clark's. Clark had scarcely touched
his breakfast. Holloway seized the salt and pepper shakers
and proceeded to season his soup with much gusto. Warmed
to his subject, Hand continued to talk after the others
had all started to drink the soup. But then he picked up
his spoon and started to eat with his customary speed.

"Hold on, Mr. Holloway!"

Hand's voice fell about the table like the shattering
of brittle glass. A spoonful of soup poised above his cup,
Holloway looked inquiringly at him.

"What say, Mr. Hand?"

"Put that spoon down!"

With a puzzled countenance, the old man gingerly
laid his spoon beside the cup. Hand snatched up the salt
shaker placed between his own and Holloway's places at
the table. It was a large one, with generous holes in the
cap. Holding it to the light, Hand peered sharply at it. He
glanced at Holloway.

"This shaker," he pointed out, "dwarfs the others on
the table. It will sprinkle salt in much greater abundance
than the others before us, too."

Holloway peered quizzically at him. "Well," he said, "it's
no bigger than my pepper shaker. I like plenty of seasoning,
and I've no patience with those dinky little shakers."

"This salt shaker, then," asked Hand, "is for your personal use?"

"Indeed it is," chuckled Holloway. "But you may use it,
Mr. Hand. You've used it already, and you notice I didn't
object."

Chuckling merrily, he picked up his spoon and dipped it into his cup.

"Put that spoon down!"

The old man started violently. His spoon clattered into his cup.

"'Pon my soul!" he exclaimed. "What are you up to, Mr. Hand!"

Hand made no immediate reply. Setting down the salt shaker, he reached over and picked up Holloway's cup of bouillon. He dipped a small quantity of the soup into his spoon and delicately tasted of it. The rest of them, in stony silence, regarded him fixedly. He reached out, set the cup in the center of the table, and placed the salt shaker beside it. Then he leaned slowly back in his chair.

"That bouillon," he said, "is poisoned."

Their eyes turned in horror upon the innocent-appearing cup in the center of the table. A dry sob escaped Sinclair.

"P-poisoned!" he chattered. "My God, I'm poisoned!"

"I think not," calmly replied Hand. "Mr. Holloway and I were the only ones who got any of it."

"I can feel it!" cried Sinclair, in a strangled voice. "I'm poisoned! It's all the same soup, I tell you!"

"Keep your head, Jasper!" snapped Holloway. "Now, Mr. Hand, what is it?"

"Arsenic," replied Hand. "It was introduced into our cups from that salt shaker. Just notice that shaker. Do you see the steel-gray, brilliant crystals mixed in with the white salt? The city chemist will give us an official verdict on it. But I am thoroughly satisfied that it is arsenic."

Forschell shot to his feet, capsizing his chair. "Mr. Holloway," he cried, "has drunk some of that soup!"

"And I, too!" said Sinclair hoarsely. "Quick, Mr. Forschell, get Dr. Hartshorne! Tell him to come over immediately!"

Forschell whisked out of the room. Hand turned quickly to Holloway. The old man sat staring at the cup of bouillon, his hands spasmodically grasping the arms of his chair.

"Don't be alarmed, sir," said Hand earnestly. "If you are in any danger then so am I, for I used that salt shaker, too. You took but a spoonful of the bouillon. I was watching you, fortunately, and I noticed an expression of uncertainty cross your face when you drank it. I knew at once when I tasted my own soup that it contained arsenic. I succeeded in stopping you before you had taken another spoonful. I am quite positive that the amount of arsenic that you have consumed is not sufficient to cause any ill effects whatever."

"I sincerely hope you're right!" said Holloway fervently.

"No doubt of it," Hand assured him. "You will feel more comfortable, though, if your own doctor tells you that. It is just as well that Mr. Forschell is summoning Dr. Hartshorne."

"I am positive," muttered Sinclair, "that I am becoming ill. Here, Mr. Hand, for heaven's sake take a whiff of this!"

With trembling fingers he picked up his bouillon cup and all but threw it across the table to Hand. Hand's eyes twinkled. He took the cup and sniffed at it, knowing full well that arsenic has no odor.

"Perfectly all right," smiled Hand. "You may drink it, Mr. Sinclair, without any hesitation."

He offered the cup back to the attorney. Sinclair refused to touch it. He pulled out a handkerchief and mopped his brow.

"Drink it?" he asked, aghast. "Merciful heaven!"

Holloway regarded Hand curiously. "How under the sun," he asked, "did you know so quickly that the poison came from the salt-shaker?"

"Because it flashed through my mind that it might have."

"It is difficult to drag a statement from you, Mr. Hand. Then, will you tell me how such a thing flashed through your mind?"

"Because I noticed that you use so much salt."

The old man grinned and gazed admiringly upon him. "You think fast, Mr. Hand," he said.

Gerrity had been frowning darkly through the whole episode. "What I want to know," he asked, shooting Hand a glance, "is whether it's flashed through your mind who put that damned stuff in the salt shaker!"

"What do you think, Inspector?" countered Hand.

"I think," snapped Gerrity, "that anybody who's been in this house today could have done it!"

"Precisely," agreed Hand.

"But, see here," exclaimed Sinclair, "surely that does not include me!"

"Yes!" growled Gerrity. "Surely it does."

"Preposterous!" cried Sinclair.

"Don't be an ass, Jasper," said Holloway.

"But it is preposterous!" insisted Sinclair. "I had absolutely no opportunity to do such a thing!"

"You didn't, eh?" growled Gerrity. "When I let you in I spent a few minutes giving the guard at the door some instructions. When I came back in from the vestibule, you were still in the hall. If you didn't go on upstairs during that time, where did you go?"

"I remained in the hall the whole time," stiffly replied Sinclair. "Having been treated like a criminal when I arrived, I thought it best to allow you to escort me up to Mr. Holloway. I have been practicing law for a number of years, you know, and I am well aware of the senseless grounds upon which policemen will base their suspicions.

I took no risks, and now you're attaching suspicion to me anyhow!"

"You're an ass, Jasper," sniffed old Holloway.

The maid came in with a tray to get the bouillon cups. Seeing that they were still all nearly full, she drew back.

"One moment, Hilda," said Holloway. "Do you gentlemen wish to finish your soup?"

"I don't," quickly replied Sinclair, "whether I've spoiled it or not!"

Even Gerrity shook his head, and Clark was emphatic in his refusal.

"I guess," said Holloway gloomily, "that Horace won't want his, either. You may remove the dishes, Hilda."

The girl stepped quietly forward. She reached for the cup in the center of the table.

"Don't touch that!" snapped Hand.

The girl nearly dropped the tray. Forschell returned to the dining-room. He was about to say that the doctor would be right over, but before he could say a word Sinclair, with a choked sound in his throat, leaped abruptly to his feet. He threw his napkin on the table.

"I cannot stay!" he cried. "Forgive me, Mr. Holloway, but the thought of putting another morsel of food into my mouth terrifies me!"

Holloway glanced up at him. He smiled, but his smile was not unmixed with contempt.

"Of course, Jasper," he said. "I can understand only too well what your feelings must be. Of course you may go; think nothing of it, my boy. But you're not the man your father was!"

Sinclair walked nervously over to the door. He halted, as if in uncertainty, and turned back. His eyes encountered those of Inspector Gerrity, bent suspiciously upon him. The lawyer hastily strode out of sight through the door.

9

IDENTIFICATION

Inspector Gerrity left Leander Holloway's house soon after Sinclair had departed. In his pocket was the salt shaker with its potentially dangerous contents. He also had with him a small phial, supplied by Hand from one of his amazing pockets, and in it was a sample of the bouillon from Holloway's cup. The inspector was bent upon turning them both over to the city chemist for an official analysis. He had arranged to meet Hand and Clark later at his office in police headquarters.

Holloway was disposed to take Hand's word for it that he had not consumed enough arsenic to harm him. He insisted, however, upon being examined and prescribed for by Dr. Hartshorne. Hand, he and Clark sat in the parlor and discussed the latest developments. Dr. Hartshorne soon arrived, explaining that Forschell's message had taken a little time to reach him. He agreed with Hand that no harm had been done. But more to reassure the old man, than anything else, he took Holloway upstairs and gave him some medicine. Hand and Clark prepared to leave the house.

As they were putting on their hats and coats in the hall, Simeon opened the door and stepped from the elevator. He scurried anxiously up to Hand and grasped him by the arm.

"Hain't nothin' the matter with Mr. Leander, is there?" he demanded. "I just took him up with Dr. Hartshorne, and Hilda says there was somethin' wrong with his soup. I'll tell the cook, by gorry, she better—"

"It wasn't the cook's fault," smiled Hand. "There's nothing the matter with Mr. Holloway, Simeon."

"You sure?"

"Positive. Don't you worry."

Simeon retained his grasp of Hand's arm. He looked searchingly up into his eyes. Hand smiled kindly down at him. Simeon briskly nodded his head, denoting that he had settled a matter within his own mind.

"You're all right," he said. "That Inspector's a fool! He won't get any place yellin' and barkin' at people like he did at me yesterday. That was before you come in. I wouldn't tell him anythin' I knew!"

"The inspector," gently argued Hand, "was probably excited, Simeon. I'm sure he didn't intend to offend you. If you know anything you ought to tell him."

Simeon energetically shook his head. "He don't deserve it!" he snapped. "But, now, maybe I might tell you. You're a nice young feller. I kind of like you."

"I'm honored, Simeon, and very curious to hear what you have to say."

Simeon swelled with importance. "All right, Mr. Hand. You better keep your eyes on Gus Staub."

"Mr. Holloway's chauffeur? Why?"

"Because he was out in the rose garden just before Mr. Robert got shot last night, that's why. The good for nothin' loafer!"

"You know that he was there?"

"I see him there. I thought Mr. Leander maybe had put him to work to clean it up. It needs it. And Gus ain't got nothin' to do; he don't hardly ever have to take the car out any more. He's a loafer. I might of known he wasn't out there to work!"

"Did you see him do anything out there?"

"No. I got other things to do besides watch Gus Staub. I work my fingers to the bone. That lazy loafer don't do nothin'!"

Hand shifted his gaze thoughtfully to a window. His gray eyes gleamed. Then he glanced back at Simeon and patted the old fellow on the shoulder.

"This is very important, Simeon," he said, "I assure you that I will make very quick use of this information"

"I hope," said Simeon, "that you don't find he ain't guilty. He ain't got nothin' better to do than to make fun of people that really work!"

His wizened face wrinkled up more than ever. His small black eyes snapped indignantly.

"We'll find out all we can, never fear," Hand assured him. "Do you know where Staub might be found now?"

"Loafin'!" replied Simeon spitefully. "But I don't know where. I'm goin' out and tell that cook a thing or two! Mr. Leander's been took. I know it, and it was her soup!"

He betook himself viciously to the kitchen. Dr. Hartshorne, tall, pale and austere, descended the stairs.

"Well, Doctor?" asked Hand.

"He's perfectly all right," replied Dr. Hartshorne. "There's a great debt owed to you for that."

"It's paid—in my own gratification," smiled Hand. "Do you suppose we could see Mr. Holloway?"

"Certainly," said the doctor. "He's upstairs in his study."

The doctor hurried away. Hand and Clark mounted the stairs. They found the old man sitting at his desk with his nose buried in a book. He glanced up and smiled at Hand.

"Clean bill of health!" he cried. "I knew it would be. You see what confidence I place in you, Mr. Hand."

"Thank you," smiled Hand. "Where can I find your chauffeur, Mr. Staub, at this hour?"

"Gus?" Leander Holloway scratched his jaw reflectively. "Heaven knows. I sent him down to the John Nash Settlement this morning. I'm a director there, you know. Mrs. Kirby Farnsworth called me this morning and said they'd need a car and I sent Gus. Taking some of those unfortunate people out into the country, it's such a lovely day. Like to have gone along myself, but I promised the Inspector I wouldn't leave the house until this mystery is cleared up."

"And I'm glad to see you keeping it. By the way, I'd keep the curtain drawn over this window. I see they've repaired it."

Hand stepped quickly over to the window and drew the curtain. Leander Holloway stared at it. Then he sighed and glanced up at Hand.

"What about Gus?" he asked.

"Simeon says he saw him in the rose garden just before Mr. Bradshaw was shot."

"Simeon says that? Why the devil didn't he say that before?"

"He wasn't feeling friendly toward the inspector. And no doubt the significance of it hadn't struck him."

Holloway frowned and shook his head. "No; he forgot about it. Absent minded beggar! Well, I don't know when Gus will be back. It ought to be before dark. He won't be back here; he only reports in the mornings to find out what I want these days. Don't know why he shouldn't keep the car at the disposal of the Settlement. Pretty good idea."

"Where does he live?"

Holloway gave them an address in West Fifty-seventh Street. They left the old man reading his book and went down to the front door. They found it open, with the policeman stationed inside the house holding amiable conversation with Stacey. At their approach he hastily closed the door and looked self-conscious.

"Open it up again," ordered Hand, "and listen to what I have to say. That's it. Stacey, you too. Mr. Holloway has a chauffeur named Gus Staub. You are not to let him into this house no matter what the reason is for his coming here. I'll tell the inspector in a very few minutes what I've just ordered you to do. If he wants to countermand it he'll let you know. Do you understand?"

They both assured him that they did.

"Tell the man at the rear door the same thing. You fellows have got to keep on your toes."

Hand hailed a cab. Clark had been acting strangely ever since they had left Holloway's study. He now turned anxiously to Hand.

"Do you think you'll need me?" he asked.

"I don't think so," replied Hand, with a quick glance at him.

"I need a haircut fearfully," Clark earnestly pointed out. "If you don't mind I'll just whisk off and get one. I really should."

"Get one, by all means. And have some of that nice-smelling stuff put on your head."

"Eh?"

"And a gardenia in your buttonhole. See you later at the rooms."

Hand sprang into the cab. He ordered the driver to take him to police headquarters. As he was driven off, Hand chuckled to himself.

Clark stood at the curb, looking after Hand's cab. "Gardenias," he grinned. "Gardenias nothing—orchids!"

Inspector Gerrity sat at his desk, frowning up at a stiff fellow in a sergeant's uniform who had just stepped up to it. The inspector fingered a record card. He glanced down at it.

"Kirk," he said to the sergeant, "you earned a promotion six months ago. Alone, you killed four men."

Gerrity's eyes shot up to the sergeant's face. If the lives he had taken six months before weighed heavily upon Sergeant Kirk's conscience, his expression did not show it. Neither did his expression show anything else, save cold, consummate unfriendliness and self reliance. His pale eyes stared unswervingly into Gerrity's. The inspector felt annoyed, or disconcerted by them.

"Well," he growled, "why don't you say something?"

"Nothing to say, sir." Kirk's voice was brittle.

"Damn!" breathed the inspector. "You're like a block of ice, Kirk. I'm not criticizing; you're just the man I want. Those fellows you knocked off were a bad lot, and nobody'll miss them. You earned your promotion. I think there's a chance for you to earn another. How would you like to get a lieutenant's bars?"

Again Gerrity's eyes darted to Kirk's face. Again they looked down, disappointed.

"It would suit me, sir," replied Kirk.

"Well," snapped Gerrity, "you might get a little enthusiastic. But that's up to you. You know this Holloway case?"

"Yes, sir."

"You don't know all there is to know about it—yet. Get this."

Gerrity went over every episode of the case for Kirk's benefit. The sergeant's expression remained as though cut in stone. His eyes never left Gerrity's face.

"Now, then," concluded the inspector, "you are going on twenty-four-hour duty at Holloway's house. You'll be in charge of six men, eight hours each, three detailed to the front door and three at the back. You are responsible for them! Nobody is to get into that house unless the old man says so. And if they get in—then your work starts. You watch 'em, Kirk, and watch 'em close! If you get the wind up on 'em, shoot, shoot first and tell me about it later! I'll take the responsibility!"

"Yes, sir."

Kirk's eyes seemed to become paler. Gerrity found himself experiencing a chilly sensation at the base of his skull. It pleased him. He smote the top of his desk.

"That's it!" he cried. "You'll do, Kirk, you'll do. You'll find the six men detailed with you in Captain Dykeman's office. You can give 'em your own instructions. You stay on duty at Holloway's until your orders are changed. That's all."

Kirk nodded and strode over to the door. There was a precision in his movements that the inspector eyed with satisfaction. Just as Kirk reached the door of the office it opened. Hand stepped inside. Kirk halted and stood aside. Hand glanced quickly at him.

"How do you do, Sergeant?" he said.

Kirk nodded curtly and disappeared through the door. Hand shot a glance at the inspector. "Holloway's new guardian?" he asked.

"That's right," nodded Gerrity. "Nothing will get by that fellow. He's a damned machine."

"An explosive one," agreed Hand. "Inspector, I seem to be on a rather warm trail. Gus Staub, Holloway's chauffeur, was lurking in the rose garden just before Bradshaw was shot."

"No! How did you find out?"

Gerrity rose half out of his seat. Hand dropped quietly into another. He kept the inspector suspended, after a fashion, in mid-air like that until he had lighted his pipe.

"Simeon told me. He saw him."

"A fine time to be telling us!"

"I believe it slipped his mind."

"Damn his mind, if he has one! Where can we find this Gus Staub?"

"He's out of town for the present. Holloway lent him to the John Nash Settlement to take some of their unfortunates out into the country. I have his address, and he ought to be home before long."

"Let's go there and lay for him!"

Hand cocked an eye at him. "Somehow," he said, "it seems like a dreadful waste of a police inspector's valuable time. Why not send a detective there to watch out for Staub. I can give him the address and the exact location of Staub's rooms in the building. Armed with a description of the man, he can let you know the minute Staub gets home."

"That's better," nodded Gerrity.

He quickly dispatched a detective to Staub's address. As the detective was leaving the office, Gerrity's phone rang. He snatched it up and spoke over it. Then he hung it up again and turned to Hand.

"The city chemist," he said. "That was arsenic in the salt shaker, all right, and it was in Holloway's soup, too. That clinches it; we can look for more trouble any time. I told Kirk to look out for everything, even poison darts."

"Yes," nodded Hand. "It doesn't appear that the case is going to wind itself up of its own accord. Bradshaw and Morley died within a short time of each other yesterday; no doubt about that. It was possible that the mischief ended there, but now I wouldn't say so."

"Not a bit of it!" concurred Gerrity. "I was expecting more deviltry all along. I'm still expecting it. I don't just see—"

His telephone rang again. Gerrity snatched it up. "Hello," he said. "What! I'll be right over."

He slammed the phone down and swung about to Hand.

"What now, Inspector?"

"They've got it! A tug fished Bradshaw's body out of the East River! It's at the morgue."

"Good! We must get McNader. If he testifies that Brad-shaw was the man who jumped over the park wall after Leander Holloway was shot at, then that's established."

"Right! And I'll get young Roderic Holloway to make the identification of the body for the family. By thunder, I'm glad they got it; that blasted corpse has been bother-ing me!"

Thirty minutes later they were at the morgue. They stood beside a slab on which rested the body of a man. It was Robert Bradshaw's body, the ghastly expression of astonishment still fixed on the face. With them stood Rod-eric. He was nervous and plainly upset. Occasionally he glanced dawn at the gruesome face, as if unable to avoid it, but for the most part he stared at the floor. They were all waiting for McNader. Hand noticed how pale Roderic was getting.

"Mr. Holloway," he said, "it isn't necessary for you to wait. If you like I'll let you know whether this man makes the identification."

Roderic stubbornly shook his head. "No," he retorted. "This means clearing my father. I'll wait."

"You won't have to wait any longer," said Gerrity. "Here comes McNader now."

The gambler entered with a couple of detectives, with whom he was on the best of terms. He was a slim little man, dressed glaringly, and he walked with a slight limp. He smiled crookedly and talked out of the corner of his mouth. He said something witty. The detectives clapped him on the shoulder and laughed noisily. Roderic winced.

"Hello, Inspector," called McNader. "Following up that tip I gave you, eh? Where's the stiff?"

"Right here," replied Gerrity. "Take a look at him."

McNader stepped up beside the slab and glanced down at the dead face of Robert Bradshaw. Immediately he nod-ded his head.

"That's him," he said. "That's Phil Holloway."

"You lie!" grated Roderic. "You filthy scoundrel, what did you mean by saying you saw my father?"

"Oh, ho, who's this?" cried McNader, eyeing Roderic.

"Never mind," said Gerrity, scowling at Roderic. "Look here, McNader, how can you be so sure this is the man you saw; his features are all distorted."

"It's the same look," replied McNader, "that he had on his pan when he jumped over the wall and landed right beside me. I was like to jump right out of my shoes. I wouldn't give you a bum steer, you know that."

"Mac's honest, Inspector," affirmed one of the detectives.

"You told it," said McNader, with his crooked grin. "I deal 'em off the top. This is the guy, Inspector."

10

AN INVITATION

Hand, Inspector Gerrity and Roderic went out to the sidewalk in front of the morgue. Kelly sat at the curb in the inspector's official car. He eyed them casually.

"Can we take you anywhere?" Gerrity asked Roderic.

"No thank you," Roderic coolly declined. "I suppose, now, I'll have to get an undertaker. Guess I'll have to make the funeral arrangements. Wish to heaven there was someone else to do it."

"Have to perform an autopsy," grunted the inspector. "But you go ahead and get an undertaker; he can make the arrangements here."

Roderic nodded. "If you want me," he said, "I shall be at the Lambs Club. I am almost always there, it's really the only home I have."

"Your sister," growled Gerrity, "provides you with a pretty good home."

"That," flashed Roderic, "is entirely my own business, Inspector. Good afternoon!"

He turned abruptly and walked off up the street. Gerrity shrugged.

"I'm glad he's gone," said the inspector. "I want to call the office and see whether Staub's back. And I didn't want to let Roderic Holloway in on that. Just a minute, Hand."

He briskly re-entered the morgue. Hand stood on the sidewalk, his eyes following Roderic's retreating figure. Another man stepped out of a doorway and strolled nonchalantly after the young man. Roderic walked along, angrily swinging his stick, thoroughly unconscious of the detective who had been his constant shadow all day.

Gerrity once again joined Hand on the sidewalk.

"Nothing heard from Staub," he said. "I told headquarters they could get me at Leander Holloway's. I want to go over there and get Kirk started right. Come along?"

Hand nodded and got into the inspector's car. Not long after, they were climbing the stairs to the second floor of Holloway's house. They found Kirk standing grimly outside the door of the study.

"How's it going, Kirk?" asked Gerrity.

"Quiet, sir," replied the sergeant.

Gerrity jabbed a thumb at the study door. "Mr. Holloway's in there?"

"Yes, sir."

The inspector rapped on the door and was bidden to enter. The old man laid aside his book and smiled up at them.

"You know," he said, "I think I'm beginning to enjoy this. I haven't had the pleasure of so much company in years. And I must say the way you two work is fascinating. What can I do for you now?"

"I have placed a new man in charge of your police guard," said the inspector.

Holloway sighed and shook his head. "Yes," he said, "you have. Or perhaps you should have said an automaton. I can scarcely get a word out of him. The other fellow was a human being. He told me all about his wife and their thirteen children. He is superstitious; so there is going to be a fourteenth very soon. He is going to name it after me, and, by Jupiter, I'll make a settlement on the little beggar!"

"Kirk isn't very congenial," grinned Gerrity. "But nothing will get by him, absolutely nothing! He's as quick as a hair-trigger. I feel perfectly at ease with him here. I just wanted to make sure that the arrangements were to your satisfaction."

"I suppose so," said Holloway. "That sergeant gives the old house a most ominous touch. But I do say that I feel more comfortable since he appeared. There seems to be a pall hanging over me. I don't care so much—heaven knows I've lived long enough. But I detest being outwitted! We must discover who is behind this dastardly plot!"

"Even though it's one of your own relatives?"

"Yes! So much the worse!"

Simeon entered. He stalked belligerently round the desk and halted before Holloway. He thrust forth a bottle and a spoon.

"You got to take it," he said shrilly. "Doctor's orders."

Holloway glared at the bottle. "Take it away," he ordered.

"No!" cried Simeon. "You've gone and got poisoned, and you got to take it!"

"Doctors!" fumed Holloway. "Always dumping something vile into your stomach. Take it away!"

"I won't!" retorted Simeon.

"Now, Mr. Hand," pleaded the old man, "you don't think I need it, do you?"

Hand wrinkled his brow. "Well," he said, "it is my conviction that the concoctions prescribed by doctors very often have almost no harmful effects."

"And about as much good ones," chuckled Holloway. "All right, Simeon, give me that wretched bottle!"

He took a spoonful of the stuff and followed it with a horrible face. Then he thrust the bottle and the spoon viciously into Simeon's hands.

"Take it away!" he cried. "Why in blazes can't they put a little rye whiskey in those things?"

The inspector had been considering. Now he nodded his head and peered at the old man.

"Mr. Holloway," he said, "I feel it is my duty to inform you that your nephew Phil Holloway has returned to New York. My men traced him to a hotel, and there he apparently disappeared as though he evaporated! It's peculiar, to say the least, that he would return without announcing it even to his own children, and it's more peculiar yet that he should disappear almost as soon as he arrived. Mr. Holloway, I think he intends to murder every one of his relatives, and yours, but his children, and then to murder you."

"You're wrong, like you always are!" snapped Simeon. "Mister Phil wouldn't hurt a dog!"

"I wasn't talking to you!" said Gerrity wrathfully. "And why didn't you tell me about—"

"Simeon's right," broke in Holloway. "I mean, he's right so far as Phil is concerned. Phil's no good. I've told him many a time that he didn't deserve such a daughter as Bernice. And he agreed with me. If he'd been any good I'd have made him a millionaire. He knew that. Phil was a fine youngster, but he never got to be anything else. He's just worthless. I'd swear he'd never hurt a soul. What do you think about this evidence the inspector brings against him, Mr. Hand?"

"I think he's innocent," replied Hand. "But of course, in the circumstances, I would be inclined to."

"Because you got a brain," pointed out Simeon.

"My theory," said Hand quickly, "is this. Phil Holloway returned to New York the day before the attempt to assassinate you in Central Park. Both his children were out of town. I think he was bent upon surprising them; therefore he did not reveal his return to anybody. And before Bernice and Roderic got back, he read in the newspapers of the attack upon you and that the police were suspecting him. His one thought then was to keep out of the way until he was exonerated. I might say that we have just now definitely proved that he did not fire the shot at you up in the park. The person who sought your life then was Robert Bradshaw."

"Robert!" Old Holloway started and glared about. "Robert! What in heaven's name makes you think he did it?"

They told the old man of the finding of Bradshaw's body and McNader's identification of it. It pitched Holloway into a gloomy reverie. Hand and Gerrity left him and went out of the house.

"They didn't call me," said the inspector; "so I guess Staub isn't home yet. Want to go down to headquarters with me?"

"I think I shall return to the rooms, Inspector. If you care to have me accompany you when you interview Staub, you can get me at home."

"All right. Get in; I'll drop you off."

Hand discovered that Clark was not home. He got into his dressing gown and spent some time sitting in the living-room, smoking his pipe and thinking. He found the new arrangement of the matches very trying. Twice by mistake he dipped his hand into the water of the goldfish bowl, to the consternation of the fish, and in the end was driven to draping his coat over the bowl and placing a handful of matches on it. Finally he went to the laboratory. He forgot to close the door and commenced an experiment that filled the whole place with nauseating odors. Hand did not notice it. It was as if one small corner of his mind was directing the carrying out of the experiment, while the bulk of his intellectual powers were functioning at top speed on mysterious matters of quite another order.

Clark did not return until after seven. He entered the living-room to be unpleasantly greeted by the foul atmosphere. He stared helplessly at the open door of the laboratory; then he walked over to it. Hand was still fussing with his chemicals, his back presented squarely to the door.

"Ah, Clark," he said, without turning about. "A very poor one, I must say."

"A very poor one? A very poor what?"

"Haircut."

"Hairc—? Oh, yes. I just had a trim. He took very little off."

"Why, confound it, I don't think you've had a haircut at all!"

"See here, how could you tell that I didn't—ah—get a chance to have my hair cut. You haven't once looked at me since I came in."

Hand set his test tubes in a rack and spun about. "I surmised," he grinned, "that three minutes after you left me this afternoon you were knocking at Miss Holloway's door."

"Then you're wrong! I went to the florist's and got—I didn't go directly to her house. And it seems to me that you took too much for granted, assuming so readily that it was I who came in just now. After that attempt on your life last night, I should think you'd be more cautious."

"My dear fellow, there's no mistaking your step, particularly when you are discouraged with me. I'm heartily sorry I forgot to close the laboratory door. I suppose it's a trifle—ah—fragrant out in the living-room."

"Yes, and my goldfish all enshrouded under your coat. Thank goodness that window is still broken or you couldn't breathe out there. What did you find out about Staub?"

"Nothing. It seems that he hasn't returned home yet. But Bradshaw's body has been recovered. McNader has identified him as the man who leaped over the park wall.

When you see Miss Holloway tonight, you can tell her that her father is innocent to that extent, at least."

Clark sighed and closed the door. He walked dejectedly across the small laboratory and dropped on a stool. "I won't see her," he said, with a shake of his head. "She has an engagement. With Forschell."

"Old boy," said Hand, "Miss Holloway is coming to mean a whole lot to you, isn't she?"

"She means the whole world to me now. It's the strangest thing; I met her only last night. No woman ever affected me before, but almost as soon as I laid eyes on Bernice I—I—Hand, I just can't describe it!"

"No, and if you did I'd not understand it. Well, old chap, Miss Holloway is a very lucky girl. There is no man on earth more worthy of her affection."

Clark grunted and glanced up at him. "That's just the trouble," he said wryly. "What right have I to think I can win her affection?"

"Most ridiculous thing I ever heard! Yes, I shall not see you go off and settle down without a twinge or two. But this is no life for you, Clark. I am really quite happy for you "

"Got me married already," grinned Clark. "Well, by Jove, you're right! If persistence can win I'll—"

There was a strident ring of the telephone. Before it had stopped Hand had leaped into the living-room and snatched up the instrument.

"Hello," he sharply answered.

"Hand," came Gerrity's voice. "Staub is back! I'll pick you up; it's on the way."

"Good. We'll be at the curb."

Ten minutes later Hand and Clark were picked up by the inspector's car. Six minutes after that they were standing with the inspector in a dark hallway outside Staub's door. With them was a fourth dim figure, the detective who had been detailed to watch for Staub.

"He's catchin' merry hell from his wife," whispered the detective. "He didn't come home in time for dinner. And he was late for dinner last night, too; I heard her yell it at him."

"Good work," grunted Gerrity. "Maybe he can explain that away for his wife, but he'll have trouble explaining it away for me!"

The inspector rapped energetically on the door. The knock did not halt the lashing of an angry female tongue inside, but a bulky young man opened the door and peered out at them. He wore a harried expression on his round face. Then he espied Gerrity and broke into a wide grin.

"If it ain't the big shot from police headquarters!" he cried. "What'd you want?"

"You," replied Gerrity succinctly.

"Me?" exclaimed Gus, his grin disappearing.

A buxom, flaxen-haired young woman stepped up beside him and peered at the ominous aggregation in the hall. Then, placing her hands on her generous hips, she turned upon her husband.

"Gus Staub," she demanded, "what you been up to? Now you got the cops here!"

"Who, me?" demanded Gus, in his turn. "You mean I got the cops here, baby? Oh, no, you got it all wrong!"

"What you been up to? Don't lie to me, Gus Staub?"

"Nothin', baby, honest! A little bottle pool, like I told you, that's all. They were suckers for me tonight. I'd of been a fool to lay off just when I was cleanin' up!"

"Were you playing bottle pool yesterday afternoon?" demanded Gerrity.

Gus glanced at him uneasily. "Sure," he replied.

"And kept the dinner waitin' an hour!" said his wife viciously.

"Baby," said Gus sadly, "you're a great help t' me."

"'S that so!" she snapped. "What'd you think I married you for, to sit home rockin' the baby and keepin' your supper hot? Let me tell you, Gus Staub, you get in a jam and lose your job and I go right back to the glue factory! And you stay here and take care of the baby!"

Gus looked sick. His wife thrust him out into the hall and shut the door with a prodigious slam. Gus dodged as though he had been hit.

"Is she sore!" he groaned. "All on account of a little bottle pool."

"Come along," said Gerity. "We'll see whether you were playing bottle pool yesterday."

Following Gus's directions, they went to a little pool room not far away. Gerrity sent the detective in to inquire casually about Gus's activities of the day before. The man soon returned to the car.

"Well, Inspector," he said, "there's three mugs in there, includin' the proprietor of the joint, who're ready to swear this bird was in there yesterday between three and seven P.M. shootin' pool."

"One 'f 'em must be Hip Blonsky," said Gus. "He took me pretty yesterday."

"Did it sound straight?" Gerrity asked the detective

The man shrugged. "You know, Inspector," he said. "Maybe it is, and maybe it ain't."

"Yes, I know," said Gerrity grimly. "We'll take this fellow down to headquarters for a little visit."

"Hey!" objected Gus. "I get an alibi and you fellas don't pay no attention to it! What do you call this? You heard what my wife said about them diapers!"

His plaintive objections did no good. The best he could do was to get Gerrity to agree to send a detective round to his wife to attest to the fact that he was not playing pool. Knowing the inspector was anxious to give Gus a grilling,

Hand refused the half-hearted offer to be driven home.
The inspector's car drove off. Hand and Clark left the spot
on foot. Presently Hand hailed a cab.

"Now where?" asked Clark.

"To Leander Holloway's," replied Hand. "I want to
make sure that Simeon wasn't just working off a grudge."

The policeman in the vestibule recognized them and
readily granted them admittance. Save for a low light
burning in the upper hall, the house seemed to be in darkness. But out of the gloom a form materialized at Clark's
elbow, causing him to recoil against the wall.

"Hello, Kirk," said Hand. "Mr. Holloway gone to bed?"

"Yes, sir."

"Where is Simeon?"

"In the kitchen getting himself something to eat."

"Thank you."

They found the kitchen brilliantly lighted. Simeon
was conducting a raid of considerable magnitude on the
ice box.

"Simeon," said Hand.

The little old man gave a violent start and spun about
to face them. "Glory be!" he exclaimed. "You scairt me!
Why don't you make a noise when you come in on a man
like that—knock over somethin', or sneeze, sort of?"

"I'm sorry, Simeon. But tell me, are you positive that it was
Gus Staub whom you saw out in the rose garden last night?"

Simeon muttered unintelligibly and went back to raiding the ice box, putting bits of this and that on a tray.
Hand and Clark waited for him to get ready to answer.

"Maybe it wasn't," he grumbled. "I see somebody, kind
of crouchin' among them old bushes."

"But you weren't positive it was Staub?"

"Thought it was. Maybe it wasn't. I got other things to
do besides watch that lazy loafer. Don't hardly get time to
eat, not till most everybody else is abed."

"I'm sorry to be so persistent, Simeon, but it is most important. Unless you could swear that it was Staub that you saw, I'm afraid—"

"Wouldn't swear to it. Maybe it wasn't him. Good night."

Having laden his tray to suit him, Simeon picked it up and stalked out of the kitchen. They followed him out to the hall, where he got into the elevator and closed the door. Kirk came down the stairs.

"Mr. Hand," he said curtly, "Mr. Holloway wants to see you upstairs. He heard you come in."

Hand and Clark quickly mounted the stairs. They found the old millionaire in the hall, wearing a faded dressing gown and a nightcap. He was rubbing his hands together, peering brightly at them, and seemed in a state of enthusiastic self-satisfaction.

"Glad you stopped in," he said. "I have developed a wonderful idea. I'm astonished that neither you nor Inspector Gerrity has thought of it."

"I am all interest, Mr. Holloway," said Hand. "What is it?"

The old man chuckled and shook a finger at him. "I won't give it away," he said. "You'll have to wait until morning. I request you two gentlemen to be here tomorrow at ten in the morning. I have a surprise for you, one the cleverness of which will take your breath away, Mr. Hand. And thereafter I shall be as safe from these scoundrels as though I were a thousand miles away from them!"

"Excellent! We shall be here at ten, then."

"Good! And I hope you rest well tonight, gentlemen. I shall expect you at ten, and you may expect the surprise of your lives. I have struck at the very roots of this outrage! Good night."

He shuffled back into his room and closed the door. Clark's face broke into a smile.

"Quite an old boy!" he said. "No wonder Bernice thinks he's wonderful."

The night being clear and invigorating, they elected to walk back to their rooms. Had Hand and Clark known it, at least one of them would have been vitally interested in a little restaurant that they passed. In it, secluded by a low partition, sat Bernice and Horace Forschell. The man leaned across the table, tensely eager, his eyes devouring the girl's face. Her eyes were cast down, watching her finger draw imaginary figures on the tablecloth.

"Bernice," said Forschell, softly, passionately, "I've got to—"

"Please, Horace," she pleaded. "Don't spoil it. It's been so nice here, and you've been a dear."

"But I can't go on like this!" protested Forschell, hoarseness creeping into his voice. "I'm not to blame. You are so beautiful, so wonderful, that you set my whole being blazing with a passionate urge for you. Bernice, why won't you listen to me?"

She sighed and took his hand across the table. He grasped it until she all but winced.

"I'm not to blame, either, Horace," she said. "You must realize how upset I am, with these ghastly tragedies. And I can seem to feel something threatening me all the time! And threatening Rod, and Uncle Leander, and the others. It's horrible!"

"All the more reason why you need someone to protect you."

"I have Mr. Hand, you know. He seems to give me confidence. I know he'll straighten it out!"

"I don't think so much of him. Or that police inspector, either. But that's not what I mean, Bernice. I mean someone whose sole interest in life is looking out for you. Darling, you know I—"

She re-captured her hands and rose with a nervous little laugh. "Don't, Horace," she pleaded mockingly. "If you start that we'll be here for hours, I just know it, and I'm fearfully tired. Come, let's go."

He rose frowning slightly and helped her into her coat. Standing behind her, he suddenly clasped his arms tightly about her.

"I'll never let you go," he said gruffly. "Some day I will make you say that you love me!"

"I'm fond of you, Horace. I'd never do anything to hurt you."

"Bernice! Tell me how—"

She broke lightly away from him and turned about laughingly to face him. But her laughter was still unnatural. She beckoned a finger at him.

"Come on, Horace," she said. "Please take me home."

He sighed and donned his hat and coat. They said very little on the way home. Forschell left Bernice and quickly returned to Leander Holloway's house.

Hand and Clark, after stopping off on the way for dinner, returned to their rooms. Hand went immediately to the laboratory and took up his experiment where he had left it off. First closing the door on his friend, Clark dropped into his easy chair. Gazing into the swirls of smoke from his pipe, he fell into a reverie, now delectable and now apprehensive.

Hand concluded his experiment. He put away his test tubes and chemicals, scrupulously neat now, and sat down before a half-finished bust of Inspector Gerrity. Digging unceremoniously into a small mound of clay, he took a handful and commenced applying the material with the thumb and ball of his hand to the facsimile of Gerrity's ample jaw. A sitting was not necessary; he knew the inspector's unclassic features as well as Gerrity's own mother did. Besides, this was the sixth bust of the inspector that he had modeled. Gerrity had been gratified when he made the first, and even the second, but since then he had suspected what was exactly the case, that Hand honored him so merely to keep his hand's busy while his mind was at grips with a problem.

And while Hand and Clark sat so quietly in their rooms, a man in another part of town also sat silently, in the sanctity of his own bedchamber. Clad in pajamas, he sat on the edge of his bed and gazed at a vicious blackjack that he held in his hands, almost caressingly. He appeared so wasted and spent that it seemed he had not the strength to wield even such a handy weapon as this. But on the morrow he intended to use it, and he intended to use it in the taking of a human life. The man grinned evilly.

11

THE SEDAN

"Well, Clark, going to sleep all day?"

Clark opened his eyes and glanced sleepily over to the door. There stood Christopher Hand, smiling and fresh. He wore pajamas and a bathrobe. Clark sat up in astonishment.

"Have you been to bed?" he demanded.

"Certainly," replied Hand.

Clark glanced at his wrist-watch. "Eight o'clock!" he exclaimed.

"That's what it is," confirmed Hand. "I've rung for Mrs. Flemming. Better hurry, if you want any breakfast."

Hastily completing the morning's preparations, Clark went out to the living-room. Hand, already dressed, was fussing about in the laboratory. Mrs. Flemming appeared with a tray laden with breakfast for two.

"Good mornin' to yez," she puffed. "Mr. Hand out ag'in?"

"No; he's in the laboratory."

"Indade! I didn't smell nothin'."

She went to work setting the food on the table. Hand came out of the laboratory behind her. He rested his arms on the back of a chair and regarded her for a moment.

"A perfect shame, Mrs. Flemming," he said abruptly. "How did it happen?"

Exclaiming sharply, she turned about and stared at him. "'Tis you, Mr. Hand!" she cried. "Always poppin' up like the cork out of a bottle o' beer. Good mornin' to yez, and how did what happen?"

"I observe," he replied, "that you have broken your mirror."

Mrs. Flemming started violently. "The second sight!" she said hoarsely.

"No; the first," grinned Hand.

"And me with seven years o' bad luck starin' me in the face!"

"I shouldn't worry about that; the theory has been thoroughly exploded."

"I'm expectin' somethin' terrible like that to happen any minute!"

Dismally shaking her head, Mrs. Flemming left them. Hand bounded over to the table and drew up his chair. He seated himself and attacked his grapefruit. Clark slowly seated himself opposite, eyeing him skeptically.

"How did you know she broke her mirror?" he demanded.

Hand dodged a sudden squirt from his grapefruit. "I heard her," he replied, "and so would you have, if you didn't sleep like a petrified forest."

"But you told her you observed that she'd broken it."

"Well, that tidy knot of hair of hers isn't tidy at all this morning. After all, it was mostly a guess on my part."

Before Clark had more than half completed the delicious circle of his grapefruit, Hand had devoured his fried eggs, toast and coffee. He pushed his chair back, sprawled out in it, and set flame to a cigarette. With the expertness born of long habit, he flipped the match into the goldfish bowl. It settled on the water with a sizzle, nudged about by the inquisitive noses of the fish. He grinned at Clark's annoyed glance.

"Sorry, Clark. But just the same, I have provided an interlude in the monotonous existence of the little pests."

Clark went back to his grapefruit. Suddenly Hand jerked the cigarette from his lips and sat tense for a moment.

"A woman's step," he muttered. "Our client, undoubtedly, Clark. I was afraid of this."

Clark bounded out of his chair and flung the door open. It revealed Bernice, rosy from the morning air and astonished at the abrupt appearance of Clark.

"Hello!" he cried joyously. "This is wonderful!"

"You must have seen me right through the door," laughed Bernice. "I came over to tell you the latest."

Clark ushered her in with much fuss and seated her in Hand's easy chair. She was wearing a green suit of tweed with a fluffy fur collar. Clark thought the living-room did not look half so drab as it had a moment before. She quietly smoothed her skirt.

"Clark complains," said Hand, with a twinkle in his eye, "that the springs of my easy chair need attention. But I'm sure you will agree with me, Miss Holloway, that it would be a mistake."

"Heavens, yes!" exclaimed Clark. "Here, Bernice, don't sit in that wretched thing; take my chair."

"No," she laughed. "Please don't bother about me, Ralph. I'm interrupting your breakfast."

"I didn't want it," lied Clark. "Hardly ever eat breakfast."

"What is the latest," asked Hand, "that you came over to tell us?"

"Uncle Leander," she replied, "has called a meeting of the clan at his house at ten o'clock. It's all very mysterious; he won't let on what he has up his sleeve."

"We have been invited," smiled Hand.

"What is it all about?"

"I am no better informed than you. But assuredly the old gentleman is going to play a very fine card."

Bernice twisted her hands together. Her brown eyes became troubled. By sheer force of will Clark resisted an impulse to take her hand.

"Mr. Hand," she asked haltingly, "I suppose I shouldn't be such a nuisance, but—but haven't you made any headway?"

Hand frowned. "Yes," he slowly replied. "Of the greatest interest to you, I think, is the fact that Robert Bradshaw's body has been found. He has been identified as the man who shot at Leander Holloway in Central Park. Your father is cleared of that charge."

Bernice sat up straight in the chair. Her lips trembled. Tears shone suddenly in her eyes. Clark took her hand and pressed it. She smiled up at him.

"Isn't that wonderful," she said. "That is worth everything. But Mr. Hand, I've been unfair to you. I haven't any money. My allowance is just enough for Roddy and me to live on. But I'll get a job. It was too mean of me to retain you when I'll have to make you wait ever so long to be paid."

"Don't worry about it," said Clark gruffly.

"I can't add anything to that," smiled Hand.

"How can I thank you?" cried Bernice.

"Unnecessary," said Hand.

Mrs. Flemming tramped into the room. Her eyes darted to Clark's unfinished breakfast and then, apprehensively, to Clark. "You've gone and took sick," she accused.

"No, really, Mrs. Flemming," he hastily denied. "I became interested in—in—"

"You've took sick!" she emphatically repeated. "You always eat up every last speck of your breakfast. Mr. Hand, now, has ate up everything. When he don't, he's just thinkin'. But when you don't, you've took sick. Some castor-oil's what you need. I'll be right up with it in lemon juice, I will!"

"Mrs. Flemming!"

She was gone. Clark turned excitedly to Hand. Bernice giggled.

"We've got to get out of here!" stated Clark firmly. "If she comes back with that awful stuff I'll have to take it!"

"She'll be back with it, never fear," said Hand.

Bernice looked at Clark with bubbling eyes. "Of course," she said, "if I didn't know that you scarcely ever eat breakfast I'd think you really were sick."

"If I drink that stuff," he retorted, "I'll be the sickest thing you ever saw."

"Then why drink it?" she laughed.

He looked at her significantly. "You don't know Mrs. Flemming," he said hollowly. "Why, she even made Hand take some of it once. Let's get out of here! It's nine-thirty, and we're due at Leander Holloway's at ten. There's no time to lose!"

Hand grinned and got leisurely to his feet. But to Clark's dismay, he went into the laboratory. A moment later, however, he was back again. He picked up the telephone. Placing the instrument to his ear, he gave the number of police headquarters. He waited a few seconds, and then:

"Captain Doyle, please—Hello, Doyle, Christopher Hand speaking. There is a dark blue sedan parked directly across the street from our rooms. Two men in it, one in front at the wheel and the other in the back. It would bear investigation. I shouldn't waste any time about it, and I suggest that you be careful— Excellent. Good-bye, Doyle "

He hung up and walked quietly over to the chair where he had left his hat and coat the night before. He proceeded to put them on. Bernice's face had gone white. She watched his deliberate movements with widening eyes.

"What is it?" she breathed.

"Come," said Hand, "or Clark gets a dose of castor-oil."

Quite as perturbed as was Bernice, Clark got into his coat and hat and followed them out to the door at the back. The shade was habitually drawn over the glass panel of that door. But at the correct height for Hand's eyes there was a small hole in it. He peered through this now, subjecting the court-yard below to a long and careful scrutiny. Then he stepped back and glanced at Bernice.

"That," he said, "was one of those things that are hardly necessary but just as well to do. Also, it is hardly necessary for you to be the last to descend the stairs, keeping yourself close to Clark's back, but that is what we shall do."

He opened the door and descended the outside stairs. Regardless of his careless demeanor, his gray eyes missed very little that was in the court-yard. Clark's eyes also darted keenly about. He took Bernice's hand, holding it tightly, and made sure that she was keeping close behind him. He was nervous about Bernice, fearful lest this mystery that he could not penetrate might bring harm to her, but he gloried in at last being her actual protector. They gained the court-yard and, wasting no time in it, crossed to an alleyway on the opposite site and emerged into the street behind the lodgings. Hand hailed a cab and gave the driver Leander Holloway's address. They all quickly got in. Bernice sat between the two men, nervously eyeing Hand.

"Why," she asked, "were all those precautions necessary?"

Hand turned his head and regarded her speculatively. "There is no reason," he said, "why I should increase your anxiety by adding to the mystery that already surrounds you. It is possible that the sedan I mentioned over the telephone to police headquarters contains two men bent upon murdering me."

"Murder!" gasped Bernice. "Why do you say that?"

Hand settled himself comfortably back against the cushions. "Just let me outline my reasons for it," he said, as though he were a professor lecturing students in a class-room. "There was an attempt upon my life the night before last. It failed, and because it failed I felt reasonably certain that the neighborhood had quickly cleared of assassins. Therefore, I took no exceptional precautions. A little clear thinking, you know, is worth a thousand precautions."

"Do you think," nervously asked Bernice, "that it had—"

"Anything to do with your retaining me? I think there can be no doubt of it. I prefer to assume, at least, that the shot aimed at me through our living-room window was meant to remove the possibility of my taking up the case. Such an assumption, you see, places me in a position to guard against a second attack."

"How horrible!"

"Horrible? Yes, perhaps, if it succeeded. But it will not succeed; they are altogether too clumsy! I have been quite on the alert since that first attack upon me. Strange to say, although there have been opportunities for following up the attack, nothing aroused my suspicion until this morning. As soon as I awoke I went to the various windows, somewhat cautiously, and inspected the several views. From the laboratory windows, which look out upon the street at the front, I saw a sedan parked across the way. The men in it, one at the wheel and one in the back, were strangers to the neighborhood. Only mildly interesting, you see."

"Why didn't you call the police?"

"Premature. I had no intention of going out at the time; I had, indeed, not yet even dressed. After dressing I again inspected the street from the laboratory windows. The sedan, with its two occupants, was still there. The matter became a trifle more interesting, particularly as the two chaps had, apparently, never shifted their gaze from my door. Still I had no intention of leaving the rooms. But then, just before we left, when I again stepped into the laboratory and saw that they were still there, I felt there was sufficient reason for suspecting that they were waiting for me to emerge from the building. I called Captain Doyle, therefore, and we left by the rear exit."

"What might they have done to you?"

"Had I left by the front way, the fellow in the back seat might have turned the contents of a sub-machine gun upon me. My demise would have been quite certain. They would have whisked away from the scene before anyone had gathered his wits about him. It is a notorious method. Also a stupid one."

Bernice cried out and started suddenly from the seat. The taxi driver glanced quickly about, and just as quickly relaxed into the stolid imperturbability of his kind.

"Oh, it's horrible!" cried Bernice. "Everywhere I turn now I seem to run into a new horror! And always I seem to be in the center of it! Mr. Hand, tell me, what does it all mean?"

Her voice broke. Clark impulsively put his arm about her and drew her gently back. She sobbed hysterically and rested her head on Clark's broad shoulder. Clark tightened his arm about her and spoke compassionately to her. Hand regarded them with arched eyebrows, thus displaying about as much emotion as he ever did. Bernice forced a smile and looked gratefully up into Clark's eyes.

"Sorry," she murmured.

"You don't need to be," he softly replied.

Hand leaned forward and gazed keenly at the girl. "You must rely upon me."

"I will."

"This is my profession—criminology. Let me do the thinking; endeavor to keep your mind off the thing in its entirety. Don't allow it to overwhelm you by attempting to embrace it in your thoughts. Leave that to me. I am weaving all of these sinister events together. When the pattern is complete, we shall see that it is not added to."

Clark had not supposed that his friend's voice could be so soft. Bernice rested her head comfortably, unashamedly on Clark's shoulder and closed her eyes. Glancing down at the delicate profile of her cheek, Clark wished the cab would never reach its destination. But it did, and Hand and Bernice had leaped out before he had time completely to readjust himself. As usual, he was left in Hand's wake to pay off the cab driver. He caught up with them in the vestibule, where Hand and Bernice were being closely scrutinized by the guard.

"You're all on the list," said the policeman, "but you'll have to get passed on by the sergeant."

He opened the door, just after Simeon had passed by it through the hall, and blew sharply upon his whistle. Simeon all but sat down. He whirled about and glared at the policeman.

"You and your whistle again!" he said harshly. "Always a-blowin' it in a body's ear! Whyn't you go out in the street and blow it?"

"Take it easy, grandad," grinned the policeman. Simeon marched truculently off to the kitchen. Sergeant Kirk materialized on the stairs.

"Well?" he snapped.

"Got some more," announced the policeman. "Mr. Hand and his pal and Miss Holloway."

"Let them in," ordered Kirk.

He slowly descended the stairs to the hall, his hand hovering near the butt of his pistol. It remained there even after he had recognized Hand and Clark. Bernice looked into his hawk-like face, his frozen eyes and thin, colorless mouth, and instinctively drew away from him.

"You are to go upstairs," said Kirk coldly. "Miss Holloway is to go into the front sitting-room. Mr. Hand and Mr. Clark are to join Mr. Holloway in the den."

"Just like that," said Bernice, attempting a flippant attitude toward him. "My goodness, is this really Uncle Leander's house?"

Kirk merely continued to eye them all as frostily as ever. He waited until they had started to ascend the stairs; then he followed them up the steps. At the top he turned to Hand and Clark.

"Wait here please," he said. "Now, Miss, if you'll just go into the front sitting-room."

A little overawed by this time, Bernice walked slowly toward the sitting-room. Kirk silently followed her. Ludovic and his mother were already in the sitting-room, and so was Roderic. The mother and son sat apart, Mrs. Holloway in a gloomy study and Ludovic palpably at the mercy of his nerves. Roderic sat by the window, one leg thrown over the other, gazing serenely out into the street. Viewed by daylight, his elegant clothes were just a trifle threadbare. But he was correct to the last detail. He gave Bernice a quick smile. Mrs. Holloway, apparently, did not notice her. Ludovic glanced up almost fearfully, as though half expecting to receive distressing information.

Out in the hall Clark turned to Hand, a gleam of resentment in his eyes. "Look at him," he sputtered, indicating Kirk, "standing there in the doorway eyeing Bernice as though she were a criminal! By Jove, this is a mighty strange business. What do you suppose the old gentleman is going to do?"

Hand nodded his head toward the sitting-room. "I fancy," he said, "that we are going to see some disappointment out there."

Kirk returned to them. He halted stiffly and indicated with a glance that he was ready for them to proceed. But at that moment Horace Forschell hurried toward them from the direction of the study.

"Hello," he said. "I say, Mr. Hand, I tried to keep Mr. Holloway out of the study, but he would go in there. He's in there now, with Mr. Sinclair."

"Well," smiled Hand, "I imagine he'll be all right."

"Have you seen anything of Miss Holloway?"

"She just went into the front room."

"Oh. Well—well, I'll be getting on."

He passed quickly on. Clark peered steadily at his receding back, without any semblance of good will. Then, religiously followed by the sergeant, he followed Hand into the study. Leander Holloway sat at his desk. Beside it, with his back to the door, Sinclair sat in the leather easy-chair. Hand strode round him and shook hands with the old man. Holloway smiled up at him. Kirk stood in the doorway and glanced keenly about the study.

"Good morning, Mr. Hand," cried Holloway. "And good morning to you, Mr. Clark."

He seemed in high good spirits. Hand and Clark exchanged greetings with him and Sinclair, in the midst of which the sergeant withdrew. Clark glanced back from the door he had closed to Leander Holloway.

"You're getting some rigid police protections now," he observed.

Holloway frowned slightly. "The fellow is too infernally assiduous," he said. "My house looks like a jail and is regulated precisely like one. At breakfast this morning Horace said—Horace always has his meals with me, you know,—this morning at breakfast he was most amusing,—

he said in a day or so he and I would be lock-stepping to the dining-room and back. Horace is really a most exceptional young man."

"I understand," said Sinclair, "that the body of Robert Bradshaw has been recovered."

"Yes," sighed Holloway. "Poor Robert. That cowardly shot was fired at him as he sat in the very chair you're sitting in, Jasper."

"My soul!" gasped Sinclair, leaping out of the chair as though it were red hot.

"Careful you don't fall out that window," mildly cautioned Holloway. "That is the window the shot came through."

"This window!" shrieked Sinclair.

Once more he leaped for a less sinister haven. He leaned panting against the wall and mopped his brow. Clark regarded him compassionately. He was afraid that Jasper Sinclair was not built to endure the weird things in life. Hand smiled at old Holloway.

"Well, Mr. Holloway," he said, "you have all the appearance of a man who is about to thrust his hand into a hat and draw forth a rabbit."

The old fellow grinned and rubbed his hands together. "No wonder," he chuckled. "Yes, Mr. Hand, very presently I shall launch a counter attack. And when I do, I think you will agree that the time has not yet come when a man can engage Leander Holloway in a desperate game of wits and expect a one-sided battle. I have reduced this situation to its most delicate points. A precise reasoner such as yourself will be delighted with my counter attack. Just now I am setting the stage. Inspector Gerrity is the last actor to step from the wings. When he does, I shall be ready."

Holloway leaned back in his chair and folded his arms, a complacent smile on his old lips. Clark regarded him admiringly. Old and feeble as Holloway was, he thought, with the immense power of the police department exerting itself in his behalf, aided by an expert whose reputation towered imposingly throughout his profession, nevertheless the aged industrialist preferred to fight his own battles. He sat there, a shattered monument of a day when Titans such as he breathed upon iron and steel and made it live,—the veritable creators of the machine age.

Gerrity suddenly opened the door and peered inside, rather as if he expected to see them all lying slaughtered on the floor. He grunted unintelligibly and stepped inside, carefully closing the door. He frowned and glanced at Hand from under his heavy brows.

"Do you want a body-guard too?" he demanded.

Old Holloway sat up and stared at him. Sinclair retreated a step farther into the corner, as though he scented something sinister in the air. Hand's eyes kindled with enthusiasm.

"Then I was right!" he exclaimed. "The sedan bore fruit?"

Gerrity became gruffer than ever, a sure sign that his emotions had been stirred up. "If you had stepped into the street this morning," he growled, "you would have been riddled with machine gun bullets! At this minute you would be stretched out at the morgue!"

THE LAST WILL

Holloway slumped back in his chair. He sighed and gloomily shook his head.

"Mr. Hand," he asked, "your life is threatened too?"

"There certainly seems," smiled Hand, "to be somebody who would enjoy seeing me reclining in the morgue
in the position that the inspector has just described. You
captured the men, Inspector?"

"Doyle did," grunted Gerrity.

"Get anything out of them?"

"Only that they were hired to knock you off. If they
pulled the trick they were to wait until the newspapers
had announced it. Then they were to have been paid off
by Richy Biordino."

"Hurn-m, that gangster! Undoubtedly the trail will
lead off into thin air."

"Afraid so, unless they pick Richy up in a hurry. Who-
ever wanted you killed dealt through him. Richy is probably lying low, and the newspapers, blast them, have got
hold of the story of the arrest. Richy will beat it."

Holloway leaned forward again. "Would you mind telling me," he asked, "how this all took place?"

Hand gave him an account of the entire episode of the
parked sedan. The old man listened with growing enthusiasm.
When Hand had finished he jabbed a crooked finger at him

"That's it!" he exclaimed. "We have got to outwit them! Your reasoning, Mr. Hand, was as subtle as that of mine which you are about to hear. We have got to outwit them! They'll make no progress against us!"

Jasper Sinclair seemed impatient to hear the subtleties that Leander Holloway had so long promised. "Mr. Holloway," he said, "don't you think it well to outline this—er—plan to us before presenting it to the others in the sitting-room? I am your attorney, you know."

"Yes," smiled Holloway, "yes, Jasper, you are my attorney. But you are not the attorney your father was! Many's the battle we've fought, side by side. Just look at you, as nervous as a cat. I've seen your father stand in court when our opponents threw new evidence like a bomb into our case, and he never so much as moved an eyelash! Ah, what a man he was. A moment to think, and he'd fly back at them and riddle them to bits!"

"I am no imbecile," said Sinclair stiffly.

Holloway grinned and shook his head. "No," he agreed, "if you were you would not be my attorney, I promise you, your father's son or no. I dandled you on my knee when you weighed no more than a gallon of beer. But you stand on your own legs when you represent me! But no mind, Jasper, you shall have my plan before the others."

"Yes, what is it?" demanded the inspector.

With an elaborate show of deliberation, the old man rested his elbows on the desk and leaned forward. "Very well, my friends," he said. "As I mentioned before, I have reduced this sinister affair to its finest points. The ultimate conclusion is that a number of persons would profit by my death. And all of these persons against whom I entertain the gravest suspicions, are mentioned in my will."

Sinclair started violently. He attracted the attention of all the others. His face flushed.

"This is incredible, sir!" he fumed. "By gad, I am mentioned in your will!"

"Yes, I know," grinned Holloway.

Gerrity turned slowly to the attorney. "How did you
know you were?" he asked.

"How did I know it?" hotly retorted Sinclair. "By gad,
I drew it!"

"Of course," said Holloway placidly, "there are a number of beneficiaries in my will who, I am sure, would never
think of hastening my death. I am sure such a thing would
never enter the heads of my fellow directors of the John
Nash Settlement, for instance."

"Then," asked Sinclair harshly, "what is your plan?"

"My plan," replied Holloway deliberately, "is to wipe
out the temptation that has placed my life in jeopardy. I
propose to draw a new will!"

"A blasted good idea," growled Gerrity. "I didn't quite
have the nerve, or I'd have suggested that very thing."

Sinclair wrinkled his brow. He pulled thoughtfully at
his underlip. Pausing, he raised his eyes sharply to Holloway.

"As your attorney," he said, "I feel it my duty to advise
you upon this important decision. I see your point, of
course, but I believe your plan might frustrate itself. You
are a man well along in years. If you were to draw a new
will now, your kin, or at least some of them, would undoubtedly at your demise seize upon your advanced age as
a means of throwing the whole thing into litigation. Yours
is an immense fortune, sir, and well worth every effort to
claim. If, as you seem to think, one of your heirs is taking
desperate measures to obtain his inheritance before your
life has run its natural course, he would not be stopped by
a will drawn at this late date disinheriting him."

"You don't think he would, eh?" smiled Holloway.

"I'm afraid that I don't," stiffly replied Sinclair. "If
you nullify your present will, the sane testament of a sane

testator, after you have passed your eightieth year, I warn you that there is grave danger that the new document might be set aside by the courts. It should be the privilege of every adult to bequeath his worldly goods as he so desires. If your will should be broken heaven knows how your fortune would be distributed. As your attorney, Mr. Holloway, I am in duty bound to warn you of that!"

To Sinclair's indignation, the old man crackled mirthfully. "A very fine speech, Jasper," he said. "Your father could not have done better. But I draw a new will! And if you wish to continue to be my attorney, my boy, you will draw it for me! Let us go into the front sitting-room."

Chuckling to himself, the old fellow got to his feet and walked feebly round the desk to the door. As he passed Hand he gave him a crooked smile.

"My legs, confound them," he said, "are as weak as toothpicks."

Gerrity opened the door. Presented squarely to them was the rigid back of Sergeant Kirk. He spun about and peered sharply at the inspector. Then he stepped back out of the way.

"That's it, Kirk," commended Gerrity. "You keep on the job like that and you won't get into trouble."

The expression of cool unfriendliness remained unaltered on the sergeant's lean face. Clark felt that he would be glad to have Kirk around if something were threatening him, but never otherwise.

Hand and Holloway led the procession down the hallway, a procession made slow by the old millionaire's halting gait. Kirk followed them all, at a distance dictated less by respect as it was by his ability to take everything in. As they entered the sittingroom, Eleanor Holloway got to her feet in a flutter and flew over to the old man. Smiling pleasantly, she took him by the arm and guided him solicitously to his chair. He scowled at her; whereupon she took alarm and retreated to her chair. Ludovic also rose. He clutched the back of his chair and, with pale lips parted, stared hard at his great-uncle. Then he sighed, as though his nerves were strained and taut, and sat weakly down again. Roderic and Bernice had also risen. But whereas Bernice smiled at the old man, Roderic gazed about in a complete air of boredom.

"Sit down," commanded Holloway, with an impatient wave of his hand. "Where is Horace?"

Forschell brushed by Kirk and entered the room. "Here, sir," he said. "I have all the data."

He set a large pile of papers in front of Holloway. The old man turned to the table and thumbed over them for what seemed an age. Ludovic's hands shook. His mother's eyes were staring. Finally Holloway raised his head.

"We are all ready to go ahead, I think," he said gruffly. "The reason that I have called you together here is that I intend to draw a new will. I want every one of you to witness it! Be seated, Jasper; you will find writing materials there on the table. I hope that you will all make yourselves comfortable; this will take a little time. Very well, Jasper, let us proceed."

The attorney's pen, scratched hurriedly over the foolscap, translating the wishes of the old millionaire into legal phraseology. Eyes were on the old than, cunning, avaricious, desperate and sad, as he portioned his millions. Sums amounting to a prince's ransom were bequeathed to charities, museums and universities. At length Holloway yanked open the drawer of the table, swept his notes into it, and flung it shut again. Not one of his relatives or any other single person had been mentioned in the will.

"That," he said harshly, "takes care of every last penny I possess. Here, give me that!"

He seized the will from under Sinclair's nose. Roughly snatching the pen from the attorney's hand, with a defiant flourish he affixed his name to the document. He lifted his head and glared from one to the other of his relatives.

"Now," he growled, "I want every man and woman in this room who has been yearning for my death to set his signature to this as a witness. We should have plenty of signatures to my last will!"

A profound, dreadful silence that followed this offer was broken by a harsh, sneering laugh from Roderic.

"I'll be damned if I'll sign it," he muttered. "Afraid, Uncle, that you'll have to get along without me."

He picked up his coat, his derby and his stick and strolled with exaggerated nonchalance out of the room. Bernice veiled her eyes to hide the pain that was in them. But she forced a little smile and rose quickly. She took up the pen and signed her name to the will. Carefully putting the pen back on the table, she patted the old man gently on the shoulder. He stared down at the floor, apparently not heeding her. Bernice picked up her coat. Clark sprang at her assistance. With eyes filled with compassion, he helped her into the coat.

"Bernice," said Holloway, without looking up at her, "your allowance will continue as long as I live."

She did not attempt to speak. Instead, she stepped up to him again and patted him affectionately on the shoulder. Then she followed her brother out of the room.

Ludovic and his mother sat dazed with horror. With a sudden sharp cry, Eleanor Holloway leaped to her feet, eyes staring wildly. She rushed up to the table, panting in her rage, and shrieked at Leander Holloway.

"You old beast!" she cried. "Giving your filthy money to strangers, and the son of your own nephew you let slowly die! And I, the widow of Randolph Holloway, am allowed to live in want!"

Holloway wearily lifted his hand. "I know you, Eleanor," he said. "You are more concerned about yourself than you are about your son. I am still considering Ludovic's case. But you get nothing from me! You have nothing to keep you here."

For a moment she stood glaring malignantly at him. The rage stamped on her own features was reflected in the wasted face of her son. Then she helped Ludovic on with his coat. Together they sullenly left the room. Kirk closed the door and followed them down the stairs.

Holloway smiled wryly and looked down at his will. "One signature," he mused. "Well, I'll need more than that. Jasper, will you sign it?"

The lawyer compressed his lips. Snatching up the pen, he hurriedly signed his name to the will, as though to get it done before achieving the strength to refuse. He stood, pen in hand, looking down at the will. Then he threw the pen on the desk and swung about with his back to the others

"It is done," he said harshly. "I did all that could be expected of me. But we'll say no more about that."

Holloway got out of his chair. He picked up the will and folded it. He laughed, and was visibly excited.

"Yes," he said, "it is done. I have outwitted them!"

"I'm not so sure," frowned Gerrity. "It's all right as far as those who were here are concerned. But there is one of your relatives who was not here."

"You mean Phil, eh?" said Holloway. "Well, Inspector, you're wrong. If he'd been here he'd have thought it was all a huge joke. He's like that. He wouldn't have my money, anyway. No, Inspector, I have a feeling that Phil Holloway is dead. You'll get nowhere by concentrating on him."

"Maybe," replied the inspector skeptically.

Kirk opened the door and suspiciously ushered into the room Leander Holloway's chauffeur, dressed in impeccable livery.

"Ah," said Hand, "I see that the police department has creaked and regurgitated Gus Staub."

"Nothin' like that happened, sir," Gus assured him.

"Gus!" exclaimed Holloway. "By thunder, step in here."

The chauffeur, cap in hand, walked respectfully into the room. He halted before his employer, grinning broadly.

"Good mornin', sir," he said. "Any orders?"

"Orders!" scoffed Holloway. "Dammit, Gus, you've hardly had a thing to do for the past two weeks. Here I am cooped up as if I'd been given thirty days for chicken stealing! The first thing you know, I tell you, I'll fix it up with your wife to have you mind the baby."

Gus grinned broader than ever. "Yes, sir," he said.

"But look here, Gus," said Holloway sternly, "what do you mean by snooping around out back when there's a murder going on in the house?"

The grin and a large volume of air slid into Gus's mouth. "I didn't," he gulped. "Simeon's been seein' things, sir. Ask the inspector; I had to get an alibi for him."

"Well, it's a good thing you had one," said Holloway. "I'm going to keep you out of mischief. You go down to the Settlement and tell them you and the car are at their disposal for all day. Report back here in the morning, just in case I may want you. And take this book down with you; I've finished it."

Gus picked up the book and departed, his grin fully restored. He was replaced almost immediately by Simeon. The old fellow started rearranging the furniture.

"Simeon," ordered Holloway, "take this will and put it in the wall-safe in the den with the old one. By the way, Jasper, I suppose I should destroy that old will, shouldn't I?"

"It makes no difference," curtly replied Sinclair. "All of the bequests in the old will are voided by the new one. I suggest that you keep the old one. It would be reinstated if the courts should ever nullify the one you have just made. As I warned you, you're not leaving a cent to your kin, and it is dangerous to—"

"Yes, yes," grinned Holloway, "you told me all that before. Take it, Simeon, and put it in the wall-safe."

Grumbling as usual when pulled out of the orbit he had
elected for himself, Simeon took the will and plodded off
to the study. He took a creased and worn piece of paper
from his pocket and squinted at the faded set of numer-
als thereon. Thus having refreshed his memory with the
combination, he opened the safe and put the will into it.
Banging the door shut again, he swung back into position
over the safe the picture that concealed it. Then, having
already forgotten about putting the front sitting-room to
rights, he went off to another part of the house.

Those in the sitting-room remained there for some
time conversing. Forschell did not take part. He opened
the drawer of the table and took out the notes he had prepared for Holloway to make the will. He sorted them out
and left to take them to his office. At length Sinclair, who
had taken no pains to be congenial, announced that he had
to go to his office and get busy.

Holloway's eyes twinkled. "Won't stay for lunch, Jasper?" he asked.

"No," firmly replied Sinclair.

"I say, Mr. Sinclair," said Clark, "you're forgetting that
it's Saturday. Surely your office will be closed by the time
you get to it."

"It will," curtly agreed Sinclair. "But I shall be working there, nevertheless, until well into the evening. I do
every Saturday. It is the only way I can keep abreast of my
work."

The others all decided to leave with him. As they
stepped out into the hall, a man in the study stiffened before the wall-safe and held his breath. He listened tensely
for several moments. Satisfied that there was no immediate danger of interruption, he went swiftly back to
twirling the dial of the safe. A few seconds later the door

swung open. He thrust his hand into the safe and took out two legal documents. He heard the shuffling step of Leander Holloway coming down the hall. He quickly closed the safe and adjusted the picture over it. When Holloway entered the study, the man was gone. The old million- aire sat down at his desk and commenced placidly reading a book. Sergeant Kirk, tireless after almost twenty-four hours of constant duty, grimly guarded his door.

13

A PIECE OF BLACK CLOTH

Jasper Sinclair took a subway down to his office. Somewhat awkwardly Clark excused himself and left Hand and Gerrity. Very soon Bernice was admitting him to her apartment. She smiled, and Clark, although he tried frantically, could not tell whether it was because she was glad to see him or because she was amused at him. From a reclining position on a divan, Roderic greeted Clark affably. Of all those whom fate had recently thrown in the young man's path, he liked Clark far and away the best. Clark was, in fact, the only one he liked at all.

Bernice declined Clark's invitation to go out to luncheon, explaining that she was standing between Roderic and temporary starvation. This Roderic heartily corroborated. But both of them insisted that Clark stay and have luncheon with them. He did, after Bernice had accepted his invitation to take her out to dinner in the evening. Immediately after luncheon Roderic departed for the Lambs Club, leaving the dishes to be done by Bernice and Clark, who insisted upon giving his assistance. At this task detested by so many of his sex, Clark was sublimely happy.

Hand and Gerrity went into the Plaza for lunch. Gerrity ate a quantity of food, befitting his bulk, and lingered over it. Hand ate sparingly and wasted no time. Neither spoke, during the meal or after it. Hand lighted cigarette after cigarette; Gerrity puffed fiercely on a cigar. When it was gone he lighted another. They sat thus in silence for over an hour, while the waiters, casting reproving glances in their direction, despaired of ever getting their table into service again. Hand stamped out a final cigarette and glanced sharply over at the inspector. Gerrity knew what he was going to be asked. He threw his second cigar stub into the ash receiver.

"Like to go over to the rooms?" asked Hand.

"Sure," grunted Gerrity.

In Hand's living-room, Gerrity picked up the telephone and gave the number of police headquarters. He wanted to let them know where they could get in touch with him. Hand dropped into his easy chair and peered up at him.

"Inspector," he asked, "are you going to put a detective on Jasper Sinclair?"

"I am," growled Gerrity.

At that moment he was connected with headquarters and got his call put through to his office. He told the sergeant there where he was and ordered a detective assigned to Sinclair. Then he turned suddenly to Hand.

"Where is that lawyer's office?" he demanded.

"Unger Building, William Street," replied Hand. "I've looked him up."

Gerrity gave instructions that the detective was to keep track of Sinclair but not to let the lawyer realize he was under surveillance. Then he hung up. He got another cigar going and stood frowning over Hand.

"Got any suggestions," he asked, "as to how we could strengthen our defenses?"

"I can think of none, Inspector; we seem to have everything covered."

Gerrity took to pacing slowly up and down, trailing heavy cigar smoke after him. "Yes," he said thoughtfully.

"And yet, I keep expecting something new to flash out of the cursed darkness that surrounds this case!"

"Your intuition, Inspector. Considered by some a doubtful blessing. It so happens that mine is not altogether dormant just now, nor has it been ever since I took up the threads of this case. A devilish thing, feeling certain that catastrophe waits on a hair trigger, but you don't know where."

Gerrity growled under his breath. He took a few turns up and down in silence. Then he halted before Hand.

"Well," he snapped, "how're we going to stop it?"

"I confess that I don't know," replied Hand. "Your guards and shadows may prevent further mischief. I doubt it. The invisible force that we are dealing with has shown himself to be far too clever to be blocked by any such superficial barrier to his macabre enterprise. As Leander Holloway says, we have got to outwit him."

"It seems impossible! A ghost would leave more clues behind him. We have got nowhere!"

"Hardly as bad as that. We have managed to dissipate a grim ruse or two that he left behind him. And we have succeeded in frustrating two or three deadly thrusts of his. Let us now, Inspector, trace through this sinister affair from what appears to be its inception. I have done it a hundred times. If there is a hidden clue along the way, or one that we have merely overlooked, I confess that I have not been able to detect it. But it would not be the first time that we have considered together with profit."

"Go ahead."

Hand sat forward, his eyes narrowing. Gerrity sank into a chair. There was a pile of burnt match sticks on the table. As Hand recapitulated the episodes in the grim series, he slid a match along the table, adding to the smaller pile as he went along.

"So far as we know," he said, "the action starts with Robert Bradshaw. He needed money."

"I've had Malloy on the mat," growled Gerrity. "It was a woman that he got Bradshaw sewed up with. She wanted twenty-five thousand to keep her from wrecking his reputation. And I can't get anything on that scoundrel Malloy at that!"

"So much for that, then. Bradshaw went after his inheritance. He did it in a clumsy fashion and failed."

Hand placed the first match aside.

"Yes," said Gerrity, "but in failing he gave someone else the idea. And this second person is a good deal more intelligent than Bradshaw was. He planned to wipe out all the other potential legatees and get all the old man's money for himself. He still plans to do that!"

"Now," said Hand, "we pass to Phil Holloway. He returned to New York and very promptly buried himself. But he made no effort to cover his tricks until the morning after Bradshaw's attack on Leander Holloway. He may have got the idea you speak of right then. No more is known of him."

Hand broke a match stick in half and placed one of the halves beside the first stick. Gerrity peered at them quizzically.

"Next," said Hand, "we take the murders of Bradshaw and Morley. Bradshaw and Leander Holloway were duped into meeting each other in the old man's study. Bradshaw was shot through the head. Either the murderer or an accomplice spirited the body away and dumped it into the river. Later it was recovered and identified as that of the man who made the original attempt upon Leander Holloway's life. Morley was shot down in cold blood. A forged note was left in his rooms to persuade investigators that the young man had committed suicide. It was also intended to persuade us that Morley had a hand in the murder of Bradshaw."

Hand placed the second half match stick beside the first. Gerrity's curiosity would not be pressed back.

"What's the idea," he irritably demanded, "of fooling with those blasted match sticks like that?"

"This one," smiled Hand, indicating the one he had not broken, "represents Bradshaw's attack upon Leander Holloway. We know all there is to know about that. This half stick is Phil Holloway; we don't know everything about him. And this other half represents the murders of Bradshaw and Morley. We know how they were killed, but we don't know who killed them."

"Go on," grunted Gerrity.

"Let us take the attacks upon me," said Hand. "The first one was followed closely by the murders of Bradshaw and Morley. I believe all three shots were fired by the same hand. Quick work, but he could have accomplished it. He came here first and attempted unsuccessfully to remove all possibility of my interference. Then he hastened to that apartment behind Leander Holloway's house and shot Bradshaw. He went directly down town and murdered Morley."

"I should say it was quick work!"

"Could have been done, just the same, and the whole thing seems to be the work of a single individual. Now the second attack upon me was crude and beneath our man's intelligence. It may eventually hang him. We have the thugs he indirectly hired to do the job, and if we can capture Biordino we may get at our man through him. But we don't know who that man is yet. This represents the attacks upon me."

He broke another match and placed a half on the little pile.

"Go on," said Gerrity.

"The next incident," said Hand, "is the attempted poisoning of Leander Holloway. The arsenic must have been placed in his salt shaker some time between breakfast and luncheon. And here we have the first episode in which the case was positively narrowed down."

"You're right!" snapped Gerrity. "That salt shaker was loaded by somebody who had access to the house that morning! Here's who they were: Mrs. Eleanor Holloway and Ludovic; Bernice and Roderic; Jasper Sinclair; Horace Forschell; Simeon; Gus Staub was there; the maid and the cook. It's one of them!"

"We really had decided before that, however, that it was someone who had easy access to the house. The whole thing has been planned almost on schedule with Leander Holloway's private habits. And the murderer of Morley certainly had knowledge of the young man's habits, too. Nevertheless, Inspector, we don't know who put the arsenic in the salt shaker. This half match does for that."

Gerrity scowled as Hand put the broken piece with the others. "All right," he said. "What next?"

"Gus Staub," promptly replied Hand. "I feel satisfied that the man was maligned by Simeon. Are you satisfied of that?"

"No!"

"Very well, another half match for our score board. And I think that brings it up to date. Let's look these match sticks over. We have six. In other words, there are six distinct episodes that have fallen under our attention. We know all there is to know about one—the attempt upon Leander Holloway's life in Central Park. It is represented here by this full-sized match. The other five episodes are all masked in obscurity, an obscurity that conceals the one who perpetrated them, or if not that, it conceals anything that might identify the individual person with the crime."

"We are almost as much in the dark as ever!"

"We have a few bits of tangible evidence—two forged notes, the pistol that killed Morley and the cartridge that made an end of Bradshaw. Then, of course, we have the bullets that Dr. Richards extracted from the heads of the two men."

Gerrity viciously knocked the ashes from his cigar. "Clues!" he scoffed. "There aren't any clues! Never saw such a case!"

Hand settled himself in his chair, burying his chin on his chest. He stared long at the wall without speaking. Gerrity cocked an eye at him.

"There are clues," said Hand slowly. "But you won't see them. They are intangible clues. Their substance is no more than the thin air, and upon them we must construct our case."

"I'd rather think," said Gerrity gloomily, "that Leander Holloway's new will has removed the incentive and there will be no more trouble."

"Yes," nodded Hand. "But in any event we have a double murder to solve. I presume, Inspector, that you have been exercising your mind on the problem. I have. Suppose we exchange our views."

"Suits me," smiled Gerrity. "You promised to have some more of your theories. Go ahead."

And as they talked, a man entered the Unger Building in William Street. The day was brisk and cool, but hardly cold enough to account for his coat collar being up, with his chin buried in it. His hat was pulled low over his eyes. The lobby of the building was deserted. The man deliberately avoided the elevators and mounted the stairs instead, floor after floor until he had reached the seventh. About to walk down the hall, he drew back and cautiously descended the stairs again a few steps. Two men, carrying brushes and vacuum cleaner attachments, had come out of an office near the end of the hall. Concealed from them by the wall of the stairs, the man listened intently. The janitors paused in the hall, engaging in a noisy altercation concerning the respective merits of two contenders for the heavyweight prizefight championship of the world. Finally they took their argument and their impedimenta into another office, their voices becoming almost inaudible.

The man on the stairs once again mounted cautiously to the hall. He satisfied himself that no one else was in sight. Then he strode rapidly over to an office door. On the ground glass panel of it was emblazoned in gilt letters: JASPER SINCLAIR—COUNSELOR AT LAW. The man silently slipped a skeleton key into the lock and just as silently turned the bolt and opened the door. Like a spectre he floated over the threshold and closed the door after him. He stood in an outer office, alone. From a coat pocket he slowly drew a stiletto, a stiletto with a keen, flashing blade. Then he glided across the floor to the door of an inner office, paused momentarily, and vanished inside. Less than three minutes later he was back in the outer office again. He opened the door to the hall and peered out cautiously. Unobserved, he crossed the hall and descended the stairs to the street. A few seconds later he was lost among the people on the sidewalk.

Not long after that a detective from police headquarters entered the Unger Building. He glanced at the directory in the lobby and then rang for the elevator. He rang several times more, finally giving it up and walking irritably up seven flights of stairs. He walked quietly down the hall. After pausing momentarily at the door to Sinclair's office, he passed on and took up his station in an alcove at the far end of the building.

The two janitors came out into the hall, still vigorously on the subject of pugilism, and carried their brushes and vacuum attachments into Sinclair's office. The detective once more settled himself as comfortably as possible in his alcove. Ten minutes later he was electrified. A hoarse shout had come from the lawyer's office. The detective sped down the hall and cautiously entered. A few moments later he was speaking to police headquarters over Sinclair's phone. He had scarcely hung up the receiver before police headquarters was calling Christopher Hand's rooms. Hand answered and then held the phone out to Gerrity.

"For you," he said.

Gerrity gave him a quick, apprehensive glance. He set his jaw and took the phone.

"This is Inspector Gerrity."

"This is Lieutenant Aldworth. Holloway's lawyer, Jasper Sinclair, has been murdered. Reported by Detective Hayzen."

"God! Hayzen's report, quick!"

"Body was found by two janitors in the lawyer's office in the Unger Building, William Street. He was stabbed through the heart from behind, although there had been a struggle. Evidently had been dead but a short while. I've ordered Hayzen to stay there to guard the body."

"Send the finger-print men right down. Also get in touch with Dr. Richards. I will be at the Unger Building in a few minutes."

Gerrity set the phone down with scant regard for the delicate construction of the instrument. Hand had risen to his feet. He was slowly pulling at his under lip. He flashed a glance to the inspector's choleric countenance.

"Our intuitions, Inspector," he said softly, "seem to have been working well."

"Damn!" exploded Gerrity. "Sinclair has been murdered!"

"So I gathered," said Hand. "Shall we go?"

Gerrity jammed his hat on his head and got angrily into his coat. He felt mightily impotent, and that always moved him to wrath. Hand quietly led him down the stairs. As they stepped out to the sidewalk, Hand's eyes narrowed and rapidly took in everything to be seen in the street.

He lost no time getting into the inspector's car. Gerrity gruffly ordered the patient Kelly to drive to the Unger Building. He had them there with his customary dispatch. The elevators in the Unger Building, at least one of them, was now in commission. In response to Gerrity's vicious thrusts of the signal button, it stopped at the street floor for them. A thin, care-worn man in a high state of nerves was operating it. When Hand ordered him to take them to the seventh floor, he very nearly swooned. He got them there, but as soon as they had left the elevator he closed the gate and shot it up to the top floor.

Hand and Gerrity entered Sinclair's outer office. There they found the two janitors, the superintendent of the building, the detective and a policeman in uniform. There were several clerk's desks in the outer office. Near the door was a telephone switchboard.

"Hayzen," said Gerrity to the detective, "how did you let this happen?"

Hayzen squirmed. "Inspector," he said earnestly, "nobody came in this office after I got here except these two men."

He indicated the two janitors, whose faces blanched with dismay.

"We wouldn't hurt a flea!" one of them cried.

"We just found him," gulped the other. "I ain't got over it yet."

"Stay here, all of you," growled Gerrity. "He's in there, Hayzen?"

"That's it, Inspector; right in there."

Quickly stepping into Sinclair's private office, Hand and Gerrity paused just inside the door. The lawyer lay on his face, his arms crumpled under him and his head buckled under his chest. From his back just below his left shoulder blade there protruded the handle of a stiletto. All about it, the back of his coat was stained a dark crimson.

A chair was overturned beside the body. Several large law books, knocked from their places on the shelves that lined the office, lay scattered on the floor. A coat rack lay on its side near the door.

Hand bounded forward. He crouched beside the corpse. Reaching under the right shoulder, he seized the lawyer's wrist and pulled his arm out straight. He looked up at Gerrity, pointing with his long finger at Sinclair's tightly-clenched fist. Between the dead thumb and forefinger a torn bit of black cloth protruded.

14

RODERIC

Christopher Hand carefully extricated the tattered piece of black cloth from Sinclair's convulsed right hand. Gerrity bent over him and squinted at the find.

"That will help," growled Gerrity. "It's really the only piece of evidence of the least bit of an incriminating nature that he's left behind him throughout the whole case. His one slip!"

Hand peered intently at the little piece of cloth. It was about two inches square and was ragged on three sides. There was a narrow hem on the fourth side.

"From the texture and general appearance of this," mused Hand, "I'd say it was torn from the lining of an overcoat."

"No doubt of it," agreed Gerrity. "The thing to do is to make an immediate check of the overcoats of everyone we suspect. Let's get started!"

"One moment, Inspector," said Hand. "Before anything is disturbed, let us make a careful note of the complete situation in this office. Sinclair has been stabbed through the back, the blade undoubtedly passing straight through his heart."

"Sure. He was probably sitting in that chair lying on its side before the desk. But he was not killed by stealth. There was a terrific struggle in here; everything is knocked about. But when that knife was driven into him, it killed him instantly."

"Precisely. Now just let us see."

Hand drew Sinclair's cuff back over the wrist. He made a slight indentation with his thumb-nail in the flesh of the wrist and carefully noted the length of time that it took to disappear.

"I'm no medical examiner," he muttered, "but I'd say this man has been dead about two hours. Rigor mortis not very pronounced, but present."

"Then, blast it, Hayzen didn't get here until after he was murdered! What luck! If I'd had him here earlier the whole thing would be cleared up now. But let's go. Here, I'll take that infernal dagger with me."

He put a glove on his right hand and withdrew the blade from the wound. Meanwhile, Hand disappeared into a small lavatory just off the office. He reappeared with a hand-towel, into which the inspector wrapped the stiletto. Then he placed it into his overcoat pocket. They then went out to the outer office.

"Hayzen," ordered Gerrity, "take those two men who discovered the body up to headquarters and have them make out statements. Make out one yourself. You, Patrolman, stay here and guard this body until it is removed. Dr. Richards will be here shortly, and so will the finger-print men."

Hand and Gerrity went out and rang for the elevator. When it arrived they got in and started down. Hand turned to the operator.

"Did you take anyone up to the seventh floor this afternoon?" he demanded.

"Yes, sir. It makes me cold all over to think of it."

"Do you know who it was?"

"Yes, sir. It was M-Mr. S-Sinclair!"

"Hell!" exclaimed Gerrity disgustedly.

"Did you," pressed Hand, "take anyone else to the seventh floor?"

"No, sir."

"Did you take anyone up to any floor?"

"No, sir."

The elevator stopped at the street floor. The operator was relieved about that; he did not like the company he was in. He reached out quickly to open the gate. Hand seized his wrist, gently but very firmly, and drew his arm back. The operator was dismayed.

"I noticed," said Hand coldly, "that there are two elevators. Is the other one operating?"

"N-no, sir. The other fellow's off. We take turns workin' Saturday afternoons."

"If anyone had rung for the elevator, you would have heard it?"

The operator was palpably uncomfortable. He glanced uneasily at Hand, and encountering Hand's gray eyes, his own quickly dropped. His face suddenly flushed.

"Nobody rung the bell, sir."

"I want the truth out of you! Speak up!"

"Uh—well—well, maybe I dozed off a little up in the superintendent's office. I guess I did."

"Then you wouldn't have seen anyone who might have been prowling round the building?"

"Oh, no, sir! I took a snooze right after I took Mr. Sinclair up. I didn't wake up until I heard about the murder."

Gerrity lost his patience. "Let's get out of here!" he snapped. "Open this thing up!"

The operator was only too glad to comply. Hand and Clark got into the inspector's car and were driven swiftly over to the apartment house where Ludovic Holloway lived with his mother. They found the detective assigned to Ludovic lurking in the hall. The one who was responsible for Mrs. Holloway, they were informed, was even then peering at them from a partially-opened door across the hall, through which he had let himself into a vacant apartment. The detective told them that neither Ludovic nor his mother had been out since that morning.

"Sure Ludovic didn't go out a fire escape, or something like that?" asked Gerrity.

"Well, I ain't sure, Inspector," replied the detective. "But that guy don't seem to be up to no gymnastics, and I can't see the lady doin' it. I think they're both in there without a doubt."

Gerrity rang the bell. Within less than a minute it was opened by Ludovic, backed up by his mother. Neither of them seemed particularly happy to see who their callers were.

"Have you been out this afternoon, Mr. Holloway?" asked Gerrity.

"I can't see that it's any of your business," angrily retorted Ludovic.

"It is, though," replied Gerrity shortly. "I don't want to be unpleasant, but I must insist upon an answer."

"Of course he hasn't been out!" snapped his mother. "He's been here with me ever since we left that old ingrate's house this morning."

"All right," said Gerrity. "Do you mind if we come in and look—"

"Of course I mind!" snapped Ludovic.

"Very well," said Gerrity. "A search warrant might be embarrassing to you. I thought perhaps you would rather not make one necessary."

Ludovic and his mother exchanged a long glance. Finally, a faint flush in his white cheeks, the young man turned abruptly and walked back into the apartment. Mrs. Holloway's eyes hardened. She glared at Hand and the inspector.

"Come in, then," she said sharply. "We have nothing to conceal."

They went immediately to the coat closet. There was but one man's coat hanging there. An examination revealed that the lining was intact. Ludovic stood close by and sneered at them.

"Got another overcoat?" demanded Gerrity.

"No," growled Ludovic.

"Mind if we look about?" gruffly asked the inspector.

Again Ludovic's pale cheeks colored slightly. His mother's eyes flashed. They both turned their backs on Hand and Gerrity. The apartment was small, and it did not take them long to determine that there was no other man's overcoat in it. The inspector thanked Ludovic and his mother quite insincerely, and they left. Back in Gerrity's car, the inspector avoided glancing at Hand and ordered Kelly to drive them to Bernice's apartment. Hand said nothing. They discovered the two detectives assigned to Bernice and Roderic foregathering together in the hallway outside the apartment. Gerrity accosted them.

"Roderic in the apartment?"

"Yes, sir. Been there about a half hour."

"Where's he been since he left the old man's house this morning?"

"Well, Inspector, him and his sister came right over here. Then about one-thirty Roderic went out. I followed him over to the Lambs Club."

"And he stayed there until he returned here?"

"No, sir. He went out and hopped the Lexington Avenue down town. He got off at Fulton Street. I trailed him over to William Street and he went into the Unger Buil—"

"What!"

"The Unger Building, Inspector."

"By gad! Where did he go in the building?"

"He went up the stairs all the way to the seventh floor. I watched him go into the office of that lawyer guy, Jasper Sinclair."

Inspector Gerrity closed his eyes and sucked in his
breath. He clenched his hands and expelled the air from
his lungs in a long, satisfied sigh. The muscles of Hand's
jaw rippled up and down his cheek. His narrowed eyes
flashed, but they were not focused on anything in particular. His mind was working furiously. Gerrity's eyes flew
open.

"Stay here," he snapped at the detectives. "Hand, my
net has closed in. Do you want to go into that apartment
with me? I understand how you must feel about this."

Once again Hand's face was inscrutable. "My dear
Inspector," he smiled, "all your men could not keep me
out of that apartment."

Gerrity nodded and grinned. He stepped over to the
door and rang the bell. Bernice promptly opened it. Her
quick smile faded just as quickly and was replaced by an
expression of concern.

"Anything new?" she asked, almost in a whisper.

Some of Gerrity's enthusiasm left him. "Well, yes," he
replied. "May we come in?"

"By all means!" invited Bernice heartily. "Mr. Clark
and Roddy are here. Come in and—and tell us."

She stood aside as they entered and closed the door
after them. Then she followed them quickly across the tiny
hall and into the living-room. Roderic lay sprawled on the
divan. Clark had risen to his feet. He glanced apprehensively from one to the other of his old friends. Roderic
languidly threw his legs to the floor and slowly rose, smiling mockingly.

"Good afternoon, gentlemen," he drawled. "What have
our two prize sleuths been trailing now."

"Roddy, don't be so nasty!" said Bernice. "Mr. Hand,
has—has something else—happened?"

Hand slowly nodded his head. "Jasper Sinclair," he
said, "was murdered this afternoon."

Bernice's hand flew to her mouth. Clark stepped quickly to her side. Roderic's artificial bearing deserted him. He gaped at Hand.

"Mr. Holloway," asked Gerrity, in a deep rumbling voice, "may I see your overcoat?"

"That's a strange request," said Roderic.

Bernice glanced wonderingly from the inspector to her brother. "His overcoat?" she asked. "What do you mean?"

"What are you up to, Gerrity?" demanded Clark.

"Surely nothing is the matter!" cried Bernice. "Mr. Hand, what is this all about? What does it mean?"

"Miss Holloway," said Hand, "never forget for an instant that I am constantly working in your interest. For the moment I shall take no part. But I should advise Mr. Holloway to answer truthfully everything that the inspector wishes to ask him."

"I want to see your overcoat," snapped Gerrity.

"Do you?" sneered Roderic. "I want to know what you can possibly want to see it for."

"Don't be silly, Roddy," said Bernice. "I'll get it for you, Inspector."

Her face was very white as she went out into the hall. Roderic shrugged his shoulders petulantly and threw himself back on the divan. Clark eyed the inspector, his apprehension growing. He had detected certain unmistakable symptoms that, in the circumstances, filled him with alarm.

Bernice returned with Roderic's coat. Scarcely breathing, she handed it to Gerrity. The inspector took it eagerly. He threw it inside out over a chair and bent tensely over it. With a yelp of triumph he snatched up the corner of it near the lapel and pointed excitedly to a spot where a portion of the lining had been torn away. From his pocket he snatched the piece of black cloth Hand had taken from the dead fingers of Jasper Sinclair. It fitted perfectly into the rent in the lining of Roderic's coat. Roderic had edged over on the couch, his eyes sharply following the inspector's movements. Gerrity spun about, glaring viciously at him, and held the piece of cloth before his face.

"Do you know where I got that?" he snarled. "Jasper Sinclair tore that out of your coat when you attacked him and killed him! That piece of cloth was found clutched in Sinclair's right hand!"

"No!" cried Bernice hysterically. "You can't mean it! It—it must be a mistake!"

Clark threw his arm about her. She shivered and drew close to him. His brown eyes perplexed and dismayed, Roderic stared foolishly from one to the other of them. Then he flushed and tossed his head.

"Ridiculous!" he cried.

Gerrity merely glared at him. The inspector took from his pocket the stiletto wrapped in the towel. He unfolded it and laid the towel, stained and smudged with crimson, out upon a table in a corner of the room. Gingerly with his gloved hand, he laid the stiletto on it.

Bernice gasped and stared horror-stricken at the deadly weapon. Roderic's face had gone livid. He glared feverishly at the stiletto. Clark's heart dropped at the sight of it. He gently turned Bernice away. She sobbed once or twice and then steeled herself. Gerrity pointed grimly at the blood-stained stiletto and frowned at Roderic.

"Where did you get that?" he demanded.

Roderic seemed not to hear. He continued to stare fixedly at the knife. But suddenly he shot to his feet and turned his back on them.

"I never saw it before!" he said hoarsely.

"No?" growled the inspector shrewdly. "Well, I think you did, and I think your sister has seen it before, too. We'll see whether we can find out!"

He strode out into the little hall. On the house telephone he called the superintendent and ordered him to present himself in Bernice's apartment. Those in the living-room remained motionless and silent. Presently there was a timid ring of the door-bell. Gerrity admitted the superintendent and ushered him quite energetically into the living-room. The little man was painfully distressed.

"I hope nothing's wrong," he said meekly.

"Your name's Snedick, as I recall it," growled Gerrity.

"Yes, sir. That's right, Mr. Snedick."

"Did you ever see this before?"

Gerrity shot the question at him, at the same time flinging out a hand to point viciously at the stiletto. Snedick peered at the knife. He recoiled and uttered a sharp cry.

"S-somebody's b-been hurt!" he stammered.

"That knife!" barked Gerrity. "Whose is it?"

"The knife?" chattered Snedick. "It's Miss—" He caught himself and glanced fearfully at Bernice. She was staring at him in an agony of apprehension. Gerrity seized the little superintendent by the shoulders and twisted him roughly about to face him.

"Whose is that knife?" he snapped.

"It's—it's—oh, don't ask me!" wailed Snedick.

Roderic whirled fiercely about. "Let him alone!" he said harshly. "The knife is mine, of course. It's been in full sight on that table for months. Somebody must have stolen it."

Gerrity grimly nodded and released Snedick. "I suppose so," he said sarcastically. "You had missed it, and everything like that."

"No," growled Roderic. "I thought it was on the table all the time."

"What have you been doing with yourself this afternoon, Mr. Holloway?"

"That's my business."

"Yes, and mine, too. So you don't want to tell me where you've been this afternoon, eh?"

"Not particularly."

Gerrity abruptly walked out to the door. "Come in here, Howlett," he ordered.

The detective who had been assigned to Roderic walked nonchalantly into the living-room, followed by the inspector. Gerrity fastened his eyes on Roderic and never removed them.

"Howlett," he said, "you have had an assignment?"

"Yes, sir."

"What was it?"

"Trailing Mr. Holloway, sir."

"This Mr. Holloway, right here?"

"That's him, sir. I had my eye on him all afternoon."

Roderic paled. But he threw his head back and smiled scornfully.

"All right, Howlett," said Gerrity, "tell us what Mr. Holloway did."

"Well, sir, he came here from the old gent's house for lunch, I guess. Then he went over to the Lambs Club. Then I trailed him down town on the Lexington Avenue. He went over to the Unger Building in William Street and walked up the stairs to the seventh floor. He went into the law offices of Jasper Sinclair. After a few minutes he came out again and walked down to the street. Then he went back to the Lambs Club for a while and finally came back here about a half an hour ago. He's been here ever since."

Clark, feeling miserable, turned to look at Roderic. He was still smiling, but his smile was mirthless and set.

"You see, young fellow," said Gerrity, "it didn't do you a bit of good to tell me that you weren't in Sinclair's office this afternoon."

"You're mistaken, Inspector," corrected Roderic; "I didn't tell you that I wasn't in Sinclair's office this afternoon. I merely told you that it was none of your business."

"But now it looks as if it is my business, eh?"

"Well, perhaps it is. But I can explain the whole thing."

"Can you prove it?"

"Yes, of course I—" Roderic caught himself, swallowed, and dropped his eyes.

"Can't prove it, eh?" taunted Gerrity.

"Afraid not," replied Roderic politely. "You see, the only person whom I know could establish my innocence is Jasper Sinclair, and you say he is dead."

"Suppose he were alive, how could he establish your innocence?"

"Look here, Inspector, I'll tell you the whole thing, and you can see for yourself that someone framed me. Jasper Sinclair called me at the Lambs Club and asked me to come down to his office. I thought it had something to do with that balmy new will of Uncle Leander's; so I hopped right down there. He was alive then, all right, and mighty surprised to see me. He said he hadn't called me at all and that there was no occasion for him to have wanted to see me. We both realized at once, of course, that the whole thing was a hoax. Sinclair was inclined to be nervous about it. But he was always getting nervous about something. I laughed it off, thought it was one of my bright friends giving me a wild goose chase. There, you can see just how it all happened."

"Oh, yes. But your story doesn't account for just two things. This piece of cloth torn from your coat lining got into Sinclair's hand, and that dagger got into his heart. How do you account for those?"

Roderic shook his head miserably. "I can't."

"Had you noticed that your coat was torn?"

"No."

"Got anything else to say?"

Roderic spread his hands and shook his head helplessly. All his bravado was gone. He suddenly appeared very young and very helpless. With a cry of compassion, Bernice ran over to him and threw her arms about him. He straightened his shoulders and smiled down at her.

"Don't worry, sis," he said hoarsely. "They're all wrong. I'll get out of this somehow."

"Of course you will!" she said tensely. "They can't do anything to you!"

Gerrity was by no means as hard-bitten as he always liked to appear. But he was a police officer, first, last and always. He took Roderic by the arm.

"Young man," he said, "you're under arrest. I charge you with the murders of Robert Bradshaw, Quentin Morley and Jasper Sinclair and the attempted murder of Leander Holloway and Christopher Hand. We'll have to go down to police headquarters now. Howlett, you take Snedick down with you; he knows that dagger belongs to Holloway, and he's going to sign a statement to that effect!"

Howlett started the badly-perturbed superintendent for the door. Hand had been leaning easily up against the wall. He straightened suddenly.

"Howlett!" he snapped.

The detective's knees sagged momentarily; then he spun about. "What?" he gulped.

"Say *sir* when you speak to me!" whipped Hand, his eyes narrowed.

"Yes, sir."

"It is possible, Howlett, that you deliberately refrained from giving a very important piece of information here. If you did, and you don't correct it immediately, I will see the commissioner and have you out on the street without a job in thirty minutes!"

Hand's voice cut menacingly; his eyes glittered. Howlett colored uncomfortably and wished he were somewhere else.

"Yes, sir."

"When Mr. Holloway entered the Unger Building, did he ring for the elevator?"

Roderic suddenly clasped Bernice joyfully to him. "Why didn't I think of that!" he cried. "Of course that shows—"

"Wait," cautioned Clark, laying a kindly hand on Roderic's shoulder.

Howlett glanced appealingly over to his chief. Gerrity stepped quickly forward.

"Wait a minute, Hand," he said. "This is my investigation, you know."

"So it is, Inspector," replied Hand, his voice reverting to normal. "But I could not be convinced that you would willingly suppress facts."

"Well—well, I wouldn't," growled the inspector. "Answer him, Howlett, and, dammit, tell the truth, if you can!"

"Did he ring, Howlett?" snapped Hand.

"I—guess so," grudgingly admitted Howlett.

"You'll do no guessing here! Did he, or didn't he ring for the elevator in the Unger Building?"

"Yes, sir."

"Waited quite a while, did he?"

"Yes, sir."

"Rang two or three times?"

"Well—yes, sir."

"I happen to know that the elevator operator was asleep. After it was certain that Mr. Holloway was going to get no response to his rings, he walked up the stairs. That right?"

"Yes, sir, that's about it."

"Now, what time was Mr. Holloway in the Unger Building?"

"One twenty-five when he got there. One forty-two when he left."

"That's all, Howlett, for the present."

Inspector Gerrity turned frowning upon his detective. "Howlett," he said bitterly, "get the hell out of here."

15

IN THE OLD HOUSE

Detective Howlett, with a much-abused mien, took Snedick by the arm and swiftly left the apartment. Gerrity started out after him with Roderic. The young man, overcome with joy at Hand's swift thrusts at the evidence that had been swung so completely around him, had forgotten that he was under arrest. Gerrity's heavy hand on his arm dismayed him afresh. He drew back. Bernice seized his shoulder and glared spitefully at the inspector.

"I suggest," said Hand quickly, "that you do anything, Mr. Holloway, that the inspector requires of you. You will be subjected to a bombardment of questions, no doubt, but I will try to secure your release before you have lost too much sleep."

"Arrested!" muttered Roderic. "I can't go to jail! My reputation—"

"I haven't any choice," growled Gerrity. "If you'll use your head, young fellow, you'll come along without any fuss."

"I think you better had," counseled Clark. "Hand and I will move heaven and earth to establish your innocence."

Bernice glanced helplessly over at Hand. Then she let her arms fall to her sides and dropped listlessly into a chair. With bowed head, her brother allowed Gerrity to escort him from the apartment. A dead silence followed the closing of the door. Hand turned briskly to leave.

"Wait a minute, Hand!" cried Clark. "Can't you give Miss Holloway some encouragement before you go?"

Bernice glanced up and smiled bitterly. "Everything has blown up," she said. "There doesn't seem to be any use in fighting, does there?"

"That's not the proper spirit," reproved Clark. "Please don't become disheartened."

She glanced up at him and met his eyes, glancing earnestly, appealingly into her own. She smiled gratefully, but the hopelessness remained deep in her eyes. She turned her head slowly and looked at Hand. He had folded his arms and was peering speculatively down at her.

"You don't think that Roddy did it, Mr. Hand?" she asked, almost pleadingly.

"Of course not!" scoffed Clark.

"No," said Hand slowly, "I don't."

"But," cried Bernice, "how can we prove it?"

"We may have to do it indirectly," replied Hand, "but I think we can do it. I believe that I have made more headway this afternoon than I have since I took up this case. Our man has overstepped the bounds of prudence. He became a bit too clever for his own good."

Bernice's eyes suddenly shone with interest. "Tell me," she breathed.

"I refer, of course," said Hand, "to this latest murder. Consider how completely the evidence all pointed to the guilt of your brother. The thing was overdone! What man would stab another with a knife that he knew a dozen people could swear was his, and then leave it behind him in the heart of his victim? In the first place he would have chosen a weapon less incriminating. That piece of cloth torn from the lining of your brother's coat is not convincing, to me. It is too small. You can't pluck a small bit like that out of a piece of cloth, unless the material is rotten. The strength necessary to rip the fabric would have torn out a sizable strip. I think the knife was stolen from this apartment and purposely left behind to incriminate Mr. Holloway. I think the piece of cloth was torn out of the lining of his coat some time recently, probably today, and placed in Sinclair's dead hand for the same purpose. It would have to be a small piece, you see; otherwise he would have noticed it at once. He didn't mention having noticed it, did he?"

"No," replied Bernice. "I wish he had!"

"Unquestionably he hadn't noticed it," said Hand. "But the fine hand of our friend went too far in another respect. There was the evidence in Sinclair's office of a desperate struggle having taken place there. On the other hand, Mr. Sinclair's clothing bore no such evidence. An autopsy will reveal whether his body is marked with bruises; I saw none on his face and hands. He was stabbed in the back. I believe that death crept up behind him as he sat at his desk; he never knew what fate had overtaken him. As I say, an autopsy will go far toward determining that, not alone by the absence of bruises, but the amount of carbonic acid in his lungs will reveal whether he was exerting himself when he died."

"Then we must wait for the awful autopsy to be sure," said Bernice.

"To be positive, yes," agreed Hand. "But I shall not wait. I am assuming on excellent grounds that Sinclair was killed stealthily as he sat at his desk. That being the postulate, it is absurd to think that your brother would, having stabbed Sinclair in the back, gone about counterfeiting the evidence of a struggle in the office. But assuming that he was calm enough to pull the books off the shelves and otherwise upset the office, it is even more stupid to think that he would have marched off and left his knife behind him. There is nothing in the whole thing that smacks of your brother's guilt. And when we take into consideration Howlett's reluctant testimony that he rang several times for the elevator, the whole case against him collapses. Yes, Miss Holloway, 1 think I can assure you that your brother will soon be back with you."

"Oh, I believe you!" cried Bernice.

"But in order to do it," cautioned Hand, "we shall have to unravel the whole puzzle. We shall have to turn over to the police enough evidence to convict the real criminal. Only thus can we disprove the fallacious circumstantial evidence amassed against your brother."

Again hope was quenched in Bernice's eyes. Clark noticed it. He glanced resentfully at Hand.

"I wish you hadn't said that, Hand," he said complainingly. "Why didn't you let it go the way it was? How long is it going to take you to get to the bottom of this?"

"I can't say," shrugged Hand. "I believe that I am nearing the solution. At least one important link is yet to be found."

"How about that new will?" cried Clark suddenly. "That didn't seem to work. Evidently it is not for Leander Holloway's money that all this blood is being shed!"

Hand's eyes narrowed, just slightly. "In a very few moments," he said, "I shall make sure of that. Wills can be destroyed, you know. Clark, you become necessary. I want you to go over to the Lambs Club, immediately. Mr. Holloway said he received a call there summoning him to Sinclair's office. Find the servant at the club who paged him and called him to the phone. Get his name and address and a signed statement from him to that effect. Then join me at Leander Holloway's house. Miss Holloway, I suggest that you stay here until you hear from me."

He clapped his hat on his head and strode out of the apartment. Clark lingered to reassure Bernice. Then he hurried to the Lambs Club.

At Leander Holloway's, Hand was accosted almost immediately by Sergeant Kirk in the front hall. The sergeant said hello in a single syllable. Hand said nothing. His curt nod and the sergeant's cold stare were the only other passages between them. Kirk returned to the upper floor. Hand went out to the kitchen. There he met the cook and the maid.

"Where is Simeon?" he demanded.

The question associated itself with nothing pleasant in the cook's mind. She tossed her head.

"So long's he keeps out of here," snapped the cook. "I don't care where he is!"

"Yes," smiled Hand, "but I do. Do you know where he is?"

"He's down stairs, in the cellar," said the cook, suddenly smiling back at him. "He's fussing with that old invention of his."

"Invention?" Hand's eyebrows raised almost imperceptibly.

"Yes," sniffed the cook. "He thinks he's inventing a new way to steer horse cars over to the sidewalk to pick up passengers."

"Horse cars? My word, they went out of existence years ago!"

"That don't make any difference to Simeon. He's been working on it for about fifty years."

"Do you think he'll have it perfected in the next half hour or so?"

"What? Oh, sir, you're such a joker. He'll never have it finished."

"Well, then, how long do you think he'll remain in the cellar?"

"Until dinner time. And the old fool always gabbing about how hard he has to work!"

"Simeon seems to have a good appetite. I saw him raiding the ice box last night."

"I know he did! If he does it again I'll fix him!"

"It's not a regular habit of his, then?"

"I should say not! The old fool hardly eats at all. I knew sooner or later he'd go pecking around my ice box to keep himself alive."

"Well, you'd better lay a trap for him. We'll let him alone for the time being, though. Thank you."

Hand left the kitchen and went up the stairs to the second floor. Kirk stepped out into the hallway.

"Where is Mr. Holloway?" asked Hand.

"In the sitting-room," replied Kirk, as usual wasting no more words than necessary.

"Is Mr. Forschell in?"

"No, sir. Been out all afternoon. Inspector Gerrity called and I told him that."

"Good."

Hand received this information with satisfaction. He knew that Gerrity, with his customary thoroughness, would have every move of Forschell's traced and verified. He went on into the sitting-room. The old man greeted him with pleasure. Hand divined that Holloway had not been told of the murder of Jasper Sinclair.

"Reading again, Mr. Holloway!"

"Yes, almost always, Mr. Hand. This is a very good book, too."

"By the way, have you destroyed the will that your new one superseded?"

"No, Mr. Hand, and I doubt that I'll do it. If they succeeded in breaking my new one, you see, the old one would again be in effect. At least, it seems reasonable that it would."

"Where are you keeping it?"

"They are both together in my wall safe in the study."

"I'm glad they are protected. Where is Mr. Forschen?"

"Horace is out on business for me. He had to spend some time at the brokers', and take care of one or two other things. Did you want him?"

"Not particularly."

"By the way, Mr. Hand, one of the things Horace is doing is to get a check certified for me. I am going to furnish Ludovic with money to go off to the mountains."

The old man's chin sank to his chest. He frowned speculatively off into space. Hand regarded him for a moment.

"I'm glad to hear it, Mr. Holloway," he said. "The young man really should be in a good sanitarium."

"Yes," sighed Holloway. "Well, he shall go to one. Horace ought to be back with that check. Ludovic will soon be here; I told him I wanted to see him at five-thirty."

"It's nearly that now. Well, I shall not interfere. That poor chap has enough to put up with without having strangers present to embarrass him at a time like this. Good afternoon, sir."

"Good-bye, Mr. Hand, and stop in any time."

Hand went out into the hallway. He stalked right by the statuesque figure of Sergeant Kirk. He entered the study. Closing the door silently, he switched on the light and glanced rapidly about. There were but three pictures on the walls, and under the second one he shifted he found the wall safe. Getting out his electric torch, he examined the knob of the safe by its strong rays. His sharp eyes immediately detected that there were no finger-prints on it, not so much as the vestiges of them. He nodded and put his torch away. Hand was always suspicious of the knob of a safe that bore no finger-prints. The inference was that they had been carefully rubbed off. People who have a right to open safes do not rub their finger-prints off the knobs.

Placing his delicate finger-tips on the knob, Hand bowed his head so that his ear was in contact with the face of the safe. The knob spun slowly, silently, this way and that. But to Hand's ear, the slow turning of the little dial was not a silent process. The faintest sound registered on his eardrum. And then a soft sigh escaped him. He stepped back abruptly. The door of the safe swung out.

Again Hand got out his torch. He directed its beam into the receptacle in the wall. Then he took out several papers and examined them swiftly. His eyes narrowed slightly. Then he put the papers back, softly closed the safe, and placed the picture back over it. Neither the new will nor the old one were in the safe.

Hand stepped over to the door at the head of the stairs and opened it. He peered down the dark staircase for a moment, his thoughts racing. Then he closed the door and swiftly inspected the small room. The walls were paneled in dark oak, extending to within a height of three feet of the ceiling. The panels, he estimated, were about a foot and a half wide. He commenced circling the room, rapping his knuckles against them. Across from the desk, in the wall toward the front of the house, he halted before a panel in the center. It yielded and rattled to the pressure of his hand. Hand was by no means too modern to suspect the room of having a secret egress. This was an old house, he knew, probably as old or older than any other in that section of New York. Architects in those days loved nothing better than to sneak a secret door, stairway, or both into their plans. On the other hand, the woodwork had dried out through the years. This panel may just have become loose. But to Hand it felt suspiciously as though it would slide. He tried to push it up, down and to either side, but it refused to budge. He stepped back and keenly scrutinized the wall around it, looking for a possible method of releasing it.

With a scrape and a rattle the panel flew up before his face. Framed in the aperture stood a man, leveling a pistol straight at Hand's head. He was moderately tall and held himself with an athletic bearing. His hair was tinged at the temples with gray, his face was bronzed and lean. His brown eyes looked steadily, unwaveringly into Hand's gray ones, which were just as steady and unwavering.

"Mr. Holloway," said Hand softly, "if I were you, I should be very careful with that pistol."

The man's black eyebrows raised. "You're a cool one," he said. "What makes you think that my name is Holloway?"

"Because," replied Hand, with the suggestion of a smile, "your children bear such a remarkable resemblance to you. Miss Bernice Holloway, in case you don't know, did me the honor of retaining me."

"But I do know. Otherwise I would not have confronted you. But I am taking no chances, just the same."

He smiled grimly and motioned the pistol toward Hand. He made no other move, merely stood there, his eyes never leaving Hand's face.

"I confess," said Hand, "that I am at some loss to understand why you confronted me at all. But suppose we leave this danger spot. I presume that you have some secret retreat back there. Let us go to it; there are a number of things I should be interested to hear from you."

Phil Holloway, still smiling, nodded his head. He stepped out into the room and motioned for Hand to precede him through the wall. Hand discovered a narrow, musty flight of stairs on the other side of it that led upward. Holloway stepped through the open panel and closed it behind him. He flashed a light up for Hand to see by. Hand leading, they mounted to a small room. There was no window in it and the air was dank and stale. There seemed to be no door or other means of getting in or out of the room besides the stairs they had mounted. Some blankets and a pillow lay in one corner. Besides them stood a

half-burned candle, standing on the floor in its own hardened wax. An overcoat and broad-brimmed black hat hung
on a peg against the wall. There was nothing else but a
cheap chair in the little room. Hand was astonished at the
lack of dust.

"You have been doing a bit of cleaning here, Mr. Holloway."

Hand stood with his back to the man, who was playing
his electric torch on him.

"Simeon has," replied Holloway.

"Ah, Simeon, then, is your guardian angel."

"Yes, and a blessed old guardian angel he is, too. I
shouldn't have known what to do without Simeon."

"He has contrived to supply you with food."

"So he has. How did you know that?"

"I saw him foraging for it last night. How on earth did
you get into this house?"

"I slipped in at the first opportunity there was. Eleanor
and that boy, Ludovic, of hers, dashed by the policeman
at the front door. There was a hullabaloo, and while it was
going on, I slipped in the house. I came up to the third
floor in the little elevator that Simeon had told me about."

"I recall the occasion. The Holloways certainly punc-
tured Gerrity's police cordon that day. You had been keeping rather close watch on the house, then."

"As close as I dared. Several times I just managed to
escape being seen by persons who knew me."

"You had been in communication with Simeon?"

"Oh, yes, for several days. I got him on the telephone,
first. Then he came out as often as he could and met me
at a rendezvous."

"Mr. Holloway, what induced you to risk stealing into
this house?"

Hand swung about and stared into the rays of the torch.
He could see that Holloway was still holding the pistol.

The light, however, blinded him from seeing the man's face.

"Mr. Hand, have I your assurance that what I may say to you here will be confidential?"

"It will be, unless I think it is to your interest to reveal it."

"Well, yes. And you will not reveal where I am in hiding?"

"Not unless I have already proved your innocence."

"Very well."

Holloway put the pistol into his pocket. He stepped over to the candle and, bending over and striking a match, lighted it. Then he extinguished his torch and turned smiling to Hand. Phil Holloway was as handsome as his son and as charming as his daughter. He bowed and waved Hand to the only chair.

"My meager hospitality, Mr. Hand," he offered.

"Couldn't think of it," grinned Hand. "Instead of stalemating each other with courtesy, let us both remain standing. Permit me to present a theory I have formed concerning you. You arrived in New York, not with ostentation and not with stealth. I fancy that it was your intention to surprise your children. Then you learned that they were away from the city for the week-end. Probably your information came from Simeon. You did not wish your children to learn of your return from others; so you swore Simeon to secrecy and kept knowledge of yourself from your relatives. The next morning you read in the newspapers of the attack upon your uncle in Central Park. The morning after that you learned from the papers that you were being suspected of having fired that bullet at Leander Holloway. Before the police had time to check up on the hotels, you left yours and hid away in the city."

Holloway gazed at Hand in amazement. "Is this a theory?" he demanded incredulously.

"Nothing more."

"It is absolutely correct! To this day I have not told Roderic and Bernice that I am back in New York. What good could it do! It would only add to their worry! And yet the suspense has been driving me crazy! Simeon knew almost nothing. The newspapers—I devoured them all—said the police believed someone intended exterminating the entire Holloway family. My one passion was to protect my children, and yet fate had placed me in such a position that it was impossible! I knew this house as a child, every inch of it, and so, of course, I knew of this secret room. I determined to gain it, in spite of Simeon's remonstrances, and now I have done it. But here I am almost as cut off from doing anything useful as I was before. I have been able merely to spy upon the study at the foot of the stairs. There is a small opening through which you can inspect the study, and everything that is said in it comes clearly through the thin panel. I have seen you in there and heard you addressed. That's how I knew who you were. But tell me, Mr. Hand, you think that my children are safe?"

In his eagerness he stepped over to Hand and took him anxiously by the shoulders. Hand regarded him skeptically.

"I can't tell," he said, "until we have cleared up this mystery."

Forgetting his courtesy, Holloway sat dejectedly in the chair and dropped his head in his hands. Then he raised his head and looked at Hand.

"But don't you think, really," he insisted, "that the whole thing is just a newspaper scare? Don't you think that the whole thing ended with the death of my cousin, Robert Bradshaw?"

Hand shook his head. "No. There was the death of Quentin Morley, palpably by the same agency. There have been attacks upon me. This afternoon Jasper Sinclair was murdered and—your son has been placed under arrest for it."

For a moment Phil Holloway sat motionless; then he bounded out of the chair and seized Hand again by the shoulders. "What?" he cried. "Roderic arrested! That is outrageous! What in heaven's name do the police think they are doing?"

"There was plenty of occasion for the arrest. Circumstantial evidence pointed directly to Roderic. But I myself am convinced that he is quite innocent. I think that I can convince the police of that before long."

"Why, the fools!" fumed Holloway. "Roderic wouldn't so much as—"

"I suggest that you calm yourself," cautioned Hand. "There is a particularly alert police officer stationed in the house. It would not help if you were to join Roderic at police headquarters. By the way, if you don't mind my saying so, you puzzle me, Mr. Holloway."

Holloway mastered his emotions and frowned at Hand. "How's that?" he asked.

"Your concern for your children," replied Hand, "certainly is genuine. I would not be the one to say that it isn't. Yet the fact remains that you deserted them for a number of years."

Holloway stepped back. His frown deepened. Before replying he paced back and forth, head bowed, several times. Then he stopped, his eyes still on the floor.

"That," he said, "was really a kindness to them. Had my wife lived, I think I would have always been a successful, decent man. But, one way or another, I got into a lot of bad ways. I was beginning to be a reflection upon my children; not a credit to them. I left them in the care of my uncle, who I knew would handle that better than I could. Then I went— I don't know why I'm telling you this."

"I don't, either," smiled Hand, "except that I asked you."

"No," retorted Holloway, "it's more than that. It's because I've taken a fancy to you; otherwise I wouldn't do it.

Well, anyway, I went to South America, and very shortly a
real torture set in from being separated from my boy and
my little girl. I think that reforming is a lot of trash, but
I have been able to get back my footing. Out of nothing I
have built up a sizable fortune down there, in cattle. Not
until I had done that would I permit myself to come back."

"Let me return the compliment, Mr. Holloway," said
Hand. "I have taken quite a fancy to you."

"Well, then, for God's sake, see that nothing happens
to that boy of mine and protect my daughter!"

"I'll do all in my power, I promise you that. There is
something else that I want you to tell me. What have you
done with those wills of your uncle's?"

Holloway glanced sharply at Hand. "You know that,
too! By thunder, there's nothing you don't know. You've
given me confidence in you."

"Well, where are the wills?"

"Hum-m. Simeon told me that Uncle Leander had
drawn a new one. I was afraid he might have cut the kids
and all the rest of them out of it. And that's what he did!
The new will, Mr. Hand, is a little pile of ashes over in
that corner. The old one I have in my pocket. And that's
where it's going to stay!"

"See that it does. And now—"

Hand's voice ceased abruptly. In the place of it there
came up the dark secret stair-well the voices of Leander
Holloway and his grandnephew Ludovic. Phil Holloway
and Hand stood tense and motionless, the light from the
flickering candle playing over their colorless faces and
glinting in their eyes.

"Now, Ludovic," came the old man's high, quarrelsome
voice, "you know that you have no right to expect a penny
from me. Not a penny!"

"I am your dead nephew's son," Ludovic sullenly reminded him.

"And look how you've served me!" cried old Holloway. "You stole! You're a thief! I put you in a position of trust, and you stole! If I hadn't made good you'd be in jail this minute! You stole from—"

"Shut up!" screamed Ludovic. "I know what I've done, and I'm through hearing you harp on it! I won't come crawling round on my knees begging you for money. I'm through with that!"

"You had better keep a civil tongue in your head, Ludovic! If I don't help you, then who will? And you have the unmitigated gall to think that I will!"

"I don't, I tell you, you old villain! I'll see you in hell before—I'll—"

"Here, Ludovic! Put that away! Quick!"

"Put it away? What do—"

"Help! Help! Murder! Murd—"

The crashing reverberation of a pistol shot snatched the old man's scream into its thunder and ended it. Then there was a dead, terrifying stillness below.

16

THE LIBRARY

Phil Holloway bounded for the secret stairs. Hand seized his arm and pulled him back. Holloway whipped about and glared at him.

"Stay here!" hissed Hand. "How do I get out to the third floor?"

Holloway nodded his head in agreement. He stepped over to the farther wall and pulled a board out of place, revealing a dark hole.

"You'll have to crawl through there," he said. "It lets you out into the attic. Hurry!"

In the attic, Hand got out his torch and quickly gained the upper hallway. As he dashed down the steps to the second floor, Clark ran up those from the first. They met in the hall on the second floor.

"What's happened?" cried Clark. "The policeman at the front door said he heard a shot."

"He did, too," replied Hand without stopping. "It was in the study. Come on."

The study door stood ajar. They rushed through it, and halted in horror. The bodies of Leander Holloway and Ludovic lay sprawled on the floor not more than two feet from each other. Kirk was at the telephone, coolly reporting to police headquarters. Hand bounded over to the old

man, who was lying on his back, as was Ludovic. He placed
a hand over Leander Holloway's heart and felt his pulse.

"Has he been shot?" asked Clark weakly. "Is he dead?"

"No," snapped Hand. "Ludovic is the one who is shot.
I'll carry Mr. Holloway into his room; you look after
Ludovic."

He picked up the emaciated form of the old man and
strode out of the study with him. Clark dropped beside
Ludovic. He felt in vain for the pulse. Ludovic's face
looked strangely calm and peaceful. He lay like a shattered
column, quiet and still. A dark stain surrounded a little
hole in the left breast of his coat.

Kirk dropped the receiver on the hook. He turned about
and glanced narrowly at Clark. Slowly, Clark rose to his
feet and faced the sergeant.

"He's dead!" he breathed.

"Yes," coldly replied Kirk.

"Good heaven!" cried Clark suddenly. "Who shot him?"

Hand turned swiftly in at the door. He halted and
glanced down at the body. Then his glance lifted sharply
to Kirk's face.

"What about it, Kirk?" he snapped. "Did you shoot him?"

"Yes, sir."

"He attacked the old man with that blackjack he's holding?"

Clark glanced down at the corpse. The right hand
gripped the thong of a murderous blackjack. Clark had
not noticed it before. Kirk said nothing.

"Well, Kirk," sharply demanded Hand, "have you any
objection to answering my question?"

"No, sir. Mr. Holloway screamed for help. I jumped
in here. The old gent was on one knee, with an arm up to
defend himself. The young lad stood over him with the
blackjack. I shot him before he could use it."

"Your aim was good," said Hand laconically.

Clark glanced at the sergeant with repugnance. "Couldn't you have stopped him in any other way?" he harshly demanded. "Instead of shooting him to death!"

"My orders," stiffly replied Kirk, "were to protect Mr. Holloway's life, not to be careful about anybody else's."

"You have reported this?" asked Hand.

"Yes, sir," replied Kirk. "Inspector Gerrity is on his way over."

Clark, with furrowed brow, paced back and forth across the study. Suddenly he halted and took Hand impulsively by the arm.

"Hand," he said earnestly, "would you object if I returned to Bernice? I feel nervous about—"

"By no means!" said Hand. "In fact, I think it a splendid idea. You are armed, I suppose."

"Yes."

"Were you successful at the Lambs Club?"

"I have the statements of the telephone switchboard operator and the steward who called Roderic to the phone."

"Good. Then run along; I'll get in touch with you later."

Clark quickly left the house. The night air was damp and misty. It struck a chill through him. Clark shuddered, remembering Ludovic lying on the study floor. The pavements were wet and shiny from the mist. Clark was glad when he turned into Fifth Avenue, glad of the company of the few people on the sidewalk there, impersonal and indifferent though it was. Clark was not a nervous man, but he was filled with strange and foreboding premonitions, mysterious and sinister presences seemed to be all about him. He quickened his pace. He turned into Fifty-seventh Street and walked briskly toward Bernice's apartment. And then he halted as though he had received a blow.

In front of the apartment house some sort of struggle was going on beside a sedan parked at the curb. The rear door of the car was open. A man standing beside it seemed to be thrusting someone else through it. Behind him on the sidewalk lay the dark, motionless figure of a man. Clark's heart seemed to burst. Gasping in a frenzy of apprehension, he raced toward the car. The man saw him coming. He leaped into the machine.

"Stop!" frantically shouted Clark. "Stay where you are!"

The automobile roared away from the curb and sped down the street. Clark rushed futilely after it.

"Stop, I tell you!" he shouted, uselessly.

The sedan shot through a red light at the corner and veered dangerously down Sixth Avenue. Clark halted and glanced wildly about for another car in which to give pursuit. Except for two cars parked far down the street, there was none nearer than Fifth Avenue. He whipped his pistol from his pocket and emptied it in a series of shattering reports into the street. A traffic officer in Fifth Avenue blew his whistle, dashed through the halting cars, and ran down toward him. Clark ran back to meet him.

"What's the idea?" panted the officer.

"Quick!" cried Clark. "We must commandeer a car! I think there has been an abduction here!"

The policeman eyed him suspiciously. "You think so, brother?" he asked. "You're actin' strange as—"

"We're wasting time!" shouted Clark wildly. "Come on, we must get a car!"

"Wait a minute, now, wait a minute," cautioned the policeman exasperatingly. "Keep your shirt on, buddy. Tell me what you think happened."

"I think a young woman has been abducted!" cried Clark. "Look, that man on the sidewalk, they've done for him, too!"

The policeman for the first time saw the body lying on the wet pavement. His eyes started.

"Did you see it?" he demanded.

"I just saw them pushing someone into the car. Then they drove off. For God's sake, can't we do something!"

"Get the license number?"

"No; I hadn't time."

"What kind of a car was it?"

"A black sedan. It turned south into Sixth Avenue."

"Do you know who it was they abducted?"

"Yes, yes, I think it was Miss Bernice Holloway!"

"Oh, the granddaughter, or somethin', of the old gent on Fifty-eighth Street!"

"Yes. But, damnation, will you do something?"

"All I can do is go down to the call-box and send in an alarm and a general description. But first I better see what happened to this guy."

"You go send in your alarm; I'll look after this fellow!"

The policeman nodded and ran back toward Fifth Avenue. Clark bounded over to the man on the sidewalk. He looked at the pale face, bathed in the wan light of the street-lamp, and his heart turned to lead. The man was a headquarters detective, and the one Clark had seen trailing Bernice. His hat lay on the sidewalk beside him. The hair on the left side of his head was matted with blood.

Clark picked him up and staggered into the foyer of the apartment house. He dumped the man on a settee there and dashed up the stairs to Bernice's apartment. Rushing up to the door, he rained blow after blow of his fists upon it, desperately hoping that Bernice would come open it. The door remained impassive. A moment later Snedick crept up behind him.

"What—what's the matter?" he timidly asked.

Clark spun about and seized the superintendent by the shoulders. "Have you a key that will open this door?" he hoarsely demanded.

"Y-yes, sir."

"Then open it, and be quick about it!"

All but rendered helpless by agitation, Snedick finally managed to open the door. Clark rushed roughly by him and dashed through the apartment. Every room was empty. Clark buried his face in his hands and groaned.

"What—what's the matter, sir?" asked Snedick.

"The telephone!" shouted Clark. "Where's the telephone?"

"Oh, my! Right over here, sir."

Clark got Leander Holloway's house on the wire and a moment later was speaking to Hand.

"They've got her, Hand!" he cried. "They kidnapped Bernice just as I turned into Fifty-seventh Street! They drove her off in an automobile, and they've completely disappeared!"

There was a momentary silence. "Well, old boy," said Hand heavily, "you can chalk this up against me, and I expect you to be merciless."

"But what can we do?" cried Clark.

Hand's voice now became as crisp as usual. "Where are you, Clark?"

"I'm in Bernice's apartment."

"Stay there. The inspector and I will be there just as quickly as we can make it."

Clark hung up and turned listlessly from the phone. Snedick was biting his finger-nails.

"This's awful," sniffed the superintendent. "She—she was an awful nice young lady."

He looked too funereal for Clark to stand his company. Clark left him and went down to the foyer. The sight of the detective swaying upright on the settee and feeling of his head was some relief. He rushed over and pounced upon the man, whom he knew.

"Cleggins," he cried. "How did it happen?"

"Oh, gar!" moaned Cleggins. "What a swat I got."

Clark shook him roughly. Cleggins looked blankly up at him. Then his face cleared somewhat.

"It's you, Mr. Clark," he muttered thickly.

"How did it happen?"

"Don' know 'xactly. Miss Holloway went out an' I followed her. Some guy give a jump at me and just about knocked m' block off. 'S all I know, Mr. Clark."

"Why the devil weren't you on your guard?"

Clark frowned fiercely and paced up and down the foyer. Cleggins sighed in self-pity and tenderly felt of his head. A few moments later Hand and Gerrity hastened into the foyer. Gerrity paused and questioned Cleggins. Hand walked over to Clark and placed a sympathetic hand on his shoulder.

"Sorry, old boy," he said. "This is entirely my fault."

"Oh, you couldn't have helped it," muttered Clark. "But what are we to do?"

"I fancy we'd get nowhere rushing wildly about looking for her. It is just like everything else in this case, we have got to get to the very bottom of it before we can be effective in anything."

"And we are no nearer the solution than we were at the start!"

"On the contrary, I am but a step from the solution."

"Hand!"

"But it is a long step, and the most difficult of all. I can't seem to find the way to take it. Yet there is a way!"

Gerrity walked over to them, peering somberly at Clark. "This is devilish!" he growled. "That traffic cop just came back to the door, Clark. He said he sent in his alarm. I don't know what in thunder else we can do. This case is giving the department one black eye after another! Blast it all, will it never end?"

"What are your plans for the rest of the night, Inspector?" asked Hand.

"For one thing," growled Gerrity, "I'm going to give this city the going-over of its life! Every snatch artist is going on the mat! I'm going to find that girl!"

"Good," nodded Hand. "If you should want to get in touch with us, Clark and I will be at the rooms."

"My God," cried Clark, "I can't sit still at the rooms! I'd go out of my head. I've got to do something!"

"There is no better way to do it, then," said Hand, "than to accompany me. We shall be at the rooms, Inspector."

Hand took Clark by the arm and walked him out of the building. Silently they walked over to Fifth Avenue and hailed a cab, Hand directing the driver to take them to their lodgings. They climbed into the cab and were driven off. Hand glanced sharply at Clark. His friend's face was pinched and drawn.

"Don't be too despairing, Clark," he said kindly.

Clark turned his face upon him and seized him by the arm. "I tell you," he said hoarsely, "that, for me, the whole universe hinges upon her safety."

"I fancy she's safe enough."

"But we don't know! It's this cursed mystery that's driving me insane! Think of all these ghastly murders!"

"We are not dealing with murder here. Death has not been dealt out in that way in this case. I am quite certain that Miss Holloway was spirited away to attract my attention away from the main body of the case."

"Hand, you must bend all your energies toward discovering Bernice!"

"Have no fear, my boy, that is precisely what I shall do."

The cab stopped before their rooms. Before leaving it, Hand carefully scrutinized the street in all directions. He ordered Clark to get across the sidewalk and into the house without loss of time, and for the first time in their career together, he paid for the taxi. They went up to the living-room, where Hand carefully locked the door. Clark turned on the table-lamp and spun about.

"What earthly good are we to do here?" he demanded. "I feel more helpless than ever!"

Hand slowly removed his overcoat and hat. He seated himself in his easy chair and frowned at the floor. "Have patience, Clark," he said.

"I can't!" retorted Clark. "I'll do whatever you tell me to, because I know that you think far better than I. But don't ask me to have patience! And look here, what about Forschell? I for one have suspected him all along!"

"Merely because he happens to be in a suspicious position. The inspector has investigated Mr. Forschell more than assiduously. There is nothing to indicate that any of his actions have been criminal. He came in just after you left Leander Holloway's house this evening. He had been detained by detectives. Every move of his this afternoon was checked upon and proved. Forschell evidently had no hand in the murder of Jasper Sinclair. Yet, I wonder whether he did."

"Ah, you suspect him, too!"

"I surely do not overlook him. My impression is, Clark, that someone has directed these murders, and someone else has committed them. It would be a person intimately connected with Leander Holloway's household who has done the directing. On the other hand, everyone in that category has been watched meticulously. How was contact maintained between the schemer and his murderous ally? Consider the whole thing in the abstract. It becomes clear that the plans of the schemer are not readily transmitted to the assassin. The evening before last the plan flared forth with two murders and an attempted one upon myself. The next day was one of quiet. Save for the attempted poisoning of Leander Holloway, no violence was instituted. That attempted poisoning is a significant thing, and one which falls out of focus. But the next day, today, the plan again speeds violently into action. Sinclair has been stabbed to death, and Roderic is arrested for it, palpably as a result of the plan. Bernice is abducted. Ludovic is slain. And the whole thing started off with a second unsuccessful attempt upon my life. Due to our activities to frustrate him, the schemer has had to devise his plans as he goes along. And then, having devised them, he has had to get them into the hands of the man who is carrying them out. There was a whole day lost somehow, and I believe that it was caused by the delay in getting the instructions from the plotter to the confederate."

"But that is all supposition, Hand! We need something more concrete!"

"Supposition? Yes, so it is, or hypothesis. It is applying the imagination to the solution of crime. That is where the police fall down so woefully. They are too practical."

"Well, if the whole plan was at a standstill yesterday, how was it that the attempt was made upon the life of Leander Holloway?"

"As I said, that is out of focus. But we can bring it into line quite simply. There was no confederate necessary to accomplish that attempt. The plotter put the arsenic into the salt shaker himself. As the inspector has said, it was a clear indication that the man we are primarily after was in Leander Holloway's house yesterday, and that was a very limited group we had there. The individual case that remains definitely out of focus is the death of Ludovic Holloway. But I have no doubt that it will clear up when we have penetrated to the core of this ghastly plan."

"Yes, when we do! But we aren't getting anywhere! There you sit! Hand, why don't we do something?"

With a gesture of despair, Clark turned and paced gloomily up and down the living-room. Hand gave him a momentary, sympathetic glance. Supporting his head on

his finger-tips, all animation left his body. He lay back
in the chair as one dead, his eyes dull between mere slits.
One would not have suspected that his mind was terrifi-
cally alert. But it was darting from one possibility to another, and when necessary it manufactured new ones, only
to discard one after another as inadaptable. Clark paused
in his aimless wanderings and glanced down at him. He
realized what was going on in his friend's mind. For the
first time in his life he doubted Hand's ability to fathom a
case. Clark shook his head bitterly and paced on. He tried
sitting down, but found it intolerable. Again he wandered
dejectedly back and forth across the living-room, for what
seemed the length of an entire night.

Hand bounded out of his chair, so suddenly that Clark
tripped over his own feet in astonishment. He whirled
about and peered sharply at Hand, who was staring at the
wall as fixedly as though an electric current held him in
its grip. The seconds ticked by; then Hand broke from his
frozen posture and thumped the table.

"Of course!" he cried. "What an imbecile I've been! It's
clear as crystal!"

Clark rushed over to him and grasped him excitedly by
the arms. "What?" he hoarsely entreated. "What have you
discovered?"

"Let me tell you."

"For heaven's sake, do!"

Hand's eyes sparkled at Clark. "There is a steady stream
of objects passing through Leander Holloway's house, and
I'll wager they all pass through that house and go to the
same place. Books, Clark, books! You recall the books sent
to the old man by an anonymous admirer. Leander Holloway reads books by the score, and when he gets through
with them, I am sure that he gives them to the John Nash
Settlement. Don't you see? The sender could conceal messages in the books that he sent to the house. The plotter

would receive them, and then in turn conceal new messages in the books. When they arrived at the Settlement, the confederate could get them out of the library there and receive his instructions. Holloway reads a book in the course of a day. No doubt Gus Staub takes it to the Settlement the following morning, now that Holloway has nothing else for him to do. Exactly a day would elapse between the time a message was sent and the time that the confederate received it, and one day has elapsed while this plan stood still! Clark, at last I am unleashed! I feel it!"

"I don't quite understand it, Hand, I don't quite understand it. My mind is all twisted up. But you give me new courage, just the same!"

"I must get to the Settlement without delay! Clark, you stay here until I—"

"I stay here? I'll do nothing of the sort! I must have action, I tell you!"

"But my work for the next hour or so is bound to be purely research. You cannot help me, my boy. If we both leave we will be completely out of touch with the inspector. You must remain here, Clark, and be a clearing house for us both."

"I'll go insane with nothing to do!"

Hand took Clark gently by the shoulders and pushed him into a chair. "Old boy," he said, "I know how anxious you are for action. But I also know how anxious you are to co-operate to the fullest extent. I tell you, Clark, you will be most valuable to me if you stay here."

"All right," grumbled Clark.

Hand snatched up his hat and coat and yanked the door open. "If you need me, Clark," he said, "you will be able to reach me at the Settlement. Don't leave these rooms until you hear from me!"

He slammed the door and rushed down the stairs. A taxicab was soon discharging him before the John Nash

Settlement. It was a rather large and gloomy building, constructed of brick. Hand entered it in quest of the night superintendent. Several men reading magazines in a large, bare lounging-room lifted their eyes and peered at him. From another room came the click of billiard balls, and from somewhere in the rear issued the roll and clatter of bowling. Hand was directed to a dingy office. There he found Mr. Peek, the night superintendent, a thin, bespectacled man with a long nose and a bald head. He had heard of Hand.

"What can I do for you, sir?" he inquired.

"Perhaps you know that I am engaged in the case that involves Leander Holloway."

"Yes, yes. Most lamentable! I sincerely hope that—"

"I understand that Mr. Holloway supplies a number of books to your library here."

"We possess a number of volumes through his generosity."

"How long has he been sending them to you?"

"A great while. Two years or more, I should say. That was about the time he became interested in the Settlement. He is now one of our directors and a heavy contributor, both financial and otherwise."

"But the books. How often do you receive them from him?"

"Nearly every day. Mr. Holloway is a great reader himself, so his chauffeur tells us. At first he used to send a number of books down once or twice a month. But about a year ago he took to sending them along as soon as he had read them. He is very much interested in our library; indeed it was through his efforts right after becoming a director that the library was established. You would be surprised at the interest the men have taken in—"

"So for some time past you have been virtually receiving a book a day from Mr. Holloway?"

"Eh? Oh, yes. That is quite so, Mr. Hand. For the past six or seven months we have been getting them from him four or five times a week, at least."

"Do you happen to know what books you have received from him lately?"

"Why, yes, the librarian could tell you. He keeps a record of the books that are donated. All that information goes into the annual report. Would you care to—"

"Yes, immediately! Find the librarian for me."

The librarian was also in charge of the bowling alleys. Mr. Peek found him. All three of them went into the library, where Mr. Small, the custodian of the place, went through his precise files and produced a long list.

"These, Mr. Hand," he said, "are the titles of the books that Mr. Holloway has sent us."

"Do you know which ones you received during the past two weeks?"

Mr. Small's smile bore the stamp of having suffered from lack of use. "About the last fourteen on the list," he replied, "are the ones received in that time. I put them down one under the other as I receive them, you see."

"Excellent! Now, is there any one particular person who seems to be anxious to borrow the books that Mr. Holloway sends you?"

Mr. Small's strained smile disappeared. He glanced a trifle startled at Mr. Peek, who regarded Hand somewhat askance.

"It's a funny thing," said Mr. Small, "but there is a young fellow here who has done nothing lately but hang around until Gus Staub brings the book down from Mr. Holloway's. Then he borrows it almost before—"

"When did he get the last one?" snapped Hand.

"Oh, my!" exclaimed Mr. Small. "Why—why just this morning."

Christopher Hand's eyes glinted. For a long moment he
held his breath. Now, indeed, the shadows were parting.
Then he shot a glance at Mr. Small, who recoiled slightly.

"I shall want your assistance, Mr. Small," he said sharply. "Get me at once all the available books that Mr. Holloway has sent you in the past two weeks."

Mr. Small hastily gathered from the shelves eleven
books. He searched diligently and fruitlessly for more,
and probably would have continued it indefinitely had not
Hand impatiently called him from the shelves.

"Give me that list," demanded Hand.

Consulting the list, Hand arranged the books in a pile
in the order that they had been received. He sat down at
the librarian's desk. Placing the initial book received in
the two-week period before him, he turned a reading-lamp
full upon it. He slowly turned the pages, scanning each
one sharply. Mr. Small watched him in bewilderment.
Having gone through the entire volume, page by page,
Hand took the next book and subjected it to the same sort
of scrutiny, again without result. Five of the books were
thus laid aside. Mr. Small had lost interest and was bored.
Hand commenced inspecting the sixth volume. As he was
scanning page 3, his whole body froze rigidly, his eyes
staring at the printed matter before them. Then he banged

his fist triumphantly on the desk and rose so abruptly that he capsized his chair. Mr. Small almost collapsed.

"Wh-what's the matter?" he gasped.

Hand made no reply. He righted the chair and sat down again. Slowly now, he turned the pages of the book, meticulously scrutinizing every word. He continued thus up to page 50. It took quite a long time, but Mr. Small held his breath throughout almost all of it. As nothing further of a sensational nature happened, Mr. Small assumed that Hand was clearly out of his head and lost interest once more. Hand ran through the remainder of the pages more swiftly, at last completing them all. He glanced up smartly.

"Mr. Small!" he snapped.

Again Mr. Small sagged perilously. "My soul!" he exclaimed. "What's the matter now?"

"I want the name and address of the man who has been borrowing these books."

"Yes, yes. I have it here in my files. I keep a record of everyone who borrows our books. Now—now here it is. And it's absolutely correct, Mr. Hand. This unfortunate young man has had trouble with the police, but I hope he's reformed. He has not been in jail for the past three months. His name is Leo Marks, and he lives at five-ninety-eight Avenue A. There you are!"

"Good. Now you may leave me, Mr. Small."

"Eh?"

"I am much obliged to you, and you may leave me alone, if you please."

"Oh."

With a good deal of uncertainty, Mr. Small slowly left the library and closed the door. Hand at once snatched a pencil and a pad from his pocket. He hastily wrote down a message he had just got out of the sixth book. Then he opened the seventh book at the beginning and commenced to examine the pages. On page 4 he fastened upon a word

in the center of the sheet. Underlining this word was a
small indentation in the paper, such as one might make
with the thumb-nail. Hand copied the word down in his
pad. Two pages on he discovered another word underlined
in the same fashion. This he copied down next to the first.
Nearly up to the middle of the book he continued to find
words designated in this queer fashion, sometimes two following on a single page, and at other times two, three and
four pages lying between the consecutive words picked
out. Then the little indentations in the paper ceased altogether. But Hand had copied out of the book a complete
message that told him much. In each of the remaining
books he found other messages just as enlightening. He
then had six books that he had taken messages from. He
put his notebook and pencil away. Then he piled the six
books together, put them under his arm, and strode from
the library. He found both Mr. Small and Mr. Peek hovering round the door. They both were more than a little
nervous.

"Ta-taking the books with you?" stammered Mr. Small
in consternation.

"Yes. There are three missing. I want the names of the
ones who borrowed them."

"Leo Marks has one."

"Get me the names and addresses of the ones who have
the other two."

Mr. Small scurried into the library. He returned presently with a piece of paper bearing two scribbled names
and addresses. Hand took it from him. He nodded and
stalked away from Mr. Small and Mr. Peek.

"He's taking our books with him," hoarsely whispered
Mr. Peek.

"Yes," hissed Mr. Small. "The directors won't like it."

"He's gone," breathed Mr. Peek.

"So he is," sighed Mr. Small.

There was a precinct police station round the corner. Hand lost no time in getting to it and approached the sergeant at the desk. He displayed his badge of honorary membership in the department. The sergeant with much interest read the name on it. He smiled across the desk.

"So you're Mr. Hand?"

"Yes. Sergeant, these books must be sent up to Inspector Gerrity's office at police headquarters at once."

"Well, now, I guess we can take care of that for you, Mr. Hand."

"I want to use your telephone."

"Sure. Here you are."

He passed the instrument across the desk to Hand, who snatched it up and gave the operator the number of his own phone. When the telephone rang at the rooms, Clark was sitting hunched over beside it. He leaped at it, filled with a mixture of terror and wild hope.

"Hello! Hello!" he cried.

"Clark, I want you to—"

"Hand! Where are you?"

"I'm at the fourth precinct station. Hire the car from Peter's Garage and meet me here as quickly as you can. Be sure you are armed."

"What's happened? What have you —"

"Your party has disconnected, sir."

"What? Disconnected! What the devil did you let—I—excuse me."

In the fourth precinct station, Hand next called police headquarters and asked for Gerrity.

"Hello," answered the inspector.

"Gerrity, this is Hand. I want you to take Mrs. Eleanor Holloway into custody right away. Detain her at police headquarters until you hear further from me. And don't under any consideration release Roderic Holloway."

"Mrs. Holloway? What in blazes do I—"

"I am sending you up some books. Lock them in your safe."

"Books? What do I want with—"

"Your party has disconnected, sir."

"Disconnected? Dammit, what's the idea of—oh, excuse me, miss." Inspector Gerrity groused around his office, wondering what Hand was up to. Clark dashed madly to the garage and hired the sedan that had served them on other occasions. He drove rapidly down to the fourth precinct station. Hand was waiting at the curb. He got quickly in beside Clark.

"Five-ninety-eight Avenue A, Clark," he said.

The sedan shot out into the street. "What has happened?" savagely demanded Clark. "I've been in hell wondering what it was, all the way down here!"

"We're closing in on them, my boy. I've found the messages that were sent from Leander Holloway's house, and I know the identity of the man who has been receiving them. We are going to call on him now."

"Then—you think that he abducted Bernice?"

"Had a hand in it, at least. If our luck holds, he has by now returned to his quarters."

Clark was suddenly seized with the worst kind of nervousness. There was but one possibility, an extremely remote one, that held out any hope for his finding Bernice; and that possibility was, that having returned from his evil expedition, the man they were tracking might be found at his home. The more he thought of it, the more hopeless it seemed. Clark could scarcely breathe.

"Um-m," said Hand. "You passed right by a red light then, my boy, and you all but clipped a pedestrian."

"I—I can't help it," muttered Clark. "If we can only find him!"

"Take it easy," cautioned Hand, "we're almost there. Better pull up here; we'll walk the rest of the way."

Clark pulled the car to the curb and jerked it to a stop. He bounded out. Hand turned off the motor and dimmed the lights; then he caught up with Clark on the sidewalk. He managed to argue Clark into exercising more caution. With the aid of directions supplied by a tenant of the building, they located the room occupied by Leo Marks. Hand tried the knob of the door, so softly and carefully that he made not a sound. Clark stood tensely beside him. The hallway they were in was dark and gloomy; almost no sound came to their ears. Hand leaned close to Clark.

"The door is locked," he whispered. "I don't think we will knock. I'll try a key."

He took his bunch of master keys from his pocket and inserted one in the lock. Still Clark heard no sound. Clark had drawn his torch and his pistol. He was ready for something to happen and hoping fervently that it would. Still without the slightest sound, the door opened and Hand floated over the threshold, closely followed by Clark. Hand flashed his torch about the room. Cheap articles of bedroom furniture leaped momentarily out of the darkness. The room was empty. Clark groaned.

"Of course!' he whispered bitterly. "He won't come back here! He won't return to New York for weeks, if not for months!"

Hand said nothing. The trail, apparently, had abruptly ended. He had expected that it might, of course, but his reasoning had led him to believe that from this point on he could make rapid strides. Hand believed that Leo Marks was nothing but a tool, a henchman to a more dangerous criminal. He had expected Marks to remain in the city as a sort of contact man, which was evidently what his function had been all along. This might still be true. The single window in the room, on the second floor, overlooked the street. Hand walked over to it and stood looking absently out, formulating what his next move should

be. Clark stood behind him in the darkness of the room,
his thoughts plunging into an abyss of despair.

Suddenly Hand's eyes were turned alert and keen upon
the street in front of the building. A sedan had drawn
up and stopped at the curb directly in front of it, about
seventy-five feet ahead of their car. There was really nothing unusual about that, but Hand watched it narrowly. A
man stepped from the car and quickly entered the building. Hand bounded from the window. By sheer instinct he
avoided colliding with Clark in the darkness and crossed
over to the door. There was no need for caution now,
haste was the essential thing. This time Clark heard the
rasp of the key in the lock as Hand secured the door. An
instant later Hand was at his side, unseen in the blackness,
clutching his arm.

"A man just entered the building, Clark," he whispered
quickly. "If it's our man, we'll give him the shock of his
life!"

He guided Clark over to the wall, where the door would
conceal them if it opened. Had there been light, Clark's
face would not have been a reassuring sight to the person he savagely hoped to confront. And then the door did
open.

A faint light filtered into the room from the hall,
enough, nevertheless, to show them a dark form enter the
room. The door closed again. The room suddenly leaped
into brilliance from an unshaded bulb in a wall-fixture,
revealing a man in an overcoat and cap. He had his back to
Hand and Clark and did not see them. Nonchalantly toss-
ing his cap on a chair, he started to get out of his overcoat.
At that point Clark stepped forward, fiercely menacing
the man with his pistol. The fellow saw him out of the tail
of his eye and whirled about, his eyes glaring. His face was
coarse and unintelligent, although it was the face of a very
young man.

"Damn you!" grated Clark. "Where have you taken Miss Holloway?"

The man gulped and stepped backward. He made no reply.

"Your game is ended, Marks," snapped Hand. "You had better speak up; it may help you some."

"Who—who are you guys?" stammered Marks.

"Never mind that!" harshly retorted Clark. "Are you going to talk?"

"No," replied Marks, with a show of defiance. "I ain't sayin' a word."

Clark leaped at him and grasped him viciously by the throat. With his other hand he jammed the muzzle of his pistol into the pit of Marks' stomach.

"Tell me where Miss Holloway is," he snarled, "or, by heaven, I'll blow your miserable life out of your body!"

Marks was terrified. He was also almost choked to death.

"I think he will talk, Clark," said Hand, "if you will release your hold on his throat. But if you don't talk, Marks, my friend will surely kill you."

Clark gave the man a thrust that sent him spinning into a chair. Then he stepped forward and bent menacingly over him. Marks glanced up at him and shrank against the chair.

"I'll—I'll tell you!" he chattered. "She's in Jersey. I could take you there. I just come from there."

"Was she safe?" demanded Clark.

"Yes," quickly replied Marks. "The boss said he got orders to keep her safe."

Hand stepped up and took Marks roughly by the shoulder. "I want," he said coldly, "exact directions as to how to find her."

"The boss'd kill me if I double-crossed him!"

"You aren't double-crossing; you're talking to save your life, and don't forget it! Quick, I want those directions!"

Marks cowered miserably before the gleam in Hard's eyes. "All right," he said hoarsely. "I'll give 'em to you. You go out alongside of Plainfield, over in Jersey, on Route 29. You take the second turn to the right after you pass the traffic light outside of Plainfield. It's nothin' but a little dirt road, and you'd do better to walk up than ride. It goes up the side of a mountain about a half a mile. You'll come to a big oak tree that's been struck by lightning. There's an old path that winds off beside the oak. You ain't goin' to be able to follow it, I'm tellin' you, because it's all growed over with grass and bushes. You better take me with you."

"This path leads to what?"

"A shack. It's up on top of the mountain, almost. You've got to go through the bushes and trees about a half a mile. You better take me along to show you."

"And Miss Holloway is being kept a prisoner in that shack?"

"That's the dope. Come on, I can take you to it."

"And escape while you were doing it, eh? You're going to the Tombs, if you ever get out of here alive. Whether you do depends entirely upon whether you are telling us the truth. I can find that out in the next few questions I ask you. Who are the men you've been working for?"

"What do you think I am? I ain't tellin' you guys nothin' more about—"

Clark seized the man by his long hair, jerking his head back painfully. He leveled his pistol with deadly aim at Marks' forehead.

"Quick!" he snapped. "Answer that question, or I ll blow a hole clear through your head!"

Marks' eyes glazed with terror. "I'll tell!" he croaked. "The only one I been teamed up with is Oily Rogers. Oily's got a top he takes his orders from, but I swear I don't know who it is!"

Hand mused over this information. He had never encountered Oily Rogers but he was well acquainted with his record—first class forger and desperate gunman. But more than that, he knew that Rogers, possessed of an education and once considered a promising accountant, had served his first time in prison because of the diligence of Leander Holloway. Rogers had had the misfortune to practice embezzlement while employed in a company owned by the old magnate. Hand glanced sharply at Marks.

"Where does Oily Rogers live?" he demanded.

"Right in this buildin'," replied Marks.

"Take us to his quarters," ordered Hand.

Clark roughly yanked Marks out of the chair and thrust him toward the door. Hand stepped quickly forward and frisked him, producing a pistol from Marks' hip pocket.

"Now, then, Marks," he said, "if you don't want to get shot with your own gun, step lively!"

Marks did. He took them up a flight of stairs and down a hallway, halting them before a door. He tried it, and sighed with relief.

"It's locked," he said. "I can't open it."

Hand brushed by him and opened the door with a skeleton key. He stepped inside and turned on a light. With a soft exclamation, he strode over to a table and picked up a book. Then he glanced over at Marks, who looked more uncomfortable than ever.

"You got this," said Hand, "from the library of the John Nash Settlement this morning. I know all about you, Marks."

Hand carefully turned the pages of the book. At about the center he stopped suddenly and bent the book sharply back, peering into the crevice between the two upward leaves at the binding. Again he glanced at Marks.

"Your friend Oily," he said, "is not quite as astute as some give him credit for. There is a black thread caught between these two leaves of this book. It was a grievous error on his part that he didn't remove it."

"What do you mean?" asked Clark.

"It's simple enough," replied Hand. "The piece of lining from Roderic's coat undoubtedly was torn out at Leander Holloway's house. It was inserted between the leaves of this book and wedged into the binding to prevent it from falling out. In that fashion it traveled to the Settlement and then fell into the hands of Mr. Oily Rogers. It would never have been noticed unless someone opened the book to read it. But as Marks was right there to borrow the book as soon as it was delivered to the Settlement, that contingency was impossible. There can be no doubt that Rogers broke into Bernice's apartment and stole the stiletto while both Bernice and Roderic were at Leander Holloway's house this morning. He killed Jasper Sinclair with it and then placed that piece of Roderic's coat lining between Sinclair's fingers to make the circumstantial evidence complete. I think Clark, that we shall find the whole plan in this book."

"Not now, Hand," objected Clark, strenuously. "We have something more important to do!"

"Indeed we have. Shall we enlist the aid of the police to help rescue Miss Holloway, or shall we go at it alone?"

"Alone. We can act more swiftly, then."

"Yes, I think so too. And now, Mr. Marks, we are going to turn you over to the police."

18

FOG

Having left their prisoner and the book taken from Rogers' room at the precinct station, with instructions that both were to be turned over to Inspector. Gerrity, Hand and Clark drove swiftly to the Holland Tunnel. Here fog hung in great luminous balls round the street lamps. But in the city there was sufficient light to dissipate it. On the other side of the tunnel it was different. Clark, who was driving, could hardly see. As much as he detested driving rapidly in automobiles even in the clearest weather, Clark now drove at reckless pace through the cloying fog. Hand began to discover that his nerves, after all, were not proof against everything. He held a map in the meager light of the instrument board and scanned it carefully, giving Clark directions of the route they had to follow.

They passed by the eerie lights of Newark Airport, gleaming faintly through the murk. They edged their way through the detours and nosed into Route 29. Clark increased the speed, although the fog, if anything, became thicker. It seemed an age to Clark before Hand announced that a red traffic light, glowing in the fog ahead, undoubtedly was the one mentioned by Marks as near Plainfield. Hand put the map away. He turned the window completely down on his side and thrust his head and shoulders through it, straining his eyes through the fog at the right side of the road. They passed one road and continued on. Clark kept glancing expectantly at Hand. At length Hand bobbed his head into the car and turned to him.

"There it is, Clark. Pull as far over to the side as you can and stop. We'll walk up that road."

They leaped out of the parked car and started trudging as rapidly as possible up the little road to the mountain. The narrow road-bed was rough and strewn with rocks. It proceeded at a gradual rise for a hundred yards or so; then it ascended steeply up the side of the hill. Both men panted from the exertion of the climb. The fog seemed to cling in heavier folds under the branches of the trees. They were forced virtually to feel their way as they stumbled up the hillside. Clark pressed on, taxing even Hand's powerful legs to keep abreast of him. But suddenly Clark halted.

"Look here," he panted. "We'll never be able to see that oak tree in this cursed murk."

"I think we will, Clark," replied Hand. "It would be a stark thing, standing quite high. You can discern objects above your head, although you can see nothing at either side. I have been following the course of the roadway by the break in the foliage over our heads."

Clark grunted and continued on. However, they did pass by the splintered oak without seeing it. Hand realized this when palpably they had reached the top of the hill. He called a halt.

"We have got to go back, Clark," he said. "Marks said the oak was below the brow of the hill."

Clark made no remark. He turned about and followed Hand down the hill. Laboriously and with every nerve on the alert, they returned a considerable distance. In the end they were rewarded, Hand discovering the gaunt stem of the oak. Then commenced the attempt to locate the path, an effort that was utterly fruitless. Clark was in despair and swore that Marks had lied to them.

"If he had lied," disagreed Hand, "we wouldn't have found the oak. He said that the path was scarcely discernible. The radius of visibility tonight is no more than five or six feet, if that much. I might suggest enlisting the aid of the state police. It would take a rather large force of men to comb this wooded hillside."

"Don't care for the idea," replied Clark. "Almost anything would tip them off that the hunt was on. They'd escape with Bernice through this fog, and we'd never find them. We know we're near them; let's follow through to the end!"

"Very well," said Hand. "As a matter of fact, I think your idea is as good as any. Well, Marks said the shack was about a half a mile through the wood, almost at the top of the mountain."

He took out a pocket compass with a luminous dial and looked at it, considering deeply.

"Now what are you doing?" impatiently demanded Clark.

"Trying to estimate the direction we should take," replied Hand. "Seems to me that if we walk due south-south-west it will take us to a point near the mountain top a half mile from here. But I may be away off. Just the same, Clark, we'll follow that course through the wood and hope to heaven we'll stumble upon the shack. We'll never see it otherwise. We must guard carefully against becoming separated. If we lose each other in this murk our chances of success are about gone."

"Come on, then!" said Clark grimly.

The trek through that dark, fog-blanketed wood was one that Clark knew he would never forget. It meant feeling their way among the trees, stumbling over roots and boulders, getting soaked from the moisture brushed off the bushes and seeing next to nothing the whole time of their painful ascent. In such conditions, it was impossible

to judge when they had covered a half mile. As a matter
of fact, they passed within seventy-five feet of their goal
and continued on far beyond it. At last they halted and
zigzagged over a large territory. It was painfully slow work
and, as it continued unavailing, Clark's spirits dropped
lower and lower. Hand was certain that they should never
be able to locate the shack until daylight aided them.
Knowing, however, that Clark would never be able to stand
the inactivity of waiting for it, he continued to press the
difficult and futile search.

The black-gray of the saturated air gradually and almost imperceptibly was tinged with light, slowly turning
to soft gray. They proceeded more swiftly now, able to per-
ceive objects at a distance of twenty-five feet or more. The
visibility increased to the maximum of the early morning,
but it was still difficult to see through the wraiths of fog.
Still, compared with what they had endured through the
night, Hand and Clark both were considerably heartened.
They felt that now, if the shack was actually where Marks
had said it was, they would soon find it. They did not
know how close to it daylight had found them. But a few
minutes later, Hand clutched Clark by the arm.

"What is it?" hoarsely whispered Clark.

"The shack!"

"Where?"

"In that tall clump of bushes. You just see a corner of it."

Clark strained his eyes through the mist. Then he saw
it. He started to bound forward. Hand pulled him back.

"Softly, Clark," he whispered. "We don't know what
we're up against, you know."

Carefully selecting each spot to put Awn their feet, they
moved forward slowly, tensely on the alert. The clump of
bushes surrounding the shack glistened dully with moisture. They entered it and started carefully to make their

way through it. Again Hand seized Clark by the arm and pulled him to a crouching posture. His eyes gleaming, Clark glanced rapidly about him, discerning nothing but the ghostly trees. Both of them remained as motionless as clods. And then Clark made out voices. They were approaching, and he could distinguish that they were the voices of two men. At last he could hear what they were saying to each other.

"We ain't never goin' to find the thing! Let's give it up, I tell you, Mack."

"Not me! This dough's too easy to pass up like that."

"Says you! I don't call it easy. We been four hours in these lousy woods, blind as a couple o' bats, and I'm soaked to the skin! And it ain't healthy to get mixed up in no kidnappin', anyhow."

"Aw, soak your head! We'll find it now that we got some light. I know where I'm at now that I can see a little. The shanty's right here somewhere close. Wait a minute! There it is! Now what'd I tell you?"

The two men hurried on, passing not more than twenty feet from where Hand and Clark crouched with drawn pistols. They were an ugly-looking pair. Clark's fingers tightened round the butt of his pistol. They hastened on and passed from view round the side of the shack. Hand and Clark stealthily crept forward. They slipped up to the rear of the shack and flattened their bodies against it. Pressing their ears to the cracked and loosened boards, they could clearly hear what was being said inside.

"Well, if it ain't Oily! All nice and cozy in his country estate."

"Lay off the funny stuff, Mack. Where the devil have you two been? This is a swell place to leave me waiting all night!"

"You ain't been lonesome with a good looker like that with you, Oily!"

"Keep your trap shut, Phips. Well, let's get going. I'm trusting you two to see that no harm comes to the girl. If anything happens, remember, I'll get you, and I'll get you right!"

"Sure, you can trust us, Oily; you know that. But when's the pay-off?"

"You get a century now. I have it for you. And you get five grand when the job's done. That's pay, and you know it!"

"When the job's done? When's that?"

"Well, I've got to knock off a dame in the big town. That's the last. I don't know how much longer you'll have to keep the girl, but it won't be long. Christopher Hand's working on this case and—"

"Yeah? I ain't so wild about this racket, Oily. It's risky!"

"You're yellow, Phips! You've got nothing to worry about. I didn't leave a thing behind me; I never do, unless its a phony to throw the coppers off. Hand's in New York running around in circles, just as he's been doing ever since he got into this."

"Yeah? I been readin' up on this job, and I noticed Hand got through your phonies all right. I mean the suicide note you left for the fellow you bumped off, and the letter of that Bradshaw guy."

"You're a wise guy, aren't you, Phips? Well; suppose he did get through them. That didn't do me any harm, did it? He's still chasing himself in circles, isn't he?"

"I ain't so sure about that guy ever chasin' himself in circles. But let it go, Oily. He's up against a tough mob now. If he butts in he'll get some hot lead!"

"Now, that's the way to talk, Phips. And I know Mack can be relied on. You two fellows are hot. That's why I picked you."

"Yeah. But now how about the pay-off? How do we know we're goin' to get the five grand?"

"Listen, when this thing's over, you'll get it. I've got the swellest lay you ever saw. You don't think I'm sticking my chin out for nothing? The guy I'm blasting for thinks I am, just about. But when I get through with him, he'll know different! I'll bleed him plenty! It's sweet, I tell you. The dough will be there, millions, and I'll get the last dime of it before I'm through!"

"All right, Oily, we know we can trust you. What's the dope?"

"You take the girl to your place. No slip-ups, now! When I want her back I'll let you know. I'll ride with you to the railroad and take the train back to the city."

"Okay, Oily. Come on, sister, I got to put a bandage over your pretty mouth. And I got one for your pretty eyes, too."

With a thrill of relief, Clark heard Bernice's voice. But the tremble of terror in it struck through his heart and filled him with rage.

"What are you going to do with me?" she asked breathlessly.

Clark paid no more attention to what was being said in the shack. He felt a hand grip his shoulder. He snapped his head round and, to his vast relief, beheld that it was Hand who had him by the arm. Hand placed his lips close to his ear.

"I've looked over the ground, Clark," he whispered. "There's a window on the left side, and the door is across from this wall. You station yourself at the window. I'll go through the door. When I do, get ready for action."

Clark shook his head. "No!" he hissed. "This time I lead the attack! I'll take the door!"

Hand looked at Clark and saw that he was beyond persuasion. He nodded in agreement. Again he leaned over to him.

"When you get to the door, Clark," he whispered, "I will be ready at the window. Leave Rogers to me; we need him."

Together they stole round the corner of the shack. They could hear Bernice pleading with the men inside. Clark was white with rage, but his every muscle was under rigid control. Hand halted at the window and glanced guardedly inside. Bernice was pressing her back against the rear wall, staring wildly at the three ruffians before her. One leering fellow was advancing upon her with a strip of black cloth in his hands. The other two were holding Bernice by the wrists.

At that instant the door flew open and crashed back against the wall. Clark leaped through, his pistol gripped straight before him. Hand struck the dirty pane of glass in the window with the muzzle of his pistol, shattering it to the floor inside.

"I'm crazy to do some shooting!" cried Clark. "Come on, you dirty rats, give me the chance!"

"Don't move!" commanded Hand coldly.

For an instant the men stood thunderstruck. Then, snarling with rage, one of the men flashed his hand into his pocket. A spurt of smoke and flame leaped from the muzzle of Clark's pistol and the cabin reverberated to the roar of the shot. Then an inferno of shots shattered the air. It was all over in an instant. Bernice crouched trembling against the wall. Two of her captors lay still in formless heaps on the floor. The third, a slim, well-dressed fellow, staggered back, his right arm hanging useless at his side. His face, handsome and a trifle coarse, was screwed up in pain.

Clark stood scowling in the doorway, a thin trickle of blood coursing down his cheek. Hand leaped round to the door and brushed by him, sticking the muzzle of his gun into the chest of the wounded kidnapper.

"Don't move a muscle, Rogers," he ordered ominously. "I'm going to need you."

Bernice flew across the floor to Clark, staring wildly at the blood on his cheek. "Ralph!" she cried. "You're hurt!"

Clark suddenly grinned. He put his arms about her and drew her close to him.

"Am I?" he said softly. "I don't care. All I know is that I have you back!"

He bent his head and kissed her. Bernice's arms encircled his neck. Then she drew her head sharply back.

"But you're wounded!" she cried. "They've shot you!"

"Never mind that," pleaded Clark. "Tell me, you—you love me? You'll marry me?"

"In my right-hand coat pocket, Miss Holloway," said Hand, without turning his head, "you will find a first-aid kit."

"Can't you keep still, Hand?" complained Clark. "Bernice, you will marry me? Say you will!"

She tightened her arms about his neck and, lifting herself on her toes, she kissed him quickly. "Oh, darling, yes! yes!" she sobbed.

Then she broke away from him and rushed over to Hand. She took the first-aid kit from his pocket and went swiftly to work bandaging Clark's forehead. The wound, she found to her vast relief, was really nothing but a scratch. Clark was extremely glad that he had it.

Hand, meanwhile, relieved Rogers of a pistol he found in the man's pocket. He snatched a pair of handcuffs from his own pocket and locked their left wrists together. Bernice had finished bandaging Clark's head. She glanced at the two still bodies on the floor and shuddered. Without a word, they all went outside. There Clark bandaged a wound in Rogers' forearm where a bullet had broken the bone. Hand had shot him as he had reached for his pistol.

Then they all started silently off through the wood, Hand and Rogers leading. Behind them came Clark, supremely happy, his pistol in his right hand and his left arm about Bernice. In spite of her harrowing experience, Bernice was supremely happy, too.

19

THE FALLING CURTAIN

They made their way to the car and started immediately back for New York. Clark drove, with Bernice beside him. Hand and his prisoner sat in the rear. Rogers had not uttered a word since his capture.

For the first half of the journey, Bernice and Clark were also silent. But then they started planning. When they emerged from the Holland Tunnel to Manhattan, they had mapped out no more than half their wedding trip. Hand was bored to death. He stopped their happy conversation by requesting Clark to phone the inspector and ask him to meet them in front of Leander Holloway's house at once. But as soon as that had been done, and Clark had started up the car again, he and Bernice went right back to the subject of the wedding trip. The horrors of the past few days were forgotten. The world was lovelier than it had ever been to them. When, however, Clark brought the car to a stop before her great-uncle's house, the material side of life was once more recalled to Bernice. She twisted suddenly about and looked at Hand.

"Oh, Roddy!" she exclaimed. "He has been released, hasn't he, Mr. Hand?"

"I don't think so," replied Hand. "But I assure you that we will accomplish that in a very few minutes. Ah, I see the inspector."

Gerrity stood near the front steps, talking to a policeman. He peered over at them. He was flanked on all sides
by newspaper men, including photographers. The inspector recognized Bernice in the front of the car beside Clark.
He was so startled that he rushed across the sidewalk,
starting a stampede of reporters after him.

"You've found her!" joyously cried the inspector. "Why
didn't you say so, Clark? And what's this? Oily Rogers, or
I'm a goat!"

Hand opened the door. Rogers avoided the inspector's
stare. Hand tugged on the shackle. Rogers reluctantly got
out, with due regard for his injured arm. Clark and Bernice also left the car. The camera men were very busy. The
reporters clamored.

"Let's get into the house, Inspector," said Hand.

They pushed their way through the small mob, mounted the steps to the vestibule, and gained the haven of the
front hall. Hand closed the door and turned to Gerrity.

"Here's your murderer, Inspector," he said, indicating
Rogers.

Gerrity bristled and glared at the prisoner. "So!" he
exploded. "We've got you! I could wring your neck for the
trouble you've given us!"

Rogers continued to avoid the inspector's eyes and say
nothing.

"I imagine, Inspector," said Hand, "that you have fathomed the case."

"Sure," growled Gerrity. "But why couldn't you have
told me how the messages were sent in the books last
night? I spent half the night ruining my eyes before I saw
how it was done! And then I got Marks to talk."

"In that last book I sent up to you," asked Hand, "did
you find the instructions for the murder of Jasper Sinclair?"

"Yes, believe me I did!" nodded Gerrity. "This murder-ing devil did it, and planted all the evidence to incrimi-nate Roderic Holloway!"

"Rather ingenious murder, that," mused Hand. "I mean the intended murder of Roderic—having the state do it with its electric chair."

"Oh, horrors!" gasped Bernice. "Is that what—"

Clark pressed her arm and shook his head at her. "Don't think about those things," he gently advised.

"But Roddy!" cried Bernice. "Have you released him, Inspector?"

"Not yet," smiled Gerrity. "But I'm detaining him now only to ensure his protection. I have your aunt, Mrs. Elea-nor Holloway, at police headquarters for the same reason. They can leave just as soon as we're through here."

"Then let's go up," said Hand. "I gather that you have taken no action yet."

"No," replied Gerrity. "I waited for you to get back, thinking that perhaps you'd have more evidence."

"Well, I have," said Hand. "If you call Rogers evidence, and I surely do. Where is Mr. Forschell?"

"Upstairs," Gerrity said. "We can go on up. But I think Miss Holloway should wait down here."

Bernice tilted her chin. "Inspector Gerrity," she said tartly, "you've been trying to keep me away from places ever since I met you."

"I know," grinned the inspector, "but I haven't had much luck. All right, Miss Holloway, no more objections from me. Let's go."

He led the way up the stairs and down the hallway to the study. Kirk stood rigidly on guard at the door. He stepped aside, and they filed through it. Leander Hollo-way sat at his desk, reading a book. He peered at them. Then he thrust up his glasses and stared.

"Bernice!" he cried. "Great heaven, they've found you!"

Bernice sobbed and ran over to him. He took her pretty hands in his withered old ones. He slumped down in his chair.

"My dear little girl," he said.

Hand jerked Rogers forward. "Mr. Holloway," he asked, "do you know this man?"

The old man peered over at the captive. "Rogers!" he cried.

"Yes," said Gerrity. "Mr. Holloway, we have, got to the bottom of this case. Every one of the murders has been explained. The only death that is not perfectly clear is that of Ludovic Holloway."

"Perhaps, Inspector," said Hand, "I can shed some light on that for you. I didn't witness the murder of Ludovic, but I overheard it. He was lured to this room, and his murderer drew him into a quarrel. Then he handed Ludovic a black-jack. The young man, in his astonishment, foolishly took it from him. Then his murderer threw himself to the floor and shouted for help. He knew that Sergeant Kirk could be relied upon to shoot swiftly and accurately. In other words, Inspector, I am afraid that Mr. Holloway engaged the services of the police department in murdering Ludovic."

Bernice drew back in horror. "Uncle Leander!"

"Leander Holloway!" gasped Clark. "He—he has been planning this —"

"Also, Inspector," went on Hand, "you know, having read the messages, the exact manner in which Robert Bradshaw was shot. Mr. Holloway shot him from across the desk, right from where he is sitting now. The open window in the house out back and the exploded cartridge beneath it were plants arranged by Rogers. Rogers lay hidden in the rose garden below here and picked up the pistol when

Mr. Holloway threw it out of the window. First, however, Mr. Holloway broke the window. He would have done it, no doubt, by partially opening it, reaching out through it, and punching the glass inward with the muzzle of the pistol. Later Rogers stole up here and spirited the body of Bradshaw away. That part of the plot clearly indicates the mind of a maniac at work, the mind of Leander Holloway, once one of the sharpest in the world of commerce, but now cast dreadfully adrift by the insidious poison of time. Look at him, this shock has completed the debacle!"

Bernice and Clark were already staring at the old man. He was leering, rocking to and fro in his chair, his eyes gleaming with ghastly mirth.

"It was all for Bernice!" he grinned. "The others—ghouls, vultures! Just waiting for me to die so they could spend my money! They're gone, gone! I have no more than a month to live; why should I worry about you, Inspector Gerrity, and your law? Bah!"

"He's right," growled Gerrity. "I spoke to his doctor."

"So did I!" shrieked Holloway, in horrible glee. "He knew better than to lie to me! A month—I had a month! Bernice shall have all my money. I put that worthless Morley out of the way! He was nothing but a fortune hunter! He'll not marry Bernice and get my money! And the others are gone! I got Rogers, the fool, to—"

"Shut your face!" snarled Rogers, starting menacingly forward.

Hand jerked him back. The inspector whirled on him.

"Keep your own face shut!" he snapped. "I'd like to know how you got in this."

Rogers sneered at him and glanced sullenly away.

"It seems," said Hand, "that Rogers is not yet willing to tell you that, Inspector. We have plenty to prove that he was in it, and I think, for the present, it is safe to conjecture how he got in it. I think that Mr. Holloway saw Robert Bradshaw fire that shot at him in Central Park, or if he didn't, it was not hard for him to suppose that it was one of his heirs. At any rate, it was the spark that ignited the whole terrible plot in his diseased mind to send his relatives to the next world before him, except Miss Holloway, the only one for whom he had any affection. She embarrassed him, if I may say so, by retaining me. After two attempts upon my life had failed, she was kidnapped to draw me out of the case. But in the first place, having conceived the ghastly scheme, Mr. Holloway naturally realized that he could not carry it out alone. He cast about for a suitable confederate. He knew Rogers of old."

The old man rocked with insane mirth. "Yes, yes," he cackled. "I saw an article in the papers that Rogers had been arrested on suspicion in connection with a bank robbery. He was released, but the papers gave his address. I wrote to him, you see, and arranged a secret meeting here. He came up the back way, just as I had him tell Robert to do later. My plans were splendid, don't you think?"

"That poison!" exclaimed Clark suddenly. "The arsenic in the salt shaker, I mean. Mr. Holloway must have put it there himself! But, good heaven, why would he try to kill himself? That stuff is deadly!"

"It is rather deadly," agreed Hand. "But it is deadly only when a sufficient quantity of it is administered. Had Mr. Holloway drunk his entire cup of soup, it probably would have had no ill effects upon him. He got scarcely any of the arsenic into his soup. But he had arranged for me to use the same salt shaker as he did, and I fancy he knew I would stop him before he had more than tasted of it. It was rather clever of him, though. I confess that it had me off the track for a while."

Gerrity stared at Leander Holloway. "I suppose," he said, "I'll have to get him committed to the state asylum."

"Oh, please do that, Inspector," pleaded Bernice. "It would be terrible to put him in jail!"

Hand glanced at the old man, who sat slumped in his chair, his chin buried on his chest. He mumbled incoherently.

"No," said Hand, "he won't go to jail; a hospital is the only place for him. Now, are we agreed, Inspector, that Forschell had no part in these crimes?"

"Yes, he's out of it," replied Gerrity. "The messages showed that. It all went on right under his nose. He'd make a rotten detective!"

"Then," said Hand, "I think the case is about wound up. There is but one more episode. Miss Holloway, I have— now what would it be? An engagement present, I should think. Yes, I have an engagement present for you."

"So!" exclaimed Gerrity, peering at Clark. "An engagement!"

Hand stalked across the study, pulling Rogers with him. He faced the blank wall, his back to the others. They regarded him curiously.

"Mr. Holloway," said Hand loudly, "I see no reason for you to remain in there any longer."

"And neither do I," replied a voice through the wall.

Bernice gasped. A panel of the wall flew up, and Phil Holloway stepped through the opening into the study.

"Dad!" cried Bernice. "Oh, daddy, it's you!"

She rushed over to her father and threw herself into his arms. Phil Holloway pressed his daughter to him. Neither of them spoke.

Gerrity swallowed a mouthful of air and stared at them. "What's this?" he demanded.

"I'll explain later, Inspector," smiled Hand.

Smiling happily, Clark gazed at Bernice and her father. Gerrity continued to appear as though he were seeing a ghost.

Phil Holloway glanced over his daughter's shoulder at the pitifully shrunken figure of his uncle. "Poor old chap!" he mused. "What a pity! What a pity!"

Hand also glanced at Leander Holloway. The old man continued to mumble meaninglessly to himself, chaos ruling his mind. Now his eyes were dull and glazed.

"There was a dramatic life!" blurted Christopher Hand. "What a tragic curtain he himself rings down upon it!"

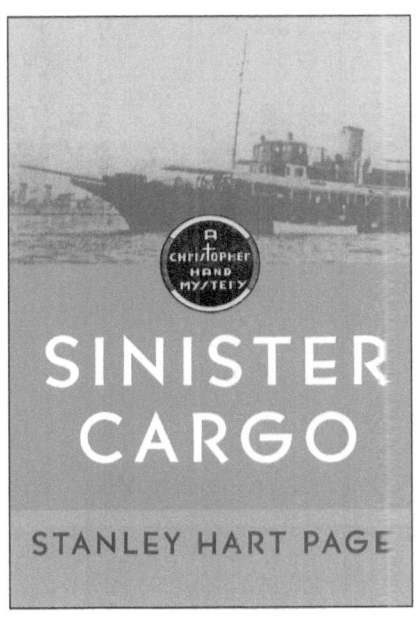

COACHWHIP PUBLICATIONS

COACHWHIPBOOKS.COM

NOVEMBER JOE

DETECTIVE OF THE WOODS

H. HESKETH-PRICHARD

MURDER
IN A WALLED TOWN
KATHERINE WOODS

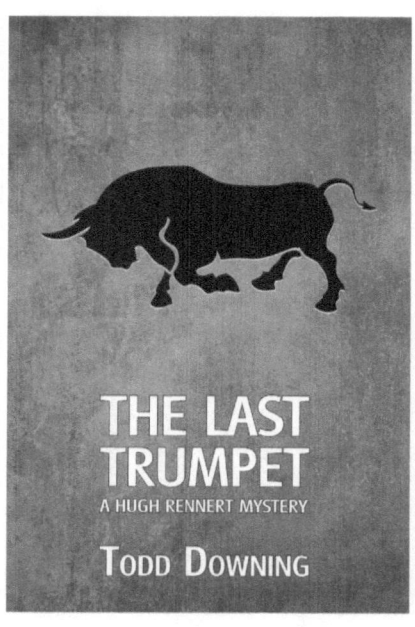

THE LAST TRUMPET
A HUGH RENNERT MYSTERY

TODD DOWNING

CLUES OF THE CARIBBEES

T. S. Stribling

COACHWHIP PUBLICATIONS

COACHWHIPBOOKS.COM

FEAR OF FEAR

FLORENCE RYERSON
COLIN CLEMENTS

MURDER IN THE FAMILY

NICE PEOPLE MURDER

Mary Hastings Bradley

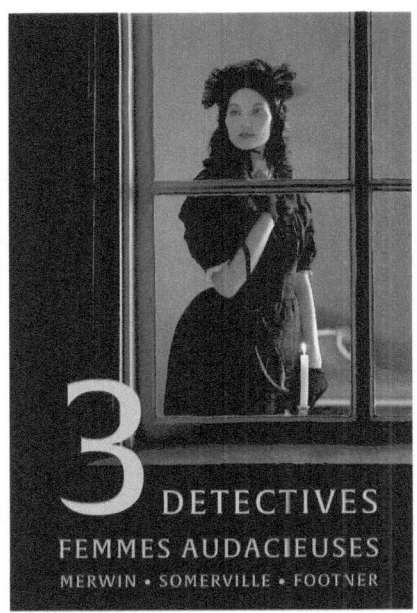

3 DETECTIVES

FEMMES AUDACIEUSES

MERWIN · SOMERVILLE · FOOTNER

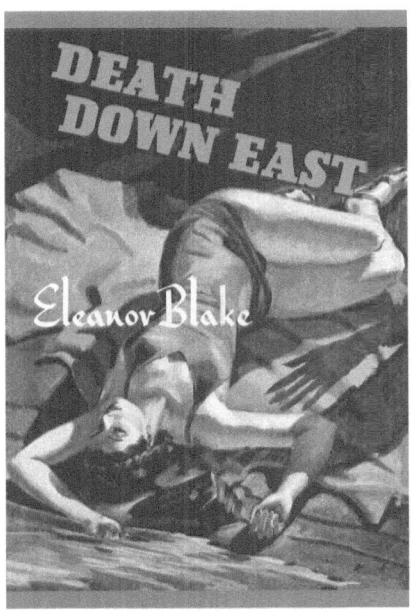

DEATH DOWN EAST

Eleanor Blake

COACHWHIP PUBLICATIONS

COACHWHIPBOOKS.COM

THE
MYSTERY
OF THE
FOLDED
PAPER

HULBERT
FOOTNER

The
Hollow Tree
Mystery

MADELON ST. DENIS

VIRGINIA RATH

FERRYMAN,
TAKE HIM ACROSS!

NO FACE TO
MURDER
EDITH HOWIE

COACHWHIP PUBLICATIONS

COACHWHIPBOOKS.COM

THE QUINNY HITE
MYSTERIES

CHINESE RED · HERE LIES THE BODY

RICHARD BURKE

I'll Hate Myself in the Morning

Murder on the Left Bank

Elliot Paul

MURDER'S COMING

GRAVE WITHOUT GRASS

BY
DONALD CLOUGH CAMERON

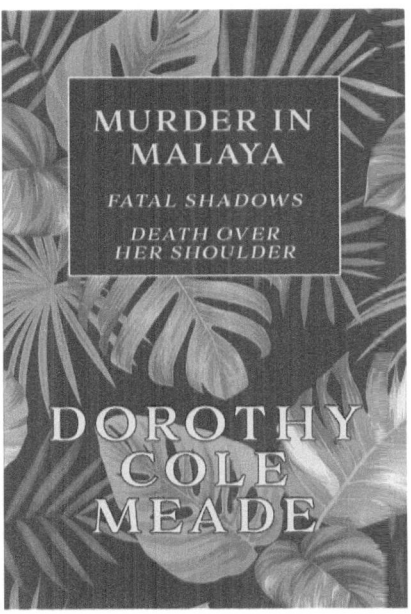

MURDER IN
MALAYA

FATAL SHADOWS

DEATH OVER
HER SHOULDER

DOROTHY
COLE
MEADE

COACHWHIP PUBLICATIONS

COACHWHIPBOOKS.COM

COACHWHIP PUBLICATIONS

COACHWHIPBOOKS.COM

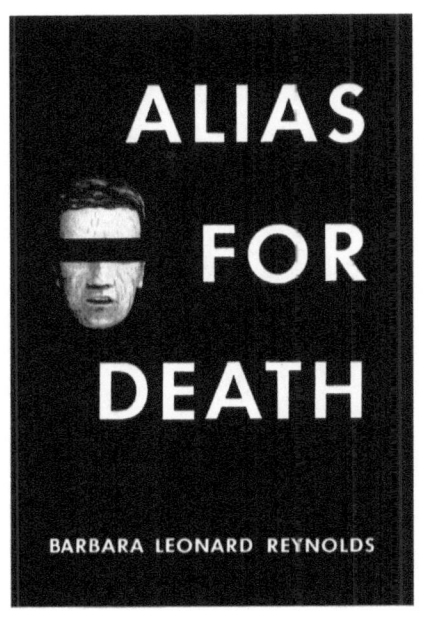

ALIAS FOR DEATH

BARBARA LEONARD REYNOLDS

THERE IS NO RETURN
THE ADELAIDE ADAMS MYSTERIES
ANITA BLACKMON

Jack Dolph

MURDER MAKES THE MARE GO

FEAR CAME FIRST

VERA KELSEY

COACHWHIP PUBLICATIONS
COACHWHIPBOOKS.COM

MURDER AT DRAKE'S ANCHORAGE

E. LEE WADDELL

MURDER AT THE KENTUCKY DERBY

CHARLES PARMER

MURDER ENDS THE SONG

ALFRED MEYERS

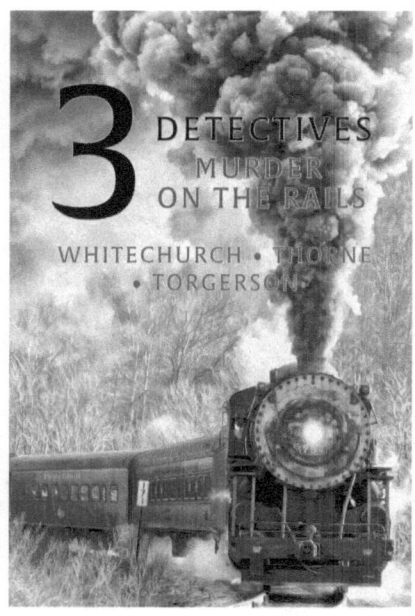

3 DETECTIVES
MURDER ON THE RAILS
WHITECHURCH • THORNE • TORGERSON

COACHWHIP PUBLICATIONS

COACHWHIPBOOKS.COM

THE FIRES AT
FITCH'S FOLLY

KENNETH WHIPPLE

DRESSED
TO KILL

Emma Lou Fetta

GRIMM
DEATH

THE
GROUSE
MOOR
MURDER

JOHN FERGUSON

COACHWHIP PUBLICATIONS

COACHWHIPBOOKS.COM

www.ingramcontent.com/pod-product-compliance
Lightning Source LLC
Chambersburg PA
CBHW031923060726
47496CB00002BB/594